THE DARKEST MIDNIGHT IN DECEMBER

LEARA RHODES

Old Fort Press
Savannah, Georgia

Library of Congress Control Number: 2024920697

ISBN: 978-1-964278–01-8 (Paperback)
ISBN: 978-1-964278–02-5 (E-book)

*To the nurses who began their training
at the St. Joseph's Infirmary
in Savannah, Georgia, in 1905
and made me want to write about them.*

*And to the nurses
who have made a difference in my life:
Stacia Price and Kris Schultz.*

THE DARKEST MIDNIGHT IN DECEMBER

The darkest midnight in December
No snow, nor hail, no winter storm
Shall hinder for us to remember
The Babe on this night was born
With shepherds, we are come to see
This lovely Infant's glorious charms
Born of a maid as the prophets said
The God of love in Mary's arms

Ye blessed angels join our voices
Let your gilded wings beat fluttering o'er
While every soul set free rejoices
And everyone must adore
We'll sing and pray that God as always
May our friends and family defend
God grant us grace in all our days
Merry Christmas and a happy end

*Fr Devereux's collection of Kilmore Christmas Carols
called "A New Garland"*

1

Sharon is tossed off the bed and into a nightmare. Only when she hears the ship's horn blasting does she know she is not dreaming. It is dark and she cannot see her hand in front of her face. She uses the bedpost to pull herself up and reaches for the cabin's doorway. She has to get out of this cabin. She is having a hard time breathing. She needs air. Her heartbeat is so powerful she feels it in her ears.

She makes it to the doorway and out into the hall. She can hear shouts up on deck. She slides her hand along the walls to guide her to the doorway leading up the deck. She isn't walking —more like holding on for dear life with the ship rolling from front to back. She feels for the door handle to the deck. She finds it and opens the door. The water coming through the doorway causes her feet to slip. She grabs the doorframe and holds on.

Voices are louder. The winds take away what little breath she has. Gasping, she holds on to the doorframe with all of her strength. Something flies past her through the air. A flash of lightning illuminates the deck. What she sees scares her even more. The ship is leaning precariously to the left. Her balance is off. Her feet slide on the threshold. Huge waves come over the side of the ship. She can feel the snarling wind snatching at her, whipping her black hair into her face and trying to toss her into the sea.

A crew member sees her and barks, "Go back to your cabin now. Put on a life jacket. There is a gale."

A gale! Why did she leave New York? To die in a gale? The push of the water knocks her off her feet. She falls back into the hallway as water flows down from the deck. She grabs at the door as she falls. Her nightgown clings to her body as she pulls herself up, using the door for balance. She hears the on-deck ship bell chime eight bells.

A crew member comes up behind her on the stairs. He is struggling to get past her. "Go to your cabin," he yells.

"What do the bells mean?" she asks. "Are we in even more danger?"

He barely pauses. "The end of a watch; it is midnight." He pushes past her and goes on deck.

Midnight. She remembers that the darkest part of the night is at midnight. There are still many long hours to wait for the morning light if the ship lasts until the morning. She turns and feels her way back to the cabin. Her first steamship experience has become the darkest, stormiest night of her life. She is being tossed and turned into the bowels of a ship. She wants more than just isolation in her cabin; she wants hope. However, with what she sees, her choice is to return to her cabin or succumb to the sea. She cannot swim. There is nowhere else to go. All she can hope for is that the ship will stabilize. Soaking wet, she inches her way back to the cabin. The door to the stairway remains open, with more water sloshing down. Another lightning flash illuminates her cabin doorway. Once inside, she pushes the door shut.

The captain's safety instructions at the beginning of the sea voyage included where to find the life jacket. It should be hanging on the door to the hallway. In the dark, she finds it easily. She takes it down from the hook, locates the straps, pulls it over her head, and then searches for the sash to tie it around her waist. The captain said the jacket was made of cottony material full of hair-like follicles containing natural oils that do not absorb water. She thought of oily fish when the captain explained. The air within the pockets gives the material high buoyancy. Two large pockets are in front of her chest, and two smaller ones are below the waist strap. Is this life jacket contraption her only hope for survival?

She hears a voice using a megaphone: "The captain has issued an order. All passengers must stay in their cabins. Please put on a life jacket. Repeat, stay in your cabins until an all clear is given." He repeats the message again and again.

Still in her wet nightgown, layered with the life jacket, she takes the chair in the cabin and puts it in the closet to keep it from sliding across the small space and hitting her. She already feels bruises from shifting and hitting the walls in the wet hallway. Her packed trunk is in the middle of the cabin, and with the roiling of the ship, it slides over to block the door. She reaches for it and tugs it back to the bunk bed. To keep the contents in the trunk dry, she tries to pull it up on top of one of the two bunk beds in the room, but she cannot lift it. Her next best thought is to put it on its side. She wedges it between the bolted-down bunk bed and the cabin wall to keep it from sliding.

Shouts from up on deck mix with the chair banging against the closet walls as the boat lurches from front to back in the turbulent seas. There are quick flashes of lightning in the cabin's porthole. Her stomach is queasy. With the bulky life jacket on, the best she can do is to sit on the bed and listen. She hears shouts on deck as wind and rain pound the steamship's side. Her adventure to find a new life may end sooner than she hoped.

There is a scream from the room next door. She does not move. Then she thinks about her valise. She does not see it on the table where she has secured her papers. The information she needs to disembark and to locate her lodging, as well as her letters of introduction for her new job, are all in that valise. She has to hold tightly to the bedpost. In the dark, she cannot see where the valise might have been tossed. She gets down on her knees and crawls over the floor; she feels nothing. Moving to the other bunk bed, she reaches under it; she feels it. Even after pulling it out from under the bed, she cannot tell if anything is damaged in the blackness of the storm. She puts it on the bed and then lays on it to keep it from being tossed again.

While waiting in the dark, she hears someone crying in the next cabin. If she thought crying would relieve her anxiety of being caught in the storm, she would cry too, but she knows it will only make her feel worse. The ship weaves back and forth in the storm. Her stomach churns. She shivers in her wet nightgown, but she cannot get changed until the all-clear is heard. She pulls the sheet and quilt on the bed over her feet. The ship's horns continue to blast. Why did she get out of bed and get so wet? She should have just stayed in the bed and waited. Then she remembers it was not her choice. She had been tossed from the bed in the turbulence of the storm. In her haste to seek safety, she left the cabin. The one thing her father said to her when she left New York was for her to be safe. Somehow, that doesn't seem to be working at the moment. She thinks about her family and her friends. For quite a while, however, she thinks of nothing. She fears the danger that is all about her in the roiling sea. She hopes to hear an all-clear. After hours of sitting and feeling numb, the ship stabilizes.

She stands without having to hold on. There is a soft light coming in through the porthole. The life jacket covers most of her, so she steps out into the hallway and carefully makes her way up the corridor to the stairs. She wants to verify that they are safe and that the ship is not damaged. Water is no longer coming down the passageway even though it is still raining. She can hear people moving on deck but there are no more shouts. She steps out onto the deck. In the early morning light, she sees how the rain and wind have damaged the ship. Ropes are everywhere. The exterior wood panels on the captain's quarters are gone. The siding has been torn, and some of it is sagging from the frames. A crew member sees her and orders her to return to her cabin immediately, but before she turns to reenter the passageway, she sees many sea birds dead on the deck, tossed there by the sea and the storm.

She returns to her cabin and hangs the life jacket on its hook. She removes her wet nightgown. Before going to bed, she had hung clothing in the closet to put on in the morning. It is now morning. She opens the closet door and finds that the clothing has remained on the hooks and is dry. Mopping up the floor with extra sheets, she piles them near the door to the hallway and then dresses.

More shuffling is heard on deck as she sits in the cabin and waits for the captain's orders. During the wait, she opens her valise. The contents are dry, though it has been on the floor under the bunk bed. On top of the papers is the oilcloth she uses to cover her hat in rainy weather. Then, the megaphone voice comes down the hallway, indicating an all-clear. Passengers are free to move about.

Sharon immediately leaves the cabin and goes up on deck to see that everything has been cleared. The birds are gone. The siding remains torn, and crews are still mopping water from the wooden deck, but all is calm. A crew member nearby tells her they are near the mouth of the Savannah River. She turns to look where he points. There is the lighthouse, which means her destination is only fourteen miles away.

2

The morning sun pushes away both the storm and Sharon's fear of being on deck. She looks out at the river leading to Savannah, Georgia. After three days of being tossed and turned in the steamship coming from New York, she is ready to have both feet firmly on land, especially after the storm. She wants to exit the ship as soon as they dock. In her haste to leave, she has done little to groom herself for her arrival in Savannah. She dressed but had not smoothed and settled her hair, which was uncombed and wet, hanging loose, black as midnight on a moonless night. As the wind blows from the port side of the steamship, she can feel the tangles increasing in her below-the-shoulder hair length.

She looks through the mist burning off as the sun rises. There is more water and muddy banks, with cypress trees dwarfed by the tangled woods and vines growing behind. Seagulls dash around the back of the boat to grab morning fish. Egrets with their talons hidden in the mud on the banks poke their beaks into the water's gurgling holes to seek crablike creatures scurrying from one hole to another. Both species of birds seem to be busy in the morning's rising sun, knowing that the heat of the day will soon slow them down. It is June in the South.

In the distance, a smaller boat, a tugboat with steam coming from its funnel, is chugging toward the steamship to guide it safely down the left river fork away from the muddy banks of the Savannah River. The steamboat waits as Sharon also waits. She left New York, her family, her business, and her friends to come down to Savannah to find a new life.

She sees this as her new beginning. She emerged from the darkness of Irish poverty from the Lower East Side of New York and made her way as a hotel maid and then as an accountant. This was all thanks to Cahey, an Irish immigrant from Galway, who was smart and handsome with brilliant red hair. She wanted to have more than a friendship or business relationship with him. Cahey, though, will never marry; he left his heart in Ireland. She learned a lot from knowing him. She learned that she has great potential when applying herself and must use her skills to build whatever future is in store for her. Cahey gave her opportunities to learn how to be an accountant—tutored by Cahey's accountant in Galway—and trusted her to take care of his finances. He encouraged her to go into the bakery business with Danielle in New York. She was a friend originally from France who married Cahey's best friend, Frederick, who was from Scotland. The friends were a mixture of immigrants who sought a livelihood in New York and found each other as a shelter from the world. Though they grew in friendship and wealth, Sharon wants more.

She remembers an Irish proverb: "*An áit a bhfuil do chroí is ann a thabharfas do chosa thú*—Your feet will bring you to where your heart is." Now, she has the opportunity to put her feet in a different place to find her heart. She applied to an advertisement in the *Irish-American Advocate* for an accountant to work in the Savannah, Georgia, offices of William Graves & Son, a mercantile shipping company of New Ross, County

Wexford, Ireland. She received a letter back asking her to join their employment. She had been consulting with Christine Ross, the first woman CPA in New York, to improve the bakery's ledgers and asked Christine what she should do. Since Christine works mainly with women to improve their finances, she encouraged Sharon to reach out and take a leap that might not seem safe at first. Without that leap of faith and trusting her abilities, she, as a businesswoman, would always be limited.

Christine told her that railroad advancements have put company finances on a continental basis and, to compete, companies need qualified bookkeepers and accountants. Many companies had been bringing accountants from Europe to fill the need. Sharon argued with Christine that without a school diploma or an apprenticeship, she would not be qualified to work for a firm like William Graves & Son, and they would find that out. Christine countered that Sharon had an apprentice-ship as an accountant by learning on the job working in many industries for Cahey and the bakery. Christine also maintained that Sharon did not need a CPA to do a good job. Men occupied the accounting field, but even they often chose not to take the new exam to become a CPA.

The letter from Graves & Son wanted her to arrive in Savannah before closing the books for the fiscal year at the end of June. Sharon weighed her options. Cahey was away at his new horse farm in Westchester more than he was in New York. He advised her to do what is best for her. He had heard that many Irish businesspeople were moving to Savannah and other port cities to advance their careers. Danielle and Frederick real-ized that the bakery restricted Sharon's advancement, and they agreed to buy her interest in the bakery. Sharon's family was doing better. All her sisters were married and had jobs. Her brothers had jobs and contributed something to the parents. Her mother and father had the rooms to themselves on the

Lower East Side. New York's June had been miserable with heat and stillness in the air. She decided to leap.

At the mouth of the Savannah River, Sharon watches the boats being hooked together. The tugboat signals the steamship with several horn blows. The steamship waits; the engines noticeably silent. Men on deck hurry to the side as the tugboat approaches the steamship. The tugboat crew throws several ropes up to the steamship crew. Using long poles with hooks, they pull the ropes over the bow and fasten securely. As a guide, the tugboat will keep the steamship in the middle of the river and away from the mudflats along the riverbank.

The Ocean Steamship Company, known as the Savannah Line, ferries passengers between Boston, New York, and Savannah. Northerners want to come south for the winter, and Southerners want to go north in the summer. Sharon has it backward. She is arriving in the middle of summer, which explains why so few passengers are on board. She learned from a crew member that the steamship would load up with cotton grown in Georgia fields and bring it to New England mills.

As the steamship is guided towards the dock, the mist rises, and Sharon sees the town. Three- and four-story tall buildings line the wharf, with a six-story building in the middle. Some of the buildings are built of red clay from the Georgia midlands. Others are grey and built with bricks made from the sandy soil of the coastlands. The bricks have become muted in color with the sun and wind off the water. There are no noticeable wooden structures at the wharf. A long brick walkway, at least three-quarters of a mile in length, lines the dock area from the first row of buildings. Various-sized ships and smaller boats anchor off the dock out on the river. Many other ships are tethered to the wharf pilings as cargo is unloaded. Along the walkway, many men push large carts of cotton bales to load on the ships. She hears their workday shouts from her place on deck. A street appears to be on a bluff beyond the buildings. Sharon hears the traffic, the wagons, the horses, and the people. The street noise is nothing like New York.

As the steamship edges closer to the dock, Sharon tries to discern where the building is where she will be working. She has the address in her valise with her letters of introduction, identification papers, and the agent's instructions on where to go when she arrives. She waits at the steamship's gate. On the stone retaining wall in front of her that keeps the sea from the wharf, ferns grow in crevices and moss covers the sides of the stones. Though the steamship has been docked for a time, going through the processing arrangements, the water still laps on the wall much like a wave would on a beach. When the ramp is lowered to the wharf, she is cleared and is off. The three days on the ship and the horrific storm made her eager to step on solid land. According to the agent, her trunk will be delivered to the boarding house near the hospital at Taylor and Habersham. She is to ask for Sister Mary Joyce at St. Joseph's Hospital, who will take her to Mrs. Schultz, the matron in charge of the boarding house.

She steps out onto the walkway. The uneven cobblestones are slippery from the recent storm, and she must slow down to ensure her steps are firm. There is a long row of buildings at the dockside of the wharf, but beyond the buildings is a wide alley with space for carts and wagons. Then, there is a tall retaining wall, at least four stories high, keeping the land in place and the sea at bay. To access the street up on the bluff are wide cobblestone ramps curving up to the street level along with stone staircases. She chooses to walk the first ramp she comes to and watches her feet to avoid puddles and navigate uneven stones. As she comes around one of the curves, she looks toward the back of the buildings and sees pedestrian bridges connecting the top of the retaining wall with the buildings' top stories on the wharf. Based on what the agent told her, Graves & Son is located in one of these buildings. She does not pause to see which one. As she walks, she can see several entrances. Suddenly, she bumps into a man standing near the ramp and drops her valise with her papers. As she hurriedly stoops to pick it up, so does the man she has run into.

"I'm sorry," she says.

"Are you all right?"

"Yes," says Sharon, pausing to look at the man with an accent similar to that of her New York friend Danielle, who came from France. He is tall, almost lanky, and wearing a suit. His brown tousled hair is stuffed under a beige linen fedora with a "press" card tucked in the hat band. He looks to be about her age. "I apologize for running into you. I need to walk after being on the ship for three days." She continues to walk up the ramp to the street, being more careful to watch where she is going.

The man steps up to pace with her. "You just arrived from New York?"

"Yes," says Sharon, still walking up the ramp.

"May I ask you a few questions?"

"I don't know anything, and I should be finding my way. Sorry," she says.

The young man persists. "I live here and know where things are. Where are you going? Maybe I can help."

Sharon pauses. Maybe he can help. She stops at a main street and does not know how to find her way. "What street is this?" she asks.

"Bay Street. The street that dead ends here is Bull Street. I'm happy to help." He pauses and smiles. "I'm Lucas Laurent." He holds out his hand.

Sharon hesitates but then extends her gloved hand. "I'm Sharon McGee."

"How can I help?"

"I need to find St. Joseph's Hospital at the corner of Taylor and Habersham."

"Are you sick," he asks, "or a nurse?"

"Neither." Sharon does not want to give information to a strange man. Her friends and family have warned her to take care of herself and not accept help from strangers. "Are you a reporter?" Sharon gestures to the card in his hat.

"Yes, I am a reporter and try to get news from folks traveling from New York and Boston. I like to hear first-hand from people about what is happening in other parts of the world." Then he takes her elbow and ushers her across the street just as a trolley stops at the corner. "Here, step up. The trolley is here, and we can take it to St. Joseph's."

Climbing up the two steps into the trolley, Sharon finds a seat in the middle and sits near the window. She shifts her cloak to her arm between them and looks out at the town. There are trees everywhere with grey silvery strands flowing from every branch of the large trees. "What's the silvery strands on the trees?" she asks.

"Spanish moss," explains Lucas. "Some call it 'tree hair.'"

The conductor walks down the aisle, collecting fees. "I have this," says Lucas, dropping a couple of coins onto the palm of the conductor, who takes his index finger and strikes the brim of his hat as a form of acceptance. He is wearing a hat badge with his title and company name. Sharon looks at the heavy blue uniform jacket he is wearing in this Savannah heat. After the recent storm, the humidity is stifling.

"Thank you," she says but continues to look out. She wants to acclimate herself to everything to make it easier for her to return to the wharf in the morning for work. She sees an allée of trees bisecting a square. The shade of the big trees is tempting in the June heat. "And what are the big trees called?"

"Those are live oaks. The biggest and oldest oak is on the northwest corner of Forsyth Park. It's the Candler Oak, 200 years old and 54 feet tall, with a circumference of seventeen feet."

Sharon turns to look at Lucas. "How do you know all this about a tree?"

"I write brochures for the newspaper to use when visitors come to Savannah," says Lucas. "And, those," he points to a tall tree with a cluster of fronds at the top, "are palmetto trees." Then he nods toward another tree with branches that curve down to the ground. "And that's a magnolia tree. Its flowers smell wonderful when they are in bloom."

Sharon looks at all the trees, which are so different from anything in New York. She was never curious about the trees in New York. With so many people and activities there, the natural vegetation was lost to her. She was constantly running from one place to another—to her family's rooms in the Lower East Side, to her friends' house in Murray Hill, to the bakery she shared with Danielle, to events in the city—constantly going, with little time to look at trees. But here, huge flowers are popping out everywhere, there are trees of all shapes and sizes, and the moss drapes down like scraggly grey hair. She understands how it got its name.

Lucas motions to the conductor, who nods and signals to the motorman that passengers want to get off the trolley. The trolley comes to a stop at the corner. Lucas leads the way down the aisle and pauses on the street to hold out his hand to assist Sharon as she exits the trolley. She is impressed with his manners.

"Is it far?" Sharon adjusts the items she carries.

"Almost there, but I mentioned Forsyth Park; it is just down the street and is worth walking about or sitting under the trees. There is a two-tier iron fountain in the middle." Then he turns down a side street. "See that three-story building there on the left side of the street?"

Sharon nods.

"That's St. Joseph's Hospital."

"Thank you. I would not have been able to find this so

easily without you guiding me, but it is not far to walk. We didn't need to take the trolley but thank you for introducing me to it. I'm sure I will need to use it sometimes while I am here." With that, she turned to walk toward the hospital.

"Wait," Lucas calls. He hurries to catch up with her. "Where are you staying?"

"I am not sure where I am staying. I must check in with the nuns at the hospital."

"I see. Well then, I will walk you to the hospital." Lucas gets in step with Sharon. She accepts his offer to guide her to her destination, but to continue to receive his offers makes her uncomfortable. She has been so sure of her adventure. She feels dependent on Lucas taking charge. Boldly, she looks over at him as they walk. His steps are sure and firm. There is no hesitation, pause, or slowing down to a leisurely walk. Walking is almost like a business he must perform. Sharon is not sure she likes the authority he has taken to get her to where she needs to go. Then again, she thinks she must be patient and learn about the area and the people here.

At the corner, Lucas stops to assess the passing traffic. He places his hand under her elbow and again guides her across the street. In front of her is a three-story brick building in the classical French Beaux-Arts style with a flat roof, a raised first story with symmetrical arches all along the front, and symmetrical but square porches on the second and third stories. The agent said that Sisters of Mercy were in charge of the hospital. She is to seek out Sister Mary Joyce.

At the entrance, she turns again to face Lucas. "Thank you for making my destination so easy to find."

"My pleasure." He gives a little bow.

Sharon turns and enters the doorway without another word. Once at the door, she looks back to see Lucas take his hat off, wipe his face with his pocket-handkerchief, and lazily amble up the street whistling a little tune.

3

Sister Mary Joyce takes a long time to come to the entry hall. Sharon notified the nun at the desk, who told her to have a seat and that Sister Mary Joyce would be with her as soon as she could. Sharon sits silently, gloves on, valise at her feet. She smooths out the green plaid skirt her mother had made for her traveling outfit and adjusts her matching green jacket. Her gloves do not quite match the green, but her sisters gave them to her as their contribution to her traveling wardrobe. She was pleased that they wanted to give her something. She pulls her hair back in a bun while waiting so she does not look so wind-blown.

Sharon watches the various people enter the hospital. Some are couriers bringing in supplies. Others, after checking in with the nun at the desk—who pulls a cord behind her to summon help—are whisked away through the open archway into rooms beyond. Sharon hears a bell chime many times and works out that the chimes tell the hour, the quarter hour, and the half hour. She stands to stretch and walks around on the open porch at the front of the hospital. When she steps back into the entry lobby, her chair is occupied and she has to change seats. After a sleepless night in the storm on the steamship, she is tired.

Finally, she sees a nun hurrying through the door, looking frantically about until she sees Sharon and heads directly to her.

"I'm late. The work here is often unpredictable and cannot be helped. You must be Sharon McGee. I'm Sister Mary Joyce." She reaches out a hand, not to shake Sharon's but to pick up the small valise Sharon had placed on the floor. "Come, I know you are eager to get settled." She turns and goes back through the door where she had entered. She turns down the hallway and exits at a side door.

Outside, they pass through a garden and an arched iron gate. Bright yellow roses climb the arch and bush out in a tangled disarray. They pass through a well-tended garden. Sharon keeps up with Sister Mary Joyce, who is heavy-set and, based on her comment about work, obviously tired from long days. Sharon has not been around nuns, especially nurses who are nuns, and notices the white habit with a leather cincture around her waist. Dangling from the cincture is a black rosary with an ebony cross. Also attached to her waist is a chatelaine holding various tools she might need as a nurse, such as scissors, a tongue depressor, and a darning needle used for mending bed linens. Her wimple is white with a long white veil.

Sister Mary Joyce talks over her shoulder to Sharon as they walk through the garden and make their way to the front of the house. They climb steep steps, cross a porch, and enter through the front door.

"You'll find everything quite simple here. The women staying at the boarding house eat at the same time every day for every meal. Wake-up time is the same, but times for the water closet are staggered and limited to ten minutes. Linens will be exchanged weekly."

As they make their way up one flight of steps and then a second set of stairs, narrower than the first, Sister Mary Joyce continues to explain. "Your lodging is on the third floor. The front door is locked after eight, but the house matron, Mrs. Schultz, is always in the parlor until ten o'clock." She points to a door at the end of the hallway. "That's the water closet," she says. "You will find a pitcher of fresh water and a bucket for disposal. The staff will remove and replenish during the day. If you need fresh water, you will need to go down to the back hallway, where additional water can be found."

Sister Mary Joyce opens a door across the hall from the water closet. The room is large, with three single beds, a chest of drawers, and a coat rack with a shelf over the top to hold hats. In the middle of the room is a table with three chairs. A single window is on the side wall overlooking the back garden, but there is additional light coming through a door leading to a covered screened-in porch that overlooks a street.

"This will be your bed." She points to the bed on the left under the window. "The bottom drawer is yours and feel free to use the coat rack."

Sister Mary Joyce puts down Sharon's valise next to her designated bed. "House rules are posted downstairs in the hallway behind where we took the stairs. Dinner is at five. The dining room is the second door to the right from the front door." With that, Sister Mary Joyce stands quietly.

Sharon looks around the room. She sees a bath towel, a hand towel, and a facecloth folded on the bed.

"Well, let me know if there is anything more that I can do for you." Sister Mary Joyce turns and leaves the room.

"Thank you," calls Sharon. She hurries to the door. "Thank you, Sister Mary Joyce."

With a quick wave of her hand in a you-are-welcome gesture, Sister Mary Joyce goes down the stairs.

Sharon goes through the room to the porch door and walks out. The square-shaped porch is screened to keep out mosquitoes. There is a chaise lounge with two matching chairs, all in natural wicker, with two small tables tucked between the chairs and a wooden footstool. She looks out over the side street but cannot see far because of the huge oak trees lining the street. She hears the street noises and feels the vibrations of the traffic, yet there is a quietness to it all compared to New York. Returning to the room, her plan to empty her trunk and get settled has to be delayed—the trunk is nowhere to be seen. Leaving her valise and hanging her cloak on the rack, she exits to ask about the trunk.

Seeing no one downstairs, she goes to find the house rules posted on the door at the far end of the hallway, just where Sister Mary Joyce said they would be. It is a long list.

Sharon knows that boarding houses hosting young women have many rules. She had been told that just to be admitted to a room, a prospective tenant must be young, unmarried, and, according to this posting, "furnish satisfactory testimonials of character, also in what employment they are engaged or intend to pursue." The company's agent found lodging for her so she qualifies. The list goes on. "If a young woman is accepted, she has to keep her room neat and clean, be present at breakfast and dinner, entertain any guests in the parlor, and adhere to a ten o'clock bedtime. She could be expelled for breaking any of these rules or for exerting an influence contrary to the spirit of the house." The idea behind the boarding houses for women is to provide a shelter for self-supporting women with good moral character in exchange for following strict rules designed not only to encourage but also to enforce good behavior.

Seeing no one, she decides to go for a walk. She must move or she will fall asleep; she has been awake since midnight. She heads for the front door. On a table in the foyer, she is surprised to see an envelope with her name on the front: Miss Sharon McGee, in care of St. Joseph's Hospital, Savannah, Georgia. Sharon picks up the envelope, opens it, and reads.

Dear Sharon,

Since you told us that you were leaving and where you would be staying, I hurriedly penned a note to you so that you might find it upon your arrival. We will miss you, and though my sisters have agreed to step in to learn the accounts, they will never have the skills you possess. All the notes you have left are invaluable. Thank you.

We don't expect to see much of Cahey. Frederick hopes he will be spending some time with us during the summer, but since he has remained at the horse farm in Westchester, we are not hopeful that he will. He seems happy among the lavender fields. Pádraig's arrival from Ireland to help with the horse farm seems to suit both of them. Cahey treats him like a younger brother, spoils him terribly, and tells everyone that he has just arrived from Galway. It is so like Cahey to take in his former employer's son and treat him like family. He has done that with all of us, I suppose, so I should not be surprised.

Anyway, I just want to let you know that I am thinking about you. We all are thinking about you. Write soon. Though you are not my sister, you are the best sister I could have.

Love,

Danielle

Sharon folds the letter and puts it in her pocket. Hearing from Danielle makes her miss the New York friends she now thinks of as family. However, she still needs to walk to stay awake and decides to find Forsyth Park. According to Lucas, it is near and has a fountain.

4

Giant trees are everywhere in the park, extending their gnarled and crooked branches out to the open sky like a hand reaching to accept what the heavens may share. The moss drapes over the branches like gossamer shawls, shielding the leaves from the coastal winds and rains. With the giant trees comes the quiet. Sharon notices a distinct difference between the noise on the street with the wagons and horses compared to the quiet under the trees in the park. A silence engulfs her and fills her with a peace she has not felt in her travels or New York. It is an unknown feeling, and she is unsure what to make of it.

Ahead, she sees a large, green-painted fountain. She also sees that on the top of the two-tier cast iron fountain is a figure of a robed woman holding a staff. Sharon smiles at seeing the figure. She remembers wearing her nightgown and the life jacket to check if there was any damage to the ship that would delay her arrival in Savannah. She didn't put on a robe. She studies the fountain. The bottom basin has a relief leaf pattern. Four triton figures hold shell horns and spout water into a basin.

Sharon sits on a bench to look closely at the fountain. She notices a pattern in how the water squirts from the statues. There is no pattern, however, in the action of the birds flying in and out, frolicking in the basin to cool off. The summer day has gotten progressively warmer, but under the tree canopy, Sharon feels a slight breeze from the river that flows softly and moves the moss on the trees in waltz-like movements. She takes a deep breath.

Until now, she has been so busy saying goodbye to family and friends in New York, packing and sorting through her affairs, that she has had no time to think about what she is doing. Why is she here? What was she thinking? She had her business with Danielle. She had her friendships with Cahey and Frederick. She had her family and a growing number of nieces and nephews. Here, she has nothing but a job. Then she smells the azaleas nearby. She feels peaceful sitting under the trees, but this is just a moment. What will tomorrow be like at her new job? What will the women be like at the boarding house? For the first time in her life, she has nothing to do with her time but wait for the sun to go down and then the morning sun to rise when she begins a brand new workday at a new job in a new city.

Church bells chime. Sharon has figured out that the bell chimes at the quarter hours, the half hour, and the hour. On the hour, additional chimes mark the time of day. She has been charmed by the fountain, and the afternoon has slipped away. She walks quickly to the boarding house for dinner as her stomach grumbles. The bell chimes five times when she reaches the front steps. She hurries to where Sister Mary Joyce had pointed out the dining room. As she enters, she sees other women sitting around a rather large table covered in a beige linen cloth. The dining chairs are as ornate as the ones at the hotel dining room where she worked as a maid. Seven of the mahogany balloon-back chairs with burgundy and beige striped fabric are occupied by young women in nurse's uniforms. They wear a long-sleeve chambray blue dress that touches the top of their white oxford shoes. They had removed their aprons and cuffs for dinner. Some women wore a cap shaped like a giant white cupcake with a cuff around the bottom.

Sharon enters at the same time as an older woman who comes from the kitchen with a large platter of chicken fried steak and a bowl of gravy. Green beans and baskets of cornbread are already on the table.

"Hello, dear," says the woman. "We haven't had a chance to meet. I am Mrs. Schultz. Please sit wherever there is a chair. Ladies, please say hello to Miss Sharon McGee."

Around the table, *hello, nice to meet you,* and *welcome* could be heard. The women sit silently as Mrs. Schultz returns from the kitchen with a large baked dish, steaming hot with browned cheese on top. Goblets with water are at each place. Mrs. Schultz surveys the table and dashes back to the kitchen to bring back a butter dish. She moves to the head of the table. As she sits, each woman bows her head.

"May this food restore our strength, giving new energy to tired limbs and new thoughts to weary minds. May this drink restore our souls, giving new vision to dry spirits and new warmth to cold hearts. And once refreshed, may we give new pleasure to You, who gives us all." Mrs. Schultz remains prayerful as she is joined by the women, who say, "Praise God, from whom all blessings flow, Amen."

Food is passed to the left, and the women eat quietly. The woman next to Sharon introduces herself. "Hello, I'm Bernice. Welcome to Mrs. Schultz's boarding house."

"I am happy to be here and to have a good meal. It has been a long time since breakfast. I have been awake since midnight," says Sharon.

"Where do you come from?" asks the woman on the other side of Sharon.

Mrs. Schultz looks at her and gives an "ahem" sound.

"Oh, I'm Katrina. Welcome."

Sharon glances at Mrs. Schultz, who smiles politely and proceeds to serve herself. Sharon turns to Katrina. "I arrived this morning from New York after a storm at sea."

There is silence at the table. Then, all the women look at Sharon, and an avalanche of talk begins with many women talking at once. "New York!" "What is New York like?" "How did you get here?" "What will you be doing in Savannah?" "Are you joining us at the hospital?" No one wants to hear about the storm at sea.

"Ladies," interrupts Mrs. Schultz. "I'm sure Miss McGee will answer your questions in good time. Let's finish our dinner. Before our Bible reading tonight in the parlor, you might get to know her better. In the meantime, let's share who we are with Miss McGee."

There are hesitant looks around the table. Each woman looks at the others.

The woman next to Mrs. Schultz begins. "I play the piano. My name is Gráinne, but people call me Gertrude." She does not smile but speaks clearly and with excellent enunciation. She is immaculate in her nursing uniform.

Sharon looks at Gertrude's hands. They are relatively small for a pianist, she thinks. There was always a lot of music going on in New York. Hearing music in the house will be a pleasure.

The woman next to Gertrude first glances at Gertrude to see if she is finished, then looks at Mrs. Schultz and back to Sharon. "I read a lot. Oh, my name is Vivian," she smiles. Her teeth are uneven, and she closes her mouth quickly and looks down at her plate.

The woman next to Vivian smiles first, pauses as if she is

not going to introduce herself, and then says, "I am Olivia, and I am stitching a sampler for my soon-to-be new home."

There is quiet at the table. Gertrude speaks first. "What are you saying, Olivia? What new home?"

"John has asked me to marry him," says Olivia. Her smile stretches across her face and dances in her eyes. The smile envelops her entire body, making Olivia shiver in her chair.

The women speak out at once and congratulate her. But Sharon notices that there is no genuine enthusiasm from the women at the table. They are polite but not curious. Olivia holds up her hand to show off her ring. There are more mumbles of congratulations.

Mrs. Schultz places her fork gently on her plate. Her dark dress, high collar, and long sleeves cover her skeletal body frame in an attempt to hide the advancing age that has creased her face around her eyes and mouth. Her lips are thin, and they form a tight, thin line when she is not talking. Her white hair pulled back in a bun, shows texture and waves over her scalp rather than lying flat. "Ladies, let's find out from Olivia how John proposed."

Olivia explains. "John came to the hospital at lunch and asked me. He had a fist full of flowers and this wonderful ring." Olivia holds her hand out again, and the tiny diamond glistens in the light from the window behind her.

Sharon has her thoughts about marriage. She wants a partnership, she thinks. Looking around the table, she sees each of these women as part of the Irish heritage she had heard was present in Savannah. The agent told her that the women at the boarding house were primarily from the low-income Yamacraw Irish neighborhood and were training to be nurses at the hospital. In return for their service, they receive full room and board. The Sisters of Mercy run the hospital and provide the living arrangements for the women. The hospital's mission is to help sick seamen and the impoverished in Savannah and train the women to become nurses.

Sharon notices that the women are indeed listening to Olivia. Even Gertrude, who sits looking at her plate, is paying attention. Sharon watches from the corner of her eye as Gertrude takes her fork to slowly move her beans around and then breaks her cornbread into little pieces. Sharon turns to her. "What will happen when she gets married? Can she still stay in the nursing program?" she asks. Sharon has not been told a lot about how the program works.

Gertrude places her fork on the plate. "We can work as nurses even after marriage, but a married woman cannot live in the boarding house. I am not sure what that will mean for her and the program. I have not thought about it at all."

"So, getting married is not what you are hoping for?" asks Sharon.

"There is not enough time to work and to practice the piano, much less to grow a family. No, I am not hoping to get married any time soon."

Mrs. Schultz is also listening, not so much to Olivia but to Gertrude. "Gertrude plays the piano beautifully," says Mrs. Schultz. She turns to Gertrude. "Will you be willing to play something for our new resident this evening?"

"Of course. I enjoy sharing music with all of you." Gertrude leaves her plate alone and places her hands on her lap.

Sharon asks the women questions about the nursing program and the house arrangements. She learns that night shifts at the hospital are handled by Sisters of Mercy unless the nurses are needed. Each bedroom in the house has three residents. The top two floors each have three bedrooms. However, on the second floor, only one bedroom is for the nurses, and two are for Mrs. Schultz's sleeping room and office. Three staff people help maintain the house: a cook, a maid, and a gardener.

Sharon comments that her walk through the garden upon her arrival indicated someone who knows what they are doing takes care of it. The women don't know who is responsible. Most women have met the maid since she provides clean linens and towels, but not the cook or the gardener. They are restricted from entering the kitchen and have not had an opportunity to meet the gardener, but they do appreciate the fresh produce provided for their meals.

Dinner ends. Mrs. Schultz stands, takes the food dishes off the table, and sets them on the buffet. Sharon observes that each woman takes her plate, silverware, and glass and places them in a bin at the door to the kitchen. Napkins are put in a basket near the bin. Any food left on a plate is pushed into a bucket on the floor for the compost pile. All of the women exit quietly. Sharon starts to exit with them but is stopped by Mrs. Schultz.

"Miss McGee," calls Mrs. Schultz, "may I speak with you for a moment?"

Sharon turns to face Mrs. Schultz, whose demeanor causes Sharon to smooth her black hair in preparation for the talk.

"Please sit," says Mrs. Schultz as she returns to her place at the head of the table. Sharon sits close by.

"I want to take a moment and review some of the items we expect of our women residents."

Sharon nods but says nothing.

"Your employer is paying for your room and board. We have space for twelve women but have a vacancy due to one of the nurses dropping out of the program."

"Yes, ma'am."

"Your employer will not pay for your laundry. All items to be washed must be placed in your basket at the foot of the stairs on Monday night. The charge is fifty-nine cents for a dozen pieces, except for dresses and skirts. The price for those is a dollar for a dozen pieces."

"Yes, ma'am."

"Breakfast is at six. The nurses have to be on duty at seven. The dinner break for them is at five. Bible reading is every Wednesday evening at eight in the parlor. All women are expected to attend unless they are working. You are not to go into the kitchen or the laundry for any reason. You may use the basement to clean your clothes; there are lines to hang clothes in the backyard. Ask me if you need something."

Sharon nods to acknowledge the litany of what Mrs. Schultz is saying.

"No food is allowed in the sleeping rooms unless the person is sick, and someone else in the house will bring food. Visitors are only allowed in the parlor and must be cleared in advance with me. The front door will be locked at eight, but I will remain in the parlor until ten should there be a need to unlock the door. All women are to be in their rooms by ten with lights out."

She pauses and continues to look at Sharon, allowing time for her to absorb the information. Then she continues. "I understand from the company's agent that you will work during the day and late into the evening. Dinner will be saved for you in the kitchen. I will be in the parlor when you arrive. I will get your plate and place it on the dining table. The agent said you would be working six days a week. I expect you to attend Mass with us on Sunday morning. Any questions?"

"No, ma'am. I read the list posted on the door in the hallway. Sister Mary Joyce indicated that I should look there for postings."

"That is correct. It will be posted there if anything changes regarding time schedules in the house." There is a pause in Mrs. Schultz's recitation.

Sharon chooses the pause to interject, "Thank you, Mrs. Schultz, for accommodating me during my transition here to a new place."

"It is our pleasure to have you, Sharon. The agent spoke highly of you and told me you owned a New York bakery."

"Co-owned," corrects Sharon. "Danielle was the baker; I kept the accounts."

"Can you bake?"

"Yes, I did learn. Everyone in a small business learns to do everything."

"Good. I will ask you to help me plan an afternoon tea for Olivia. Her mother has spoken to me. She sensed that Olivia would be marrying John and asked if we would give a tea to Olivia and her workmates as well as a few women from her parents' neighborhood and John's mother and sisters. Will you help?"

"Of course, anything at all."

"Great. Well, I know you must be tired after your long trip." Mrs. Schultz smiles.

Sharon realizes that the conversation is over. Though Mrs. Schultz is all business, Sharon also feels a softness about her.

Upstairs in her room, she is relieved to see that her trunk has arrived. First, she washes her face and hands in the water closet. Then, she begins unloading items in the trunk, including the damp nightgown. She had wrapped it in the same oilcloth that had protected the papers in her valise so the other items in the trunk remained dry. She thinks about where to place things in the room shared with two others. Growing up with all her sisters, she knows how important it is to keep her things confined to small spaces. Cushioned among her clothes is a photo that Frederick had made of all of them the night he proposed to Danielle. They were out to dinner. Frederick had arranged it all. She picks up the photo, and as the six o'clock chimes ring from the bell tower, she goes out onto the porch to enjoy the still-bright evening. It is too early for bed. Though tired, she must attend the required Bible reading this evening.

As she stands looking out over the street, she hears the

sounds of people rushing home after work or from errands. She sits in one of the chairs and breathes in the hot, sultry air. Her mind wanders to her friends and family in New York. She has thought of them often today. She feels so far away. She *is* so far away. She thinks about the people who know her and who know her capabilities. Here, no one knows her. She will need to prove herself in every area of her life. She looks at the photo. Danielle has a smile that appears to last a lifetime, and with Frederick by her side, why not? Cahey is smiling only with his business smile, the one where his eyes do not smile. Her smile, however, is hopeful. Then Sharon hears women's voices in the room. Before she can move, she hears the two women talking about her!

"I'm glad the sisters let us go early this evening. There are a few errands I need to run."

"I'll go with you, but let's change out of these uniforms."

"I don't see our new roommate from New' Yawk,'" says one of the nurses.

The tone Sharon hears in the accent of the word "York" sounds like a snobbish person is saying it. Both women laugh.

"I overheard Mrs. Schultz say that the company she works for is paying for her room and board."

"Yes, from how she dresses, no wonder. I expected clothes from a draper, not handmade ones."

"To be from New York and have such bad taste is not what I expected."

"Me either."

"Hopefully, she won't be a pain to live with."

"Here's hoping."

"Come on, hurry up. If we are going to get the shopping done, we must go before the Bible reading."

"I'm coming."

The women leave. Sharon is frozen on the porch. She glances down at the photo she is gently holding, just like she is holding her friends in her heart. Now, she has real concerns about what she should wear on the first day of her job with this new focus on her clothing. She and Danielle had packed her dresses carefully with the idea of a new job, new people, and first impressions. How can she know what is appropriate when the only women she has seen up close have been Mrs. Schultz in black conservative dress, the sisters in their white habits, and all the women at dinner in a nurse's uniform?

Sharon doesn't have a uniform anymore. She remembers wearing a black skirt and black blouse covered with a white ruffled apron at the hotel as a maid's uniform, but her uniforms were not starched like these nurses' uniforms. Still, what was she thinking? That she could dress and live the way she did in New York? That these women would welcome her quickly into their lives? Her resolve to make something of her time here is strengthened. She must find a way to make friends or learn to live without them.

5

After hearing her roommates discuss her clothes, Sharon searches the house for privacy. Downstairs, she sees no one. She finds the parlor. It is like no place she has ever lived. The parlor is opulent with burgundy velvet settees and deep gold brocade chairs. Two of the settees face each other in front of a large fireplace. Over the mantle is a mahogany-framed mirror. The front windows are covered in brocade draperies to match the burgundy and gold fabric on the furniture. Angled against the wall near the windows is a piano.

As she looks around the room, she sees an escritoire desk in mahogany in the far back corner. She crosses over and sits down at the desk. There are eight cubbies and numerous drawers where she finds sheets of paper, fountain pens, ink bottles, and an ink blotter. She will write Danielle. She will write to her parents even though they cannot read; she knows someone nearby will read the letter to them. She begins to write. Not long after she starts, Gertrude comes into the parlor. Out of the corner of her eye, Sharon sees her standing near the piano. Her body stance indicates that she wants to sit down but feels she must say something first.

"Excuse me," she says when Sharon looks up and sees her. "Would I interrupt you if I play?"

"Not at all, please do; I would enjoy the music."

The petite woman is in a yellow summer dress with a white belt accenting her small waist. Her hair is rolled away from the front of her forehead, with golden curls framing her blemish-free face. Sharon envies Gertrude's skin tones as she watches her prepare to play.

Gertrude runs her fingers up and down the scales. The rhythm of the scales creates a blank backdrop, and Sharon begins her letter to Danielle. However, when Gertrude begins to play a calm and expressive piece that Sharon has never heard, she listens instead of writing. Five minutes later, Sharon is still in reverie over the poetic sounds she is hearing. When Gertrude pauses, Sharon interrupts. "That is the most beautiful tune I have ever heard. What is it?"

"'Clair de lune' by Claude Debussy."

"The lilting melody will stay with me for a long time. It flows so beautifully. Has it been easy to learn?"

"No. It has its fair share of challenges. The fingering is difficult, and thinking through the layers and harmonies is not easy. It has taken me a long time to be able to play it confidently."

"You play it well. Why did you choose that piece to learn?"

"If I want to be a concert pianist, I must play more challenging pieces. Debussy has written several pieces for the piano. I loved this one the first time I played it."

"Me, too. I do not know much about Debussy, but I like this tune," Sharon says.

"He took the title of this piece from a poem by the French poet Paul Verlaine, and, according to the notes that came with the sheet music, the tune depicts the soul as somewhere full of music 'in a minor key' where birds are inspired to sing by the 'sad and beautiful' light of the moon."

Sharon is mesmerized by Gertrude's description and sits pondering the tune, running it through her head. She says nothing. Gertrude rummages through her satchel.

"Here, I have found it," she says. "I have the poem that Verlaine wrote. Would you like to hear it?"

"Oh, yes," says Sharon, who prepares to listen.

Gertrude sits erect on the piano bench and reads.

"Moonlight.
Your soul is a select landscape
Where charming masqueraders and berga-
      maskers go
Playing the lute and dancing and almost
Sad beneath their fantastic disguises.

"All sing in a minor key
Of victorious love and the opportune life,
They do not seem to believe in their happiness
And their song mingles with the moonlight,
With the still moonlight, sad and beautiful,
That sets the birds dreaming in the trees
And the fountains sobbing in ecstasy,
The tall, slender fountains among marble
      statues."

"The suite does examine the images in the poem, don't you think?" asks Sharon.

"Oh, yes, yes indeed."

"I have never heard of a bergamasker. Do you know who they might be?"

"No idea. I have to assume that it has something to do with a carnival type of setting," says Gertrude.

"Maybe we need to find someone French who can explain."

"In a town full of the Irish? Good luck," says Gertrude. "I see you have stopped writing. I didn't mean to interrupt your writing."

"Not at all. I am just letting the friends and family in New York know that I arrived safely and have a roof over my head."

The women continue to talk. Gertrude comes over and sits near Sharon and asks her about her family and friends in New York and how she came to Savannah to work. Then Sharon asks about Gertrude's piano learning.

"I have been playing since I was a little girl," says Gertrude. "My mother taught me."

"Your mother plays as well as you?" asks Sharon.

"No, she taught me all she knew, which were the basics. She plays mostly by ear. But then a neighbor arrived from County Wexford who had been a piano teacher. He heard me play and offered to teach me. My parents could not afford the lessons, but the piano teacher bargained with them. He was a widower who had to manage his meals. If they would allow him to have dinner with them, he would teach me."

Sharon hears how Gertrude's dreams of becoming a concert pianist began to take shape. "And he taught you to play so beautifully!"

"Though he helped me greatly, his skill was limited. I ordered sheet music, paying for it by sewing odd jobs for neighbors. I ordered 'Clair de lune' and he could not help me. So, I taught myself."

Sharon is amazed at her tenacity and ability to teach herself, and she said so. "I hope I am as successful as you are," she says.

"And you don't possess the same thing? You, who was a maid and learned how to keep books so that a major company brings you down from New York?" Gertrude smiles for the first time. "After the darkness we experience, there is hope," she says.

Sharon smiles, too, and thinks about all those nights in the dark with a candle, learning what she needed to know to be an accountant.

Women begin to enter the parlor in twos and threes. Time is closing in on the Bible reading, and Mrs. Schultz will be coming in soon. Gertrude moves back to the piano bench. Sharon stays at the desk, eager not to be noticed. Since she did not see her roommates when they were in the room, she does not know who to avoid.

Mrs. Schultz enters and sits near the door in one of the gold brocade armchairs. There is a pair of them with a lamp table between them. She reaches for a Bible on the little shelf that is part of the lamp table, looks up briefly at the women, opens the book, and begins to read Mark 10: 46-52 and Luke 18:35-43.

Mrs. Schultz glances around the room as she finishes her reading. She looks over to Gertrude and nods. "The sisters asked us to sing 'Faith of our Fathers.'" Gertrude begins to play a song Sharon does not know. The women in the parlor sing softly.

"Faith of our fathers, living still
In spite of dungeon, fire, and sword,
O, how our hearts beat high with joy
Whene'er we hear that glorious word!
Faith of our fathers! Holy faith!
We will be true to thee till death!"

"Amen," says Mrs. Schultz.

"Amen," echo the women in the room. Each one then silently rises and exits the parlor.

Mrs. Schultz remains. It is 8:30, and she will read in the chair until ten.

Going up the stairs, Sharon catches up with Gertrude. "Please, I would like to ask for your help."

_ "How so?" The women continue up the stairs with several others gently going around them.

"I am going to my new job tomorrow and would like to know what I should be wearing to make a good first impression. You make dresses. Maybe you can help me choose from what I have?"

"Okay, but first, you must get permission from your roommates so that I can come into your room. I am on the second floor at the other end of the hallway. Come knock when you are ready."

Sharon goes to her room, but her roommates are not there. They must have gone out again. She goes immediately to Gertrude's room. "They are out and I cannot ask, so please come. I have only a few things. It won't take long."

Gertrude follows Sharon out and up to the room. Opening the trunk, Sharon begins to pull out dresses, blouses, and skirts. Soon, an array of clothing and accessories is scattered over her bed and on the table in the middle of the room. Gertrude eyes the clothing and begins grouping items. They talk about colors and accessories: hats, gloves, and scarves, while they arrange four outfits. Sharon is a bit overwhelmed. She never had to think about clothes when she wore a maid's uniform. At the bakery with Danielle, she worked alone in a back office and was seldom seen by customers.

"When you have a little money saved, we can get some fabric, and I will help you make some skirts that will go with this jacket and these two blouses. Then you will have adequate clothing to last a week," offers Gertrude.

"Thank you. This is so helpful. I wish there was something I could do for you."

"No problem. In exchange, maybe you can come and listen

to me play sometimes. I could use an audience who enjoys tunes that are not hymns."

"It was wonderful hearing 'Clair de Lune.'"

"I have many more," says Gertrude. "Well, I must go and prepare for tomorrow. I have to be at the hospital immediately after breakfast."

Sharon stands, goes to the door with Gertrude, and watches her walk down the hallway. As she returns to the pile of clothes, she carefully places them on the clothes rack and in the bottom drawer of the chest of drawers. She grabs her toiletries and finds the water closet empty. Changing into her nightgown, she returns to her room and pushes the trunk to the side of the bed to use as a table. She turns off the light and slides between the ironed sheets for her first night in Savannah. As the bell tower chimes ten o'clock, she hears her two roommates enter, tiptoe across the room, and undress in the dark. There is time tomorrow, thinks Sharon, to find out who they are.

6

Early to rise, Sharon dashes into the water closet, dresses there, and goes back into the room to leave her toiletries and gown. Having been a maid, she straightens her bed and tucks the corners. Every wrinkle is gone. Her roommates are still asleep. She hears the clock strike five. Breakfast at six. She has time to finish her letters and maybe get them in the post on her way to work. She eases the door shut and goes quietly down the stairs to the parlor.

The first letter she writes is to her family. Briefly, knowing that someone else is reading the letter, she assures them she has arrived safely and is settling into the boarding house with the nurses. She finishes with a short recitation of what she saw on her trolley ride through town. Though she describes the boarding house, she doesn't mention her roommates. She has not seen them, for one thing, and does not want her parents to question her move to Savannah. She does tell them that she will be forwarding some money once she has her pay.

Next, she finishes the letter she had started to Danielle. She shares more about her arrival than what she told her family. She includes meeting Lucas and that his accent sounds like

Danielle's. She also tells what she knows about the other women living in the boarding house with her. In particular, she writes about meeting Gertrude and the piano practice that turned into a "getting to know you" conversation between the two women. She shares how Gertrude helped her with her clothing choices—she didn't tell Danielle why; the snub is still too new. As she finishes writing, she hears the bells chime for the second quarter-hour. She hurries to put the letters into envelopes, addresses both, and places them in her satchel to post on her way to work.

With a few minutes before breakfast, she goes into the dining room to see if there is anything she can help with. No one is there. She can hear footsteps above and muffled conversations. She goes to the kitchen door but remembers that she is not to go into the kitchen. Mrs. Schultz had been clear. As she turns to leave, she sees a stack of plates, napkins, and silverware on the sideboard. She sets the table. Just as she is putting the last setting together, Mrs. Schultz enters from the kitchen.

"My goodness, you are early and helpful. Thank you. Did you sleep well in a new space? Or are you early because you could not sleep?"

"I slept just fine, thank you. The trip was long and tiring, and I fell asleep right away. I have always awakened early. I like the morning and the quiet."

"I do, too." Mrs. Schultz places the platters of eggs and bacon on the table. She walks over to the windows and pulls the curtain back. "Come, take a look."

Sharon goes to her and looks out the window. Above the trees, there are streaks of pale pink in the sky. The color grows into a deep burgundy as the two women watch the sunrise. "I love this part of the day," says Mrs. Schultz, "when the colorful light is pushing the night away and the surprises of the day have not yet happened."

They stand silently, and Sharon is pleased to share this time with Mrs. Schultz. No one has ever included her so quickly in their thoughts. In this pleasant moment, Sharon feels a welcome she had not thought she would have so soon. Her inner spirit calms.

"I am sure you will have a busy day today, but remember what a peaceful moment this has been." As the nurses begin coming into the room, Mrs. Schultz turns and goes into the kitchen.

Sharon straightens the curtains and finds a seat at the table. Breakfast is subdued. The women are dressed and ready for their shift at the hospital but still groggy from sleep. They eat in silence with only an occasional, "Please pass the butter." As each woman finishes, she cleans her place and leaves the dining room. Within minutes, everyone finishes, including Sharon. She is eager to start her day. With her satchel and papers in hand, she is ready to step out into the new workday. As she passes the parlor, two women stand there.

"Hello," they say almost in unison. "We had hoped to see you before the day began."

Sharon pauses to look at the two. They had not introduced themselves at the dinner table the night before. "Yes?" she says, secretly hoping that this will be quick.

"We are your roommates," one of the women says. She points to her friend. "This is Sarah, and I am Alice."

"Nice to meet you." And without more conversation, Sharon takes a step toward the door.

"We hope we didn't wake you when we came in last night," says Alice.

Sharon looks at one and then the other. Both women have brown hair, but Alice's face is freckled, whereas Sarah's is clear and pristine, and there is no blemish to be seen. Neither wears a cap, which indicates that they are new to the boarding house and new to nursing.

"Not at all," says Sharon, taking another step toward the

door. "I really must leave now for my work." With that, she is out the door and down the steps. She pauses at the bottom of the steps and takes a deep breath.

The city is laid out in squares. Sharon thinks that if she turns right and walks straight toward the river, she can find her way to 8 East Bay Street easily enough.

A brisk fifteen-minute walk brings her to Broughton Street. She remembers that Lucas told her that there are shops and eateries along here. She takes a left turn and walks a few blocks to see what might be there. Hearing the quarter-to-the-hour chime, she turns right and hurries the few blocks to Bay Street. The offices are at the river. She remembers seeing the pedestrian bridges connecting the buildings with the bluff. In front of her is City Hall, big and bold at the end of Bull Street, or the beginning, depending on which way one might be going. Offices are on both sides of the building; Number 8 must be inside.

Her shoes make a clicking noise as she crosses the pedestrian bridge over the alley far below. A quick look over the side gives her a moment to collect her thoughts and get her bearings. There are wagons and drays loaded with bales and bundles. The businesses below are busy even in the early morning hour. She holds onto her hat as the brisk wind off the river nearly tosses it into the alley below. She goes up to the double doors, opens one door, and enters the vestibule. In front of her is the stairway going up and down. Arrows point down to floor three and up to floor five. To the left is a naval store office. Around the side of the stairway is a sign giving directions to the harbor master's office. To her right is a sign for Graves & Son. She's here. Again, she pauses and takes a deep breath.

7

Inside the office, women are seated at wooden tables scattered throughout the room. At the side of the room, across from the door, is one long table where a woman with cinnamon hair piled loosely in curls on top of her head sits with a stack of papers in front of her. She stands up immediately and crosses to Sharon.

"You must be Sharon McGee." She reaches out to shake her hand but pulls it back. "Do women in New York shake hands on first greeting?"

"Of course," says Sharon, extending her hand.

"I'm Marleen Walsh, the office manager, and I will show you around. When we finish, I am to introduce you to the accounting director. He will fill you in on what you will be doing."

Marleen talks as she walks but does keep pace with Sharon. They walk through an open space where pocket doors can be closed and into the adjoining room where more desks, tables, and chairs fill the space. At least five men are engrossed in their work and do not even look up as Marleen and Sharon enter. Marleen points to two offices. The first one is where the accounting director works, and the other one is a work area used as a confer-ence room. Marleen winds her way through the desks and goes to an empty desk in the far corner of the room nearest the windows. The location pleases Sharon; she can at least look out at the sky. The windows are massive, and the view is the pedestrian walkway with the green lawns, trees, flowering shrubs, and path-ways on the other side where she walked in from Bay Street.

"Put your things down, and let me show you where the women's water closet is and introduce you to the folks in the Naval Store office. We have to go through their space to access the toilet."

Sharon follows Marleen back through the offices. She makes a mental note of what Marleen is wearing: a simple white blouse with puffy sleeves and a long brown skirt. Her only accessory is a brown leather belt.

On their return to the office, Marleen leads Sharon to the accounting director. "His name is Mr. Tadhg McGuire," she whispers. "We call him Tad." The door is open, but Marleen knocks gently on the side. She steps into the room and beckons Sharon to follow. "Mr. McGuire, Miss McGee has arrived."

Sharon steps into the room and meets her boss for the first time.

She spends all morning with Mr. McGuire, going over the procedures, the postings, and how all are managed throughout the office. She is relieved to be able to answer questions about what she knows. The morning session turns into more of a conversation than a teaching exercise.

Finally, Mr. McGuire stands. He pushes down his cream-colored shirt sleeves and fastens his cuffs. He is thin but appears fit and healthy, and the light-green striped pants, obvi-ously a local style, actually look good with his height and fair skin. His blonde hair is swept back from his face. "It's time to take a lunch break, Miss McGee."

Sharon stands. She has forgotten about lunch. "Please, call me Sharon," she says.

Mr. McGuire crosses to the office door and reaches for a matching suit jacket on a hat tree. It is a four-button jacket with the same green stripes as his pants. He does not have to reach up far to get his bowler hat on the top of the hat tree. "And call me Tad. Meet me back here after lunch. We will continue going over what you need to know to get started."

Sharon moves quickly through the doorway and makes her way over to her desk. The office is empty. All the men working there earlier have gone to lunch, too. She picks up her purse and passes through the outer office. Only two women are at their desks. They nod, and she leaves.

Not knowing where to go, she heads to Broughton Street as suggested by Lucas. The traffic is busy on Bay Street, and she waits near the corner of City Hall to cross the street when a man suddenly takes her elbow.

"Let's go; this is when we can cross."

As they cross to the other side of the busy thoroughfare, she sees that it is Lucas.

"Where did you come from? Were you watching for another ship to unload?" She smiles at his distraught face.

"I tell you, miss, I was working in City Hall Chambers, covering a story of some importance." Then Lucas bows. "I am at your service." The clock bells chime. "That is until the bells chime again. Where are we going?"

Sharon laughs. "I am off to find some cheap lunch. I do not know yet when I will get paid."

"My lady," says Lucas, "I can certainly accommodate that since I, too, am on a budget. Here, let's go to the dining room in the boarding house right around the corner. Cheap, decent food, and pie. What's not to like about pie?"

With that, Lucas guides them quickly down the sidewalk as

he chatters away. "How have you spent your morning? You have been successful, I hope."

"I don't know how successful I have been, but I have learned a great deal about the business I am working for. I am excited that I have a chance to use what I know and also to learn."

"Oh, you are one of 'those,'" Lucas says as he continues to walk.

"And what does being one of 'those' mean to you?"

"All work and no play," says Lucas.

"On the contrary, Mr. Laurent, I have been known to dance a fast one at *cèilidh* in New York."

"Now, I have to see this to believe it, not that I know how to dance like the Irish."

"And do you dance where you are from?"

"My lady," says Lucas, "my accent has not fooled you into thinking I am from the South. My French family would be pleased."

Sharon smiles as Lucas opens the door to the boarding house. She is pleased that she was right that his accent is similar to Danielle's. They are ushered to a table in the middle of the room. Six other people are at the table. Bowls of beef stew are set before them, and a basket of bread is handed around the table. A server tosses down two glasses and, with her water pitcher in hand, begins filling the glasses on the table. People eat and talk. The noise is so loud Lucas and Sharon motion that they will eat and talk later. The stew has root vegetables and a good broth but little beef. There is another round of passing the bread basket. As a bowl empties, servers whisk the bowl away.

The server replenishes the water glasses and asks, "Peach or lemon?"

Sharon chooses peach, and Lucas chooses lemon.

Lucas repeats, "What's not to like about pie?"

Lunchtime is not long since everyone has to be back at work. As they near the door, Lucas turns to say something to the man in line behind them. Sharon digs out her change purse. "How much?" she asks.

"Twenty-five cents," says the cashier.

Sharon takes out a fifty-cent coin and gives it to the cashier. "That's for both of us," she says. Lucas turns around as Sharon hands the coin over. "No, I will get this," she says. "You helped me with the trolley; this is my treat."

Lucas grins. "Any time, Miss McGee, any time."

The walk back to City Hall is quick. Lucas chatters and points out various shops and businesses. Again, he takes her elbow and gently ushers them through the traffic to the front of City Hall. "I must bid you farewell for now. The city government cannot run until I sit in the meeting. Where do you work?"

"Just there, at Graves & Son."

"You came all this way to work as a secretary or a maid for a shipping company? Were there no jobs in New York?"

Sharon immediately responds with words chosen carefully. "I am not a maid or a secretary. I am an accountant."

"A woman accountant? In Savannah? Now that is something I do need to write about." Lucas is almost swaggering toward the door of City Hall. He continues to laugh and repeats himself, "That is something, my, my." He takes his hat off and bows. When he replaces his hat, he says, "Women are not accountants. They can be bookkeepers, but not accountants." He turns and bounces up the steps into City Hall.

The red color on her face brings a heat that she has not known for quite a while. She holds her gloved hand up to hide the blotches. She turns quickly and walks to the end of the block, where a green lawn offers her quiet under the trees. She had no problems being a maid. Her family needed the money, and it was an honorable job. However, as she has advanced in learning, she wants to be recognized for her brain and not her physical ability to clean. She needs time to let her face calm down before going into the office. The breeze from the river cools her, but she keeps walking until she sees a tall light post. It stands alone on the bluff overlooking the wide river below. She is also alone. The light post, she thinks, must be here for a reason; then so must she. What that reason is—she will have to wait and see. Adjusting her hat and smoothing her gloves, she walks back to Graves & Son to finish her day as an accountant.

The afternoon goes by quickly. Tad is quite clear on the processes she needs to learn. Around five o'clock, when the bell chimes, Marleen pushes a tea trolley into the outer office. The men immediately stop and gather around the trolley to get a cup of tea. Marleen pours each cup carefully. The men help themselves with sugar or lemon slices. Sharon smiles to herself, relishing the fact that the tea is part of working for an Irish company. She goes over to get a cup. The men move back but hover, silently sipping their tea.

"I suppose you have all met Miss McGee, Sharon McGee?" Marleen says.

The men nod to Sharon. First, one speaks up, and then the others chime in.

"Nice to meet you, Miss McGee. I am William Masterson."

"Nolan Shaw."

"Jack Michaels."

"Sean O'Reilly."

"Matthew Dunn."

Then, the men resume sipping their tea in silence. Sharon smiles at all of them, a genuine smile that lets the snub from Lucas fly out the window with the river breeze. These men are all bashful around a woman. She has not had that happen in a long time. "Good to meet all of you. I am excited to be working with what Mr. McGuire tells me is an outstanding team of accountants."

The men again nod, almost in unison, finish their tea, place their cups on the tea trolley, and return to their desks. Sharon glances up and sees Marleen smiling behind the hand that she is holding in front of her face. Sharon joins her with an "only women understand" kind of smile.

At seven o'clock, when the bell chimes, the men stand, stretch, pick up their hats, and one by one wish Sharon a good evening. It has been a long day, but Sharon is energized by what she has learned and sees that there are many great things she will be learning each day.

Tad interrupts her thoughts when he comes over to her desk with his coat and hat.

"This has been a productive day, I hope," he says.

"Thank you for all the instructions."

"I'll see you in the morning. You will be given a ledger book and receipts to begin your day." And with that, he tips his hat and leaves.

Marleen is still in the outer office when Sharon passes through.

"Good, you are the last one, I will lock up now. But you have a message. Here it is." And Marleen hands Sharon a folded sheet of paper.

Sharon walks into the vestibule and then out onto the pedestrian walkway so Marleen can lock up the office. The sunlight is still bright at seven o'clock as she reads the handwritten note.

Dear Miss McGee,

I feel I responded badly to the news of your employment and offer my apologies. Since you are new to the town, I would like to offer my tour guide expertise on Sunday to show you how splendid Savannah can be for any new member of the local working society. Please accept my offer

by meeting me at the entrance of St. Joseph's Hospital at two
o'clock. I will be the one with my hat in my hands.

Sincerely,

Lucas

Sharon reads the note twice, not because she does not
understand but because she does. With renewed energy, she
focuses on walking back to the boarding house. A plate of food
is waiting for her, and she needs to be rested for the work she is
expected to do in the morning.

8

A routine develops over the next couple of days. Sharon is the first one up to use the water closet and the first one out the door after breakfast. On the way to work, she stops at a market on Broughton Street and purchases fruit, cheese, and a freshly baked roll to have for lunch. On clear days during lunch, she walks to the strand. She asks Marleen about the strand and is told that it is Emmet Park, named for Irish orator Robert Emmet, who never came to Savannah. Colloquially, the park is known as the Irish Green.

There is a bench near the light post where she has a good view of the river. Marleen explains that the light post is a beacon light, though it looks like an ordinary street lamp. It is used as a rear range light for the Fig Island Lighthouse to steer ships coming into the port at Savannah away from the sunken vessels in the river channel downed by the British during the Revolutionary War.

Sharon is happy to know that they both have a purpose: the light marks a spot; hers is to do a great job and be promoted. On days when rain squalls come quickly and then go quickly, she eats her lunch at her desk. The window offers her a change of scenery from looking at the ledgers all day to a secret view of life going on outside the office.

At the end of the day, she walks back to the boarding house. She feels her back, her arms, her neck. They all want activity. These short fifteen-minute walks hardly compare to her long-distance walks in New York. However, it is a way to clear her head of all the numbers she has seen during the day. The steps at the boarding house come too soon, but her stomach rumbles. It must know her dinner is waiting.

Mrs. Schultz gently puts the plate down at a single spot at the dining room table and then leaves her to eat alone. This is the part of the day she likes the least. She walks alone, works alone, interacts only when someone brings her receipts to post, eats lunch alone, and her roommates are almost always gone when she is in the room in the evening. She is not sure where they are spending their evenings, but they do not return until the bell chimes at ten o'clock. They tip-toe into the room and undress in the dark. Since her arrival on Wednesday, she has barely spoken to anyone in the boarding house. Breakfast is quick, and people are quiet or not fully awake.

It is Saturday, and her routine is the same with one change. As she straightened her desk at the end of the day, Tad came around to everyone's desk and handed each of them a pay envelope. Hers is not much since she only worked three days that first week, but it is better than she had imagined. She heads back to her room. As Mrs. Schultz is setting her plate on the dining room table, they hear Gertrude running scales on the piano in the parlor. Mrs. Schultz pauses and looks at Sharon.

"Would you like to eat your dinner in the parlor and listen to Gertrude? It is Saturday night." The smile she offers Sharon warms her heart.

"Yes, please."

Sharon picks up her silverware and water glass. Mrs. Schultz carries her plate into the parlor and sets it on a table next to a green brocade settee. As they both settle in, Gertrude pauses, sees them, and immediately begins playing "On the Beautiful Danube" by Strauss. As she finishes and pauses at the piano, Sharon and Mrs. Schultz both applaud.

"That was beautifully played," says Mrs. Schultz.

"Yes, indeed, and was that tune also inspired by a poem?" asks Sharon.

"It was," says Gertrude. "Strauss had been asked to compose a song for Austria, but he delayed and did not. Then, when Austria was defeated by Prussia in the Seven Weeks' War, Viennese morale was at a low. Strauss was asked again to write something that might cheer the people. He recalled a poem by Karl Isidor Beck where every stanza ends with the line: 'By the Danube, beautiful blue Danube.' Thus, the name of the waltz."

With that, Gertrude begins to play another song. "Do either of you know this one?" Her fingers fly over the keyboard. When she finishes, she looks up to see Sharon and Mrs. Schultz clapping along with the beat.

Both women laugh. "I do not know it, but I like it," says Mrs. Schultz.

"I don't know it, either, but it is a delightful song. Tell us about it," says Sharon.

"The music guild has scheduled a musical melody just for its members at the end of the summer. The tune is 'What the Brass Band Played' by Theodore Morse." She pauses and then talks as she flips through some sheet music on the piano. "What I think is fun is he and his wife often performed together, the violin and piano, and became successful writing songs for Tin Pan Alley. Her name was Theodora. Isn't that interesting?"

"Absolutely," says Sharon. Mrs. Schultz agrees with a nod.

"Sharon, did you hear any of the popular songs from Tin Pan Alley when you were in New York?" asks Gertrude.

"I did. My friends and I would have dinner at one of the

clubs in the city. Often, the bands would play the songs. My friends Danielle and Frederick would dance, but Cahey and I would sit at the table and enjoy the songs."

"Cahey didn't dance?"

"He danced Irish but not the popular dances. I took him to *cèilidhs* where my father would play, and he was a masterful Irish dancer."

"Ah, you like the *cèilidhs* then," says Gertrude. "I'm sure you can find one happening here. It's likely that some of the Irish organizations and pubs in town would have sessions on the weekend."

"Thank you, I will ask," says Sharon, content to stay and listen to Gertrude, but then Mrs. Schultz interrupts her thoughts.

"You will be joining us for Mass tomorrow at eleven o'clock? St. John's is just down the street. We'll leave here at a quarter till, and you can walk with us to see the way."

"Yes, thank you. I will be ready."

Gertrude stands as Sharon does. "I'm heading up as well; it has been a long day at the hospital."

The two women say goodnight to Mrs. Schultz, who has settled into her regular chair to read. The women walk slowly up the stairs and say their goodnights. Sharon retires to her room, which is once again empty.

9

Sunday morning, Sharon awakens to thunder, shattering the stillness with flashes of lightning, making the morning sky white and then fading to blackness again. She awakens with a jolt and is relieved that she is not on the steamship. She glances over at her still-sleeping roommates. With the bright lightning and thunder, she can't sleep. She grabs her clothes and toiletries and heads to the water closet. The thunder is so loud that she jumps as she opens the door, startled in a way that storms had not affected her in New York. The thunder is loud and constant, and the flashes of lightning are fierce in the sky. The boom and the light appear to be in the room with her, not outside. No one is in the hallway. The water closet is empty. Another pounding of thunder makes her pull the door shut quickly.

Returning to the bedroom, she hurries, placing everything neatly in her space. Her two roommates have not moved. Sharon hears the bell chime at the quarter hour. Time to spare before breakfast. She slowly descends the stairway and sees Mrs. Schultz standing on the porch with the door open.

"Is anything wrong?" Sharon asks.

"Have you heard the storm?"

"Yes, how could one not hear it?"

Sharon stands in the doorway and looks at the rain falling in torrents, splashing and puddling in the yard out front. Rivulets form on the walkways and make a course of their own over the cobblestones. The water moves swiftly. The thunder is repeatedly louder and louder. The lightning is brighter and brighter. There had been soft breezes blowing off the river, but now the wind was blowing from the land side and pushing the moss on the trees almost horizontally to the ground. Smaller trees are bent at a sharp angle, and the branches of the larger trees wave in the rain like children trying to get attention in a crowd.

Suddenly, Sharon hears a groaning sound. The sound is small at first, but it grows until there is a crack, and right in front of the house on the other side of the street, a tree breaks in half and falls to the ground, blocking the street. The river of water backs up behind it at first, but as the rain continues to pound, the water begins to flow under and around branches of the downed tree trunk. Sharon steps back into the house. "I'm going back in. The storm is too much for me to watch."

Mrs. Schultz joins her and says, "I know I said the kitchen is off limits, but you are a baker, and I could use some help this morning. The cook is always delayed when there is a storm."

Sharon nods, and they go through the hallway to the kitchen rather than through the dining room. The massive room has two stoves—an electric and a wood-burning. It also has two ovens, two ice boxes, one of which is electric, and a long-oversized sink in front of a pair of windows that look out over the garden. In the middle of the room is a wooden table, well-used with only two mismatched straight-back chairs tucked under. Mrs. Schultz goes to the pantry and returns with two aprons. One she hands to Sharon while she dons the other.

"Do you bake biscuits?"

"I do," says Sharon, who goes to the sink to wash her hands and returns to begin mixing the biscuit dough. Mrs. Schultz had already gathered the ingredients, bowls, and baking pans.

As Mrs. Schultz dashes about the kitchen preparing other dishes, Sharon measures and mixes. She's ready to knead the dough. This is the part she likes. Her mind always wanders, and time passes quickly when baking bread. Her hands pull the dough back and forth. She turns it, puts a dab of flour on the top, and turns it again. She works her fingers deep into the dough. As she turns and folds the dough over and over, she realizes that sharing food with her friends back in New York was one thing that brought all of them close together. She pats out the biscuits, having learned to roll them by hand instead of cutting them, and places them on the baking pan.

While the biscuits bake, she begins helping Mrs. Schultz with other food preparation. Both have ignored the storm. While they are getting everything together, in walks the cook. Mrs. Schultz introduces her as Edwidge. She is darker than anyone Gertrude has ever known. She wears a bandana around her hair, which hides its color. Her skin has no wrinkles to show her age, but Sharon guesses she must be in her middle years. She has good, strong, dark brown eyes that communicate that she is in charge of the kitchen. She grabs her apron and suggests that everyone leave and let her get on with her work.

One by one, the women sit down for breakfast. They comment about how the biscuits are different—good but different. The women surmise the storm must have changed how the cook makes biscuits. Mrs. Schultz and Sharon share a glance and a half smile.

After breakfast, Sunday morning is free until Mass so Sharon hand-washes as many of her clothes as possible in the vats located in the basement. She takes her clothes back to her room and spreads them discreetly on the wicker furniture in the screened-in porch off the bedroom so they cannot be seen from the street. Once again, her roommates are gone.

She changes into something she thinks may pass as church-going. She has little idea of fashion. Her mother hand-sewed all of her clothes. She did own one good dressy gown bought with funds from Frederick to attend the dinner and revue arranged by Frederick the night he proposed to Danielle, but it was a New York-type gown that had little hope of being used in Savannah.

When the bell chimes at ten thirty, she is ready and goes to wait in the parlor. As she skims through several books on the shelf above the writing desk, she looks at the titles. Most of them she has never read, such as Herman Melville's *Moby-Dick*, Henry David Thoreau's *Walden*, Walt Whitman's *Leaves of Grass*, Louisa May Alcott's *Little Women*, Harriet Beecher Stowe's *The American Woman's Home*, and Stephen Crane's *The Red Badge of Courage*. She will at least have something to read in her spare time. Mrs. Schultz enters.

"I see you are ready to go. Some of the women have been called into the hospital this morning due to the storm. There has been major damage, with trees falling and ships capsizing due to the wind and water. The seamen have been brought to St. Joseph's. The sisters have called in all the available nurses. That is to say, I believe it will be only you and me off to Mass today. Shall we go?"

Sharon nods and follows Mrs. Schultz out the front door. Work crews are already sawing and moving limbs from the street. The downed tree they saw crash earlier that morning is in pieces, and a cart nearby is loaded with limbs and twigs. The water has abated. Though the stones are still wet, there are no large puddles for the women to have to navigate. Just as they reach the cathedral, the bells chime three-quarters till the hour.

Made of brick, copper, and terra cotta, the cathedral covers two city blocks. Its spires soar into the Savannah sky that is clearing from the morning storm. Sharon sees a large rose window high above the entrance. Nothing prepares Sharon for the absolute splendor of the inside of the cathedral. The stained-glass windows are more colorful than the red and white flowers blooming in the squares.

As they choose a pew, Sharon turns briefly and looks at the rose window. From inside, she can see it is a quatrefoil with St. Cecilia, the patroness of music, in the center. Appropriately, it is located directly above the organ. The window is at least twenty feet in diameter with ten radiations from the center, each containing celestial figures singing and attending to musical instruments. This is not her first view of a rose window. In New York, one was installed in the Cathedral of St. John the Divine on Amsterdam Avenue. She and her friends had attended the evening service with hundreds of people. The service was held outside with the lights on inside the cathedral to shine through the stained-glass window.

Following the Mass order is easier than Sharon expected, even though she has been away from the Church for many years. Before all of her sisters and brothers were born, Sharon, as the oldest, was taken to Mass in New York. Once the family grew, it became harder and harder to gather the family off to Mass. Finally, her mother would go and leave the family to their own devices, meaning Sharon would mind her brothers and sisters in her mother's absence. Her father would be still in bed or off to play cards with his fellows.

Sharon lets her thoughts wander, standing when others stand, kneeling when Mrs. Schultz kneels. At communion, when it is her row's turn, instead of going with the others, she moves to the exit door. She has been away too long to be ready for the taking of communion without going to confession. She must see the priest soon.

At the end of the service, Sharon waits for Mrs. Schultz, who makes eye contact but says nothing. They walk in silence back to the boarding house. Mrs. Shultz retires to her room. Sharon is undecided as to meeting Lucas. Should she meet him at the hospital entrance at two o'clock, as he asked? Or should she find other things to do with her time? She chooses to take a walk. Forsyth Park is close and made her feel peaceful on her first visit. She'll return and see if its magic will work again.

Wandering through the park, she sees the damage the storm did with broken limbs and twisted bushes. Soggy puddles fill many of the dirt paths. Walking around them is laborious but necessary. She constantly looks at her feet. She makes it to the end of the park and begins the slow walk on the other side near where Lucas said the oldest tree is growing. She finally sees a giant oak tree. It is indeed a massive tree, taller than the buildings behind it, with a trunk circumference so big that Sharon's arms could not even begin to go around it. She sits down under the tree and leans back on the trunk. It's limbs shield her from the sky.

The bells chime at the two o'clock hour and awaken Sharon as she had nodded off under the tree. Scrambling to her feet, she straightens her hat and walks quickly to the hospital. She has decided to meet Lucas after all. She knows she is late, but not by much. No one is at the entrance. She looks inside. Lucas is not there. She hears the quarter-hour chime. She waits. When she hears the half-hour chime, she turns and heads back to the boarding house. There are better things to do with her time than standing around waiting for Lucas.

As she approaches the boarding house, she hears another

bell, a loud gong that continues for many minutes. Mrs. Schultz is standing on the front porch and listening.

"What's with the big gong bell?

"There's a fire. That's Big Duke, the fire department's warning of a fire."

"Are we okay here?"

"One can never know. Savannah has burned twice due to too many wooden houses and too many careless people. We just don't know."

"Are you watching to see what happens?

Mrs. Schultz sits on one of the rockers on the porch. "Yes, the hospital will need as many hands as possible if it is a bad fire. And I want to make sure all of my women are safe if the fire comes near us."

"What can we do if it does?"

"Every square has a cistern. We can help with the water."

Sharon sits in a chair next to Mrs. Schultz. They sit in silence, watching the street and scanning the skyline. There is a definite smell of smoke in the air. Due to their nervous energy, both women begin to rock. The motion causes them to get in sync and rock as if they are one unit. No one is on the street. The women remain as the bell chimes the quarter and then the half hour. Down the street comes a young man running through puddles and across lawns. He approaches the porch and looks as though he will not slow down.

"Hello," he says as he gasps for breath. He places both hands on his knees and takes multiple breaths before continuing. "I've come with a message for Olivia," he says.

"She is at the hospital. The nurses went in due to the capsized ship in the harbor and the seamen they brought in for care. What is the message?"

"She is to come to the fire quickly; John has been injured." Having delivered the message, the young man turns and, though slower than before, still at a quick pace, goes back the way he came.

Mrs. Schultz descends the front steps and heads to the hospital. Sharon remains on the porch to watch for signs that the fire is getting closer. Sharon paces the length of the porch, over and over and over, watching the skyline. The smoke is denser. She takes a handkerchief from her skirt pocket and holds it over her face. She had seen a few fires in New York, but she hadn't been alone. She remembers when the Vanderbilt American Horse Exchange burned in Manhattan. Cahey was working there and rescued many of the horses that were running wildly around Manhattan. That fire was one for the records. Vanderbilt rebuilt the Exchange, and Cahey's reputation gained strength and approval from animal lovers throughout the region. However, the smell of the burning horses and the burning building will always be a part of Sharon's memory.

Mrs. Schultz returns alone. Sharon is still pacing on the porch but stops when Mrs. Schultz dashes into the yard. She does not come up the steps but projects her voice to Sharon.

"I found her. The fire is over in the ward where Olivia is from, Yamacraw Ward. She headed over there. The police and fire telegraph system have notified the sisters at the hospital to expect many injured firemen. Sister Mary Joyce asked that I assist at the hospital, so I must return. Can you go find Olivia and see if there is anything to be done?"

Sharon stops pacing. "Yes." And with that, she quickly heads up town and to the west. Her walks about town have improved how she navigates the streets. She sees the storm damage to Savannah's trees and houses. As she nears the west side, the smoke permeates the air like a morning fog with an odor. People are moving away from the area even as she moves closer to the blaze.

She sees a group of people and heads toward them. A

fireman shouts to her, "Stay clear." She sees a woman in a nurse's uniform being pulled away from a bulky form under a blanket on the side of the street. The woman is trying to free herself from two men who are holding both her arms and are dragging her away from the fire. The woman screams, "No!" And Sharon realizes that the woman is Olivia. Without thinking, Sharon pushes through the people evacuating the area and reaches Olivia.

"Let her be," she says and grabs Olivia's shoulders. The men back-off as Olivia crumbles into Sharon's arms. Her fainting causes Sharon to ease her down to the ground. "Water, give me some water." Sharon grabs the trouser legs of a man standing near her. He quickly snatches a bucket and hurries it to Sharon. Lifting the hem of her skirt, she douses the cloth into the bucket and smooths Olivia's face. Then, with a cupped hand, she trickles water into Olivia's mouth. Olivia opens her eyes and coughs.

"There, there," says Sharon as Olivia attempts to rise. Sharon puts her hand on Olivia's arm and keeps her on the ground. "Let's wait a minute and see if you can stand."

The bucket has disappeared, and Sharon knows she needs to get Olivia away from the blaze and the form under the blanket. The young man who came to find Olivia is in the bucket line, feeding water buckets to the others to help the firemen put out the fire. Sharon calls to him. "Young man, help me, please."

When he sees Olivia on the ground, he runs over. "Olivia, Olivia." She looks up at him and begins to cry.

Sharon has been kneeling but now stands. "Help me get her standing. Let's move her away from the fire."

Together, they grab each of her arms and position her so she is on her feet. She is weak and still crying, but they manage to move her down the block. A large group of women are huddled on the corner. When they see Sharon and the boy walking Olivia toward them, they open their arms and take in

Olivia, covering her with their shawls. As a group, they walk away, and Sharon stands alone in the street. She has no idea who these women are, but they must know Olivia.

Sharon is suddenly exhausted. Her efforts to help Olivia have sapped her energy. She backs up to a low stone wall and sits down. She looks down the street and sees that the fire has been subdued and is now just embers and smoke. The firemen continue to work and put water on the charred wood structure. They will not leave until every ember is cold.

"Sharon? Is that you, Sharon?" Lucas stops in front of her and kneels beside her. She looks at him, and suddenly, there is nothing to do but cry. The tears start slowly but then turn into loud sobs. Lucas sits on the wall, puts his arm behind her, and cradles her head onto his shoulder. She sobs louder and louder. There is no stopping the torrent of tears, and as she cries, she begins to cough. The smoke has gotten to her. She is finding it hard to breathe. Lucas, with his arm around her, raises her and begins walking down through the streets, heading toward the hospital where he had taken her that first day. Finally, the air clears as they move away from the fire, and she can breathe more easily. Lucas continues to hold her gently as they walk.

"Where are we going?" he asks.

"To Mrs. Schultz's boarding house near the hospital." She is aware that his arms are around her. He has strong arms and has been kind to let her cry so heavily on his shoulder. However, she is nervous about anyone seeing her in public being dependent on him. She stops. "I am fine," she says. She loosens her arms from his grip, straightens her skirt, and runs her fingers through her hair. As Lucas leans closer to her to look at her eyes, she says, "Really, I'm fine."

Slowly, the two walk to Mrs. Schultz's boarding house. Lucas asks, "Why were you at the fire? Most people go in the opposite direction."

"We got a message that Olivia's fiancé was hurt in the fire.

Mrs. Schultz was needed at the hospital, so I went to find Olivia and see if I could help. I found Olivia in front of a form on the ground covered with a blanket. I got her to some women who knew her and ushered her away from the fire." Sharon turns to Lucas. "You were there. Do you know who was under the blanket?"

Lucas takes his notebook out of his coat pocket and flips over several pages. "Yes, John Flannery."

10

Monday morning, the week begins as usual, with the nurses coming in quietly for breakfast, all except Olivia. The nurses are silent. Sharon sits with her hands in her lap. She knows why Olivia is not present, but she doesn't know if the nurses know why Olivia is missing. Then, as the food platters are passed around, they are interrupted by Sister Mary Joyce coming in through the kitchen door. Every woman looks up. Sister Mary Joyce stands with her hands folded in front of her. The whiteness of her habit stands out against the ornate dining room with its brocades, satins, and linens. Sharon places her hands on the table on either side of her plate. Though she knows the news the nun intends to share, she wants to brace herself.

"My dear ladies," begins Sister Mary Joyce, "you may have noticed that Olivia is absent today. Olivia is with her family. Yesterday, during the fire, her fiancé, John Flannery, died of smoke inhalation. He had gone into a burning house for a second time to rescue another person."

Katrina stands up abruptly, knocking over her chair and rushing out of the dining room in tears. Vivian stands but says to the women at the table, "Excuse me, I need to see about Katrina." As she leaves, Mrs. Schultz nods to Sister Mary Joyce. "Please go on. Katrina and Vivian are Olivia's roommates."

"This is a time when we need to be together. Some sisters will be in the parlor tonight, offering support you may need. The funeral is planned for Wednesday." Sister Mary Joyce bows her head. "May God bless John's family and Olivia during this time of loss and give all of us the strength we need in this difficult time. Amen."

Sharon slowly walks to work. Because of the heat, she eats her lunch at her desk. She thinks about love and loss. She remembers hearing Cahey express his grief at having lost Micil to tuberculosis before he left Ireland. Cahey had recited the sentence from Tennyson's elegy to his friend: "It is better to have loved and lost than to never have loved at all."

Her thoughts get complicated. She needs more time to process; therefore, she walks a different way back to the boarding house that evening. She receives a note from Lucas asking to talk with her. She throws the note in the trash bin. She does not know what love is, and she certainly does not know the kind of loss that Cahey and Olivia have experienced. She knows she needs to concentrate on her job and learn the business quickly. She has no time for love. She has nothing to say to anyone about loss.

The funeral is on Wednesday, but many of the nurses cannot go because they are needed at the hospital to tend to the burns and cuts many men had gotten in taking care of the fire. Mrs. Schultz goes but has little to say at the Wednesday Bible reading in the parlor. All she says is, "Life can be unpredictable and challenging." She asks Gertrude to play "It is Well with My Soul."

Gertrude pauses, looks down at the keyboard, and begins to play. The women sing the first verse and chorus but cannot sing more.

"When peace like a river, attendeth my way,
When sorrows like sea billows roll
Whatever my lot, thou hast taught me to say
It is well, it is well, with my soul

"It is well
With my soul
It is well, it is well with my soul."

Gertrude continues to play but switches to just the chorus as many women silently stand and form a circle in the parlor, standing close to each other. No one is singing. When Gertrude stops playing, the women walk silently out of the parlor to their rooms upstairs. Mrs. Schultz remains sitting in her chair. As Sharon walks to the door, she sees tears running down Mrs. Schultz's face. She stops.

"Mrs. Schultz, how are you?"

"I'm fine," she says as the tears fall.

Concentrating on work, Sharon is more confident that she is grasping the shipping company's concepts and is now keeping up with her colleagues in posting receipts. Each man in the office focuses on their work and leaves as quickly as possible when they hear the seven o'clock chimes. She knows that dinner is waiting in the oven for her, and since she has nothing else or anyone waiting for her, she finishes her tasks. She is eager to do well and maybe even gain more responsibilities. Though she has talked with more of the nurses in the boarding house, and they have invited her to go with them to visit Olivia on Sunday to see how she is getting along, she decides not to go. This is a time for close friends and family. Immediately after Mass on Sunday, the nurses leave to see Olivia. Mrs. Schultz and Sharon walk back to the house.

There on the porch is Lucas. He stands abruptly when the two women walk up the steps.

"May I help you?" asks Mrs. Schultz.

Sharon turns to Mrs. Shultz. "This is Lucas Laurent, a reporter for the *Savannah Morning News*. I met him on my first day here. He helped me with directions."

"I will go to my office then and prepare next week's menus." She exits quickly.

Sharon has not yet gotten up on the porch. "Why are you here?"

Lucas takes off his hat with a flourish. "You will not answer my note, and I want to talk to you. Please, sit and give me a minute." He points to the chair next to him.

Sharon steps up and crosses to sit in the rocking chair. Lucas places his hat on the side table and sits beside Sharon, who is looking at him, waiting.

"I am confused. Why would you not agree to meet with me? Please tell me why. Is it something I said or did?"

Sharon looks away from Lucas to focus on the street, where people are busy going about their Sunday afternoons. Couples walk arm in arm. A young boy pedals a bicycle languidly alongside a woman pushing a perambulator. Two elderly men stroll and talk furtively as though their thoughts must not be said aloud but shared only with the other. She is watching the scene unfold in front of her, but inside, she is thinking. How does she tell Lucas that she is afraid of what can happen to someone when their heart is broken? What happens to her when her heart falls for someone who doesn't feel the same way, like

Cahey, or they die, like Olivia's John? How does she tell Lucas that her fear is deep-rooted?

She was born in poverty on the Lower East Side of New York but has been given a great opportunity to build a career and to make her way independently in a society that says she should choose a husband. She came all this way to be strong and on her own. She has this chance to concentrate on her career and does not want to lose it. Once she is financially secure, then she can think about having someone in her life.

With his eyes still watching her, she turns to him. "I thank you for reaching out to me after the fire." She sees Lucas watching her with his eyes slightly closed, his face tense as he struggles to hear and understand what she is saying. She sees his struggles but continues. "Everything is new for me here in Savannah, so different from my life in New York." Lucas starts to speak, but Sharon raises her hand in a gesture to wait. "I came for a new job and a new way of life. I must put my energies there and learn about Savannah." She pauses and looks back out into the street.

"And since I know Savannah, I can help introduce you to what makes Savannah special."

Sharon keeps her eyes on the street. Lucas leans forward and places his hand on hers, resting on the arm of the rocking chair. She looks at his hand covering hers and gently pulls her hand away, placing it in her lap with her purse.

Lucas stands abruptly. "I see." He takes two long strides to leave the porch. He remembers his hat, stalks back, grabs the hat, pulls it tightly on his head, and then exits down the steps. As he stomps down the street, Sharon remains sitting and refocuses her eyes to see that the street is suddenly empty. No people are strolling, walking, riding, talking. The street is empty, and so is she.

"Lucas," she calls. "Wait!"

He pauses but does not turn towards her.

"Please, let's talk." Sharon goes down the steps and catches up with him. She tucks her arm in his and gently pulls him to walk with her. Lucas is reluctant and ambles beside her instead of striding as he normally walks. Sharon starts slowly and reiterates her need to stay focused on her job. However, she suggests a plan. She will spend her workweek learning and focusing on work. On Sunday, they will meet up after Mass to see Savannah. At the corner, Lucas picks up the speed of their walk.

"This is Sunday; let's see Savannah," says Lucas.

"Not today. I have not prepared for the work week yet. Next Sunday, I promise."

Lucas pats her hand tucked under his arm. "Okay, next Sunday."

11

Their first Sunday outing is to Johnson Square.

"Johnson Square was the first square laid out in the city. You see the Germania Bank over there?"

Sharon does see a tall building with another taller building next to it. Both are banks and though their architecture may be unique, Sharon is bored.

"And that big white building on the corner of Bull and St. Julian Streets is the Pulaski House Hotel. Visitors to the city stay at the Pulaski or the DeSoto Hotel."

The hotel gets her interest. As they walk past the Pulaski, Sharon peers in through the front door. On the wall next to the door is a four-page pamphlet, framed and posted behind little glass doors. The first page is a photographic image of the hotel taken from across the street. After that, there is a menu of what is offered in the hotel restaurant, a wine list, and finally, a schedule of arrivals and departures of trains and boats.

"They have a tonsorial parlor," Lukas boasts.

Sharon raises her eyebrows. "And what is a tonsorial parlor?"

"A place where men can have a shave and a haircut."

"That's a barber shop."

"Yes, okay, a barber shop."

They walk to the riverfront, and Sharon learns about its history and the fires.

Lucas is precise. "The bluffs along the riverfront have a series of retaining walls that overlook the Savannah River constructed by Michael Cash. It is called the Factor's Walk Wall and is composed primarily of ballast rocks from Ireland."

Sharon gestures to the far end of the dock. "That's where I disembarked from the steamship."

"That's right." Without a connection, he continues with his information. "Cash was from County Wexford, Ireland. There are seven carved markers on the wharf bearing the legend' M. Cash Builder.'"

"Why is it called the Factor's Walk?"

They are walking down the cobblestone Factor's Walk and looking at the storefront businesses facing the retaining walls built by Cash. Lucas had written an article on the importance of the merchants and businesses along Factor's Walk after the last time the buildings burned. The newspaper wanted to emphasize the businesses' strengths located along the river-front as responsible for Savannah's financial growth. These businesses relied on the factor system.

"The factor system developed between the West Indies and England made it possible for a wealthy man to set his son up with a plantation in the West Indies. An agent in Liverpool or London would secure everything needed to have the plantation up and running before the son even arrived. These factor agents are involved in many industries, but the cotton factors are king in the South. They set the price for cotton, and cotton planters rely on them to sell their crops." He stops midway down the walk and points up. "See the iron bridges overhead?"

"You mean the pedestrian bridges?"

"Yes, okay, the pedestrian bridges. These were constructed

so that the factors could stand above the wagons of cotton and estimate price and amounts."

"These were not constructed to assist workers in accessing the riverfront buildings' upper stories?" asks Sharon.

"No, originally, it was only for the factors to use. Other walkways were constructed later to connect them. And that brings us to the stores below the iron bridges. Since the factors also purchase supplies for the planters, they need warehouses to store goods. That's what these lower stories of the buildings along this walkway are for."

Lucas explains that cotton is the crop that allows the factor system to be the most developed and powerful. He supports his comments with local historical evidence. Eli Whitney's invention of the cotton gin in 1793 on a plantation outside of Savannah made Georgia's economy blossom, and Savannah, as a port city, grew financially.

Sharon tries to listen as Lucas continues talking during their long walk. She understands how important cotton is to the South's economy. She did not equate its importance to the fact that it is a nonperishable product that can be at sea for long periods, can be exposed to the elements, and is not destroyed with long delays. She also did not know that Georgia is one of the leading cotton producers in the country. And, as Savannah is a major seaport on the Atlantic, it has a reputation of being ranked as the top cotton seaport.

Sharon hides a yawn behind her hand and tucks behind her ear a strand of her black hair that has come loose from the breeze from the river. Sharon wants to know more about Savannah than just the squares and architectural history. Where are the stories about the people? She remains silent.

Lucas explains that the ties between the cotton factors and the planters are intimate, confidential, and lifelong. Millions of dollars have been advanced by Southern factors upon the mere personal word of the planter, with no formal security at all and with only a memorandum to witness the amounts involved. "And as an accountant, I think you can figure out that based on this relationship, a unique basis of agricultural credit has been established."

Lucas got her attention with the money part, but she finally had to ask, "What about the people who work in the fields or load the agricultural products into the ships? Are they part of the system? Do they have a say in the market?"

"Of course, we all have a job to do, don't we?"

"So, what you are saying is as long as people have a job, the system is good for all?"

"Exactly!"

"My family works. My sisters work in a shirt factory in New York. Their wages cannot pay the rent, food, and clothing for their families. They have a job but no say in the long hours, the conditions, and the lack of child care so they can work. They have no voice in the market."

Lucas clears his throat. "I'm just describing how the system works."

"And what is your role as a reporter in this economic system?"

"I provide people with information to make political or economic decisions."

"And who gives you this information, these facts?"

"Why, the businessmen themselves. They are very upfront and available to explain. By knowing the facts, people can vote in elections or expand their businesses."

"You mean men can vote, but, as a woman, I cannot vote. Since I no longer have a business interest, why should I be invested in learning the news printed in the newspaper?"

"Well, we also print advertisements and notices of sales and entertainment. That should be good for you. Women don't need to know information like men do."

Lucas slows his gait to match Sharon's now much slower

walk. Her eagerness to learn about the city has been dulled by Lucas' strong opinions on the role of women in society. Though she did not have the right to vote in New York, the men in her life, Cahey, Frederick, and her father, always talked with her about politics, business, and the direction the society needed to go. The conversations were never just with the men. She was always included, and her opinions seemed to matter.

What one does or even what gender you are should not matter when decisions are being made for society's good, thinks Sharon. All people need to have a voice. She pauses at the end of the Factor's Walk. There are stone steps, dozens of them leading up to Bay Street. She thinks about what it must be like to walk up these steps with packages and goods in long skirts, as many before her must have had to do during their workdays.

Lucas pauses. "We can turn here and walk back the way we came so it will be easier for you."

Though Sharon is happy the pedestrian bridges and ramps have been created, she starts up the steep steps. "I can do this if you can," she says over her shoulder.

She and Lucas walk up the steps, all thirty-two of them, and turn back toward Bull Street. She is not out of breath thanks to all the walking she has done in New York and all the stairs she has climbed as a hotel maid. As they approach her workspace, Sharon thinks about the fire that ended John's life, the fires that burned the riverfront buildings, and the one that burned the cathedral. Lucas has remained silent.

"I'm told that the building I work in is fireproof, a new standard."

"In Savannah? Nothing is fireproof," says Lucas. "Be careful. Stay by the window."

Encouraged by her inquiry, Lucas points to the building where she works and begins his "touring voice."

Sharon stifles another yawn hidden behind her gloved

hands, but Lucas is oblivious to her body language. He points out her workspace, the brick building with the mansard roof, ornamental crossings of iron with the balconies, and window caps made of the same iron. He flourishes his hat to indicate the building in front of them. "The whole building has all the modern improvements of gas, water, vaults, etc., and no expense has been spared to make it complete in every respect."

"Sounds grand," says Sharon.

"And those words were published in the *Savannah Morning News*."

"I see, and I assume you wrote those words."

"One can only guess who wrote them since we do not use bylines."

"You write nicely."

"Thank you, ma'am." Lucas bows.

Next, they look at the Savannah Cotton Exchange, which was built in 1886 and was one of the first major buildings to be constructed over a public street. The building is red brick with a terra cotta façade, iron window lintels, and copper finials and copings. An example of the Romantic Revival period, the Exchange's massive front pocket doors are red oak and, according to Lucas, weigh about 450 pounds. In the front of the exchange, an elaborate iron fence with detailed medallions of famous statesmen and authors encloses a statue of a griffin and a landscaped fountain.

Since City Hall is at the head of Bull Street but is closed on a Sunday, Lucas starts to usher her up through one of the three wide-arched ways when Sharon interrupts. "Can we find some water? I am thirsty."

"There's more." Lucas takes a breath and leaps down the steps to point out designs outside the building. "There is a considerable amount of ornamentation in the way of statuary."

"I'm sure there is, but we don't have to learn about it all today."

Lucas puts his hat back on. "Let's go get some refreshments." He takes Sharon's elbow and leads her to Collins-Grayson Company, a grocer and candy factory on the southeast corner of East Broad and Liberty. They sit at the counter and have a lemonade. Then, they muse through the rows of produce and candy jars. As they start to leave, Lucas sees an advertisement tacked on the wall near the front door.

Collins, J.S. will have a picnic at his pasture near Collinsville, the Meadows, on July 15.

He points to the advertisement. "A picnic! We'll go."

Sharon stares at the advertisement. "How will we get there? How far is Collinsville?"

"Not far. We'll take the trolley."

A picnic might be nice out in a meadow. She could see some of the areas around Savannah. "Okay, I will put together the picnic."

Lucas smiles and escorts her out onto the Savannah streets.

As the weeks pass, Sharon is true to her word and joins Lucas to meander from square to square, park to park, and building to building. One Sunday venture has them going to the Trustees' Garden in the Old Fort Post ward. There, he points out Kehoe Iron Works, which employs 150 men, covers ten acres with river access, and was built by a tenant farmer from northern County Wexford, William Kehoe. With his accumulated wealth, Kehoe built not one but two residential mansions on Columbia Square using iron architectural accents from his business. There is a lot to talk about and not much to see, so Lucas has them sit on a bench in the square as he shares what he knows about Kehoe.

"He was very active here in the Irish community belonging to the Hibernian Society of Savannah and a branch of the Irish National Land League. He's a member of your Cathedral of St.

John the Baptist, and when the fire destroyed much of the cathedral in 1898, Kehoe served on the rebuilding committee and contributed to the new font."

Sharon is hungry. They have walked about and stared at architecture for as long as she can bear. "Where can we get food?"

"Ah, I see you are after my riches."

"No, I am after something to put in my stomach."

"Sean's Bar is around the corner."

"I am suggesting food, not drink."

"Come and learn."

They walk to the next block and around the corner to Sean's Bar. The double wooden doors at the entrance have carved designs of monks on the door. They enter into a well-lit main room with a diamond-shaped bar taking up most of the room. The tables and bar are well-polished oak that reflects the overhead lights and sunshine from the windows. Matching oak chairs with high backs are filled with men and women. There are two stools empty at the bar. Lucas leads the way.

"Two beers, please."

Sharon sits stiffly at the bar. She wants food. When the drinks arrive, so does the food: two bowls of soup, a boiled egg, and a reed bird, fried and crisp. Sharon eyes the food.

"See? I said I would show you. In saloons, you order a beer, and food comes with it—all for five cents." Lucas takes the beers and one of the soups but pushes the other soup, the egg, and the bird to Sharon. "Would you like water?"

"Yes, please."

12

On the Sunday of the picnic, Sharon stops by a grocery and purchases cooked sausages, two baguettes, cheese, pickles, and cookies. She borrows two mason jars for water, napkins, and a blanket for a ground cloth from Mrs. Schultz. Her steps are quick. She is to have an excursion out of town and away from work.

She meets Lucas at the station, and they take the next trolley to the Meadows. Lucas explains that he believes that Collins, as a businessman, is having the picnic to encourage folks to invest in a new housing development being considered in the Collinsville area. Lucas is eager to see it as well.

Sharon is confused. "I thought the picnic was for fun," she says.

"It'll be great. You'll see. Just wait."

Sharon's basket is smaller than the baskets of families who crowd into the trolley car. An older couple both smile at her, but then they both look away. Their two young girls make faces at each other. Dressed in matching frocks with their hair in braids and adorned with ribbons, the girls giggle and hide behind their parents.

At the end of the trolley line, everyone disembarks. Lucas carries the basket and blanket, guiding Sharon through the crowds and onto the meadow. Along the entrance into the meadow are tents with tables piled with brochures. Men and women stand nearby and hand brochures to those who pass by and say, "Welcome to Collinsville."

Sharon doesn't read any of the brochures. She accepts them and keeps following Lucas. She sees a tent representing the county. A large map illustrates the planned neighborhood's lots, streets, and lighting. One of the representatives says to Sharon, "I'll be happy to answer any of your questions about building codes." Sharon says nothing and continues to walk.

"See? I was right. Collins wants folks to build out here and create a new neighborhood," Lucas says as he spreads out the blanket in his chosen spot in the meadow.

Sharon places the brochures on the blanket, sits, and opens the picnic basket. Her attention, though, is attracted to a flatbed wagon in the center of the meadow with a small group of musicians tuning up. As more and more folks settle in, the musicians begin to play. Sharon is suddenly transported back to New York. The band plays songs written by George M. Cohan. Her friends in New York had taken her to see one of Cohan's Broadway shows, *Little Johnny Jones*. She hummed the tunes from that show, "Give My Regards to Broadway" and "Yankee Doodle Boy," for days afterward. And now here is a band playing these very tunes.

She hums along with the band as she brings out the picnic food. Though she is happy to have a friend like Lucas, who has graciously shown her around Savannah, she misses the camaraderie developed among the New York immigrants who banded together to create a new identity. Without their support and encouragement, she would not be here today with a new job, a new place to live, and new responsibilities.

"Sharon, you seem off in another world. Where are you?"

Sharon shakes her head a little to dislodge the memories she has conjured during the band's opening numbers of Cohan's songs and glances at Lucas. "I'm here; I'm just caught up in the music. It's from a Broadway play my friends and I went to last year. It was fabulous—George M. Cohan's *Little Johnny Jones*."

"Well, my dear, *Little Johnny Jones* was here this spring! We are not so far behind the fabulous New York scene."

Sharon's smile hints at more than just relating to the music from a Broadway show. She acknowledges that having been raised in New York, the rest of the world will always be compared to what she had experienced there. A thought flickers through her brain. Can that be the same way people see the country where they were born? Is that why her Irish friends are so loyal to memories of Ireland? The same is true for her parents. Her mother is doing exactly what she did in Ireland— taking in sewing and washing for others. Sharon is well aware that her father has mourned leaving Ireland and has spent too much time with his pals in the pubs reminiscing and telling tales. Although, he does bring in a little money by playing music in the pubs. This new insight helps her understand.

Lucas picks up the brochures and begins to share information with Sharon. The brochure is for the Aladdin Kit Home company out of Bay City, Michigan, for "pre-cut" home kits to build cottages. The next one is for the B. C. Mills Timber and Trading Company on home kits and commercial buildings. A third one is for the Bennett Home and Lumber Company for Better-built Kit Homes & Ready-Cut Kit Homes. He looks at some of the photographs and floor plans.

"The companies selling housing kits suggest that they save the 'would-be home builder' money by spreading an architect's fees over a thousand similar house plans and by being the only source for all the necessary building materials, including nails and two coats of finish paint. The designs are standardized to maximize efficiency and reduce waste in materials and labor," he reads. "Sales pitches. I told you Collins wants to build out here."

Sharon nods and looks out at the crowds.

Lucas continues to read. "According to the brochures, lumber and hardware are purchased in bulk. The factories have skilled employees and special machines to cut difficult pieces such as rafters and staircases. Lumber is pre-cut to length, guaranteed to fit, ready to nail, and labeled for easy assembly."

Sharon is not even listening as Lucas drones on and on, reading the brochures out loud. She hears flashes of words: "Floor joists, sub-flooring, studs, rafters, shingles, stucco, plaster, columns, blah, blah, blah, blah . . ."

Lucas stops reading. "I must say, they seem to have thought of everything," He looks at Sharon for agreement.

Her nod is all she offers besides the plate of food. They are silent for a while. The noise level escalates with so many people all around them. Sharon does not want to discuss new houses for families, so she changes the subject.

"I saw the theatre when we passed by the square. Do you see the shows?"

"Occasionally, I have to review a lecture or a reading that is held in the theatre. We have a staff reporter who sees the plays and reviews them. The tickets are a bit pricey. Tickets are a dollar and a half or even two dollars. You do know that a newspaper reporter does not make much money? Two theatre tickets would cost me twenty percent of my weekly wage."

Sharon is taken by surprise. She did not know how much money anyone made but her. No one ever discusses salary. She feels her fair skin turning red, not from the sun but from being ignorant of what things cost. She knew in New York but not here, and often Cahey or Frederick, who were businessmen, paid for their friend's outings.

"I understand," she says. "I would need to save up for

several weeks and not have any other expenses if I were to purchase a theatre ticket. And, I have heard that my paycheck is half what the other accountants earn in the same office," she says.

"That's right and as it should be." Lucas is breaking bread into bite-size pieces.

Sharon stops eating. "Why do you say that?"

"Well, a man has to take care of his family and house expenses and whatever may fall their way."

"You are a man who has no family and no house expenses. Why do you earn more than a woman doing the same job as you do?"

"Sharon, a woman can't be a reporter and cover the events I cover. She can't be out at night at meetings and lectures by herself. A reporter must get all the details right and be able to write. Being a reporter is a man's job."

"That's what they told Christine Ross about being a CPA, yet she passed the exam at the top of the class and has been a licensed CPA for eight years in New York."

"I'm sure there are exceptions. And since I don't know the exam, they might have even given her an easier one." Lucas breaks off another piece of the baguette and begins to eat.

Sharon sits silently and brushes off her skirt. She stands. "I need to stretch my legs." She walks toward the musicians.

At the meadow's edge, she is just behind the flatbed wagon. She feels the music in her feet when the band plays a fast jazz number. She has missed music since coming to Savannah. She tries to be in the parlor every evening after dinner to hear Gertrude practice. The pieces Gertrude plays are often mellow and moving. They are classical and not like the ragtime from Tin Pan Alley in New York or the Irish tunes her papa plays with the bands in the *cèilidhs* on the Lower East Side.

Out in the meadow, Sharon looks about her and sees families, couples, and groups of children running and playing tag among the people sitting and standing. Some people in the meadow look out toward the trees with the lot map in front of them. Others are reading the brochures handed to them. There is nothing peaceful about the people occupying the meadow; it feels chaotic. The people didn't come to share an afternoon of music and food in the country but to bid and declare which lot they wanted to purchase. Most are not even aware of the music.

The noise is more discordant walking behind the wagon with the band. A sudden shriek from a child running near her makes her jump. The music is loud and boisterous. The cacophony of people talking over the music and shouting to others, the flurry of people moving, and children running pell-mell about her makes her dizzy. She clutches her skirt and moves toward the trees.

How could people live in a meadow and spend their whole day inside one house without stores nearby for daily shopping and only getting information from the newspaper or neighborhood gossip? Her breath gets more uneven. She is sure she is about to faint when Lucas approaches. He catches her elbow and she leans into him.

"Sharon, are you all right? You don't look well."

She says nothing. She looks frantically around her. Lucas moves her gently back to their blanket and assists her to sit down. "Here is some water. The sun is probably too much for you out in the middle of this meadow."

Sharon sips on the water but knows that it has nothing to do with the sun and everything to do with not fitting in. This is not what she wants.

13

Sharon returns to her work and the boarding house. The nurses are seldom seen even in the evenings, as there is much to learn at the hospital, and each seems to want to graduate. All of them are from the Savannah area and have family nearby. The program takes two years and includes classroom work and a lot of experience working in the hospital. Her interactions after hours are with Mrs. Shultz and catching a practice session by Gertrude in the parlor in the evening when she spends a few minutes writing letters to New York.

Sharon has little contact with her roommates and the other women in the boarding house. Breakfasts are short and quiet, with each woman preparing for her day. Olivia returns to the program but is withdrawn and seems to concentrate only on what she has to do at the time. The memory of the fire and John's death seems to hang over the women. Sharon has no idea what to say to Olivia and remains silent, too.

As the heat of the summer increases in August, she gets word from her boss that an officer of Graves & Son will be arriving soon and they must prepare. She needs to work with this officer to transition the accounts from the Savannah office to the County Wexford office. In the meantime, Sharon works with Tad to create a plan for the transition. She must learn the accounting procedures used by the firm. She does not know how long preparation will take, much less what he might want to know. Therefore, she needs to understand the current system to be able to answer any questions he might have. She counts the number of ledgers the firm has. She divides by the number of days she has before the officer arrives. She must master these many pages each day to finish in time. For a moment, she stares at the wainscot in the office as though it will assure her that she can get this done right. She shakes her head and begins.

By the time she finishes, the day is gone, and another late hour has been clocked.

Marleen comes to her one morning. "Tad told me to give you a key since you seem determined to stay late. I'll show you how to lock up."

With the late hours and tedious work with the numbers, by the time Sharon gets to the boarding house in the evening, she is too tired to eat and retires to her room. At breakfast, she finds her dinner from the night before wrapped in a tin pail next to her plate. She looks at Mrs. Schultz.

"For your lunch. Food is not to be wasted, is it?" Mrs. Schultz smiles and turns her attention to the other women at the table.

After the meadow excursion, Sharon offers numerous excuses to Lucas for not spending Sunday with him. She has much to do to prepare for the workweek. Gertrude has graciously been working with her on patterns for the two new skirts for the office. They need time on Sunday to sew and plan for other accessories. Sharon needs new hats. Then, on Wednesday after work, she passes by Foye & Eckstein on her walk back to the boarding house. She is window shopping by looking at the garments displayed in the store window and sees a poster on the door. There is to be a reception from eight to ten on Thursday night. Sharon rushes back to the boarding house to find that the women are just ending the Bible reading. Pulling Gertrude aside, Sharon shares the news. Gertrude quickly agrees to meet Sharon at the shop the next evening.

True to her word, Gertrude is waiting outside Foye & Eckstein when Sharon arrives. The friends share a brief hug. As they enter the store, young girls are at the entrance with rattan flower baskets over their arms and present a carnation. Instinctively, Sharon puts the flower to her nose for a whiff of fragrance. She sees a small orchestra tucked around the back of the double staircase leading to the second floor. The musicians are playing a soft but upbeat tune.

Gertrude leans into Sharon's ear and says, "They are playing Haydn's 'Divertimento in D Major.'"

Sharon nods like she understands what Gertrude is telling her. She makes a mental note to follow up with her.

The two-story atrium of the store has been decorated for the reception. Suspended from the second floor and swinging out in front of the entrance is a replica of what a fairy would look like driving a dozen white doves. Throughout the atrium and arranged within the potted greenery are twenty-five canaries strutting their little yellow bodies in elaborate golden cages. The spectacle gets the women's attention, but they focus on why they came to the reception: to buy accessories and fabric for Sharon.

A directory helps the women locate the items. Dress fabrics of wool, silk, and washable fabrics with laces from the cheapest to the finest are on the first floor. Sharon walks by and fingers the skirt fabrics. She looks at the prices, too. Ready-made skirts are ten to forty dollars each. More than she can afford, but she looks them over for style. They find the fabric they both like for the skirts. They choose a thread to match.

The millinery section is on the second floor. As the women walk up the staircase, they see a reception area on the bottom floor behind the orchestra. Gertrude touches Sharon's arm and nods toward the food. They reach the next floor to find hats on shelves and models who walk around and wear the latest fashions. There are buckle hats with garnitures of malines or chiffon and a large buckle or small roses in a nosegay in the front. Other hats are Queen Anne style with pink chiffon streamers tied with rosettes of pink baby ribbon. Sharon slowly walks through the many choices. Finally, Gertrude shows Sharon a wide-brimmed light green wool hat decorated with a plume of peacock feathers. It has a good, solid style that could last through several seasons.

"What might work is to get a basic hat like this, then choose some ribbons and laces and different colored feathers and streamers that can be replaced easily."

Sharon agrees. She purchases the hat but then needs to return downstairs to locate laces and other notions. The women choose various colors to match the skirt fabrics. Sharon decides to wait for more feathers. With the wind and rain in Savannah, she thinks fewer feathers might be better. The orchestra is taking a break, and the canaries can be heard singing melodic songs that they are trained to sing. Only the males sing; the females chirp. The bird songs fill the atrium, and Sharon slows down while she walks to enjoy the birds. The scene makes her feel like she is in a fairyland, and she wants to relish the moment and extend the delight.

She slowly walks, following Gertrude to the reception area. Food is elegantly displayed along several long tables. There are tea sandwiches, white and wheat bread, no crust, and cut-in star and moon shapes to keep with the fairy theme established in the atrium. The sandwiches are filled with flavored butter and cream cheese. Orange and lemon sponge cakes are iced and decorated with green leaves and vines. Chocolate muffin cakes are frosted to look like mushrooms with red and yellow dots. There are popcorn balls and small squares of fudge. A fruit punch is served by several women dressed like fairies. The entire setting is dream-like and Sharon is enchanted.

"What do you think about all of this, Gertrude?"

"I have never seen such extravagance!" she says. "I look everywhere and see something new each time."

The orchestra begins playing again, but Sharon is tired at the end of the day and Gertrude agrees to head to the boarding house with Sharon's purchases. Gertrude talks nonstop to Sharon as they walk back. The reception lifted Sharon's spirits, and she was happy to have Gertrude's company. "Thank you for meeting me."

"I would not have wanted to miss this for the world. The other nurses will be so jealous that they missed it."

"We need to hurry. It's almost nine-thirty."

Once inside the house, they part in the hallway. Sharon finds a vase in the water closet, puts in some water to keep the carnation alive as long as possible, and places it in the middle of the table in the bedroom. Her roommates are nowhere to be seen.

14

The next morning at work, Sharon is called into Tad's office earlier than usual.

"Sharon, I have received word that Connor Murphy will arrive on Sunday morning and will be at the office on Monday. We have only two days to finish the transfer plan."

Sharon nods, pulls her chair up to the desk, and opens a notebook with one of the ledgers. They work through the morning, taking tea at the desk, eating lunch at the desk, and proceeding through the afternoon.

At one point, Tad stands and walks to the window. He stares out at the river. "I should rearrange my desk to be able to look out at the river. I do like all the activity happening out there."

Standing and looking out behind Tad's shoulder, Sharon agrees. "I like having my desk near the front window because I can see the people's traffic and hear the city noises as I work. I feel I am a part of the commerce machinery that makes Savannah function."

Tad turns suddenly and looks at her closely. "I have to say, I was not excited when the company told me they were hiring a woman from New York as part of our accounting team. I had never had a woman accountant. Secretaries, yes, but not an accountant. None of us were that excited to have you join us."

Sharon's face shows her stunned look. Deep red blotches creep up her neck and reach her cheeks. She can feel the heat.

Tad continues. "I had even decided that one of the men on the floor would head up the transition." Tad pauses and walks over to where he keeps a kettle of hot water. He pours two cups of tea.

Sharon is glued to her spot, looking out the window at the river.

Tad brings the tea cups over, places one at Sharon's spot, and goes around the desk to sit with his cup. "However," he continues, "it was evident from the first day that you have mastered most of the procedures. What you needed to learn, you learned quickly. That is when I knew you should be the one to head up the transition." Tad takes a minute and then looks directly at Sharon. "I have not been wrong."

"Thank you." Sharon sits and reaches for her tea. "Shall we continue?"

Tad smiles. "Yes, we should."

On Saturday, they continue to work, pushing through on all the accounts until they have a clear plan for making the transition work. At the end of the day, but early for Sharon, Tad stands up. "That's it, we are ready," he says. "Let's go home, have dinner, and relax until Monday morning. Can you be here a little early?"

"Absolutely." Sharon closes her notebook, stacks the ledgers on the desktop, and stands up to straighten her back. Tad crosses to the hat stand, puts his jacket on, and positions his hat. She laughs at how eager he is to leave. "Go on, say hello to your family. I'll get my things and lock up."

Tad doffs his hat to her. "Have a great walk back. I'll see you early on Monday morning."

Slowly, Sharon walks to her desk in the main room. She has just a few things to do, like straighten the materials on her desk, pick up her satchel, and exit the building. The Naval Store is open until ten most evenings, so being the last one to leave is not a problem with other people around. She sees the security doorman for the Naval Store and wishes him a good evening. However, she notices a change in the light; it is getting darker earlier. She is pleased to be heading back to the boarding house for an earlier-than-usual dinner. As she exits, however, she sees Lucas leaning on a tree across from the pedestrian bridge. He is waiting and smiles when he sees her. She approaches. He begins talking immediately.

"I know that Sunday outings were occupying too much of your time, but I was hoping you were enjoying getting to know Savannah." He stops and waits for Sharon to speak, but she doesn't. She waits. "So, since it is Saturday night, I thought maybe I could walk you back to your room."

Sharon sees the shift in Lucas as he leans first one way and then another on the tree. She has not seen him so agitated. He is always in control, and to her, that is part of her problem with him. She does not want someone else to be in control. She has enjoyed seeing Savannah with Lucas but feels that Lucas wants more of her than she is willing to give. There is still so much more to learn about her career and about who she is.

"Lucas," she begins but sees the frown on his face. "I would very much like you to walk me back. We need to talk."

The frown does not leave his face even though he stops leaning on the tree and adjusts his hat. "Then, let's talk." They begin to walk toward the boarding house.

During the walk, Sharon starts explaining. "I came to Savannah to broaden my career opportunities. I want to get experience working for one company rather than multiple businesses that require different accounting approaches." She glances at Lucas, who is plodding next to her and looking at the ground in front of them. She clears her throat and continues. "I have been taking care of family and friends for many years. I didn't mind and did it freely, but to have a chance to be myself and work to improve myself rather than just make money to pay the bills interests me." She stops talking again. She had hoped this would be a give-and-take kind of conversation, but Lucas was saying nothing.

Then he says, "What do you want as far as a relationship with someone?"

Sharon stops walking, and so does Lucas. "I'm not sure. I come from a large family and understand the obligations and demands that any family has for a woman. I am not ready to make that commitment without a partner who understands me."

As they near the boarding house steps, Lucas stops, takes her arm, and turns her to face him. He kisses her softly at first, then more aggressively. She lifts her face to his and then lowers it so that he cannot see her eyes. Taking his hand, he lifts her chin so that he can see her face. "I hear you, and though I don't like the words I hear, I will wait. Not forever; just long enough for you to see that we might have a life together, a future." With that, he turns and walks away.

Sharon watches him leave. But this time, she doesn't stop him.

15

Sleeping in has never been what Sharon has done. She is up for breakfast and eager to take a walk before Mass. Because of being so occupied with Lucas on Sunday afternoons, she has had to get her clothes and room cleaned before Mass to allow time. Now, she has all day to do exactly what she wants. She decides the first thing is to walk again in Forsyth Park. She needs the enchantment the trees and fountain give her.

The day is to be hot, so she dresses in her coolest linen skirt, an ivy green one with a light green long-sleeve blouse trimmed in green lace at the neck and matching green ribbon bows covering the buttons down the front. Her new hat is perfect with the peacock feathers. She has a brooch with a bright ivy-green stone that she fastens at her neck. Feeling almost giddy at the ridiculous time and effort she has made to be more fashionable, she leaves the boarding house and goes to the park. Strolling along the paths, she finds herself near the bench she had sat on during her first visit to the park. Her favorite part is to watch the birds play in the water.

As she sits, she hears the water splashing and the birds

singing. In her head, she hears an old Irish folk song, a song her mother used to sing to all of the girls at home. Sharon sings out loud.

> "Little bird on my window
> won't you sing me a song
> When you fly over the meadow
> will you bring me along
> La, la, la, la, la, la."

Sharon's face relaxes. She settles into her memories and leans back on the bench. Then she hears a man's voice from behind her.

> "There are beautiful flowers
> to see from up high
> will you please take me with you
> little bird as you fly
> La, la, la, la, la."

She doesn't turn to look at him; she takes the moment and joins him in harmony, as she did with her father.

> "Little bird on my window
> may your songs never end
> I will tell you a secret
> you are my very best friend
> will you please take me with you
> little bird as you fly."

Sharon claps her hands together in her enjoyment of singing the child's song. She turns to look at the man singing with her. He bows. He stands tall in his three-piece beige linen suit. A tan bowler hat covers the top of his red hair. His chiseled jawline and strong brow line make her look at his eyes, green eyes that seem to look inside of her and know who she is without an introduction.

"Hello," he says.

"Hello," says Sharon.

"I remember learning that song as a child."

"Me, too. I also like the song because my father told me that a bird on my window indicates a change is coming."

"Like a sign?"

"Exactly. Maybe even a message from heaven that angels are watching over you."

"Has there been a bird on your window?"

"Not that I have seen, but I keep looking." Then Sharon hears the bells chime. She must hurry or be late for Mass. "I must go." She stands quickly. "Have a good day."

She walks out of the park and to the cathedral. Mrs. Schultz is already there and has saved her seat. Sharon hurriedly straightens her skirt and touches her hair to verify that all the strands are under her hat. Then she sees him again. The man singing with her in the park walks down the side aisle of the cathedral and sits on one of the front-row boxed seats. During Mass, Sharon can barely concentrate and memorizes every movement he makes. She watches how he sits, how he stands. Then Sharon is aware that he is looking at her. He smiles. She smiles back, then ducks her chin and pays more attention to the psalm being read. At the end of the Mass, she joins Mrs. Schultz, and they exit to return to the boarding house. Sharon is disappointed that she does not know who he is, but at least he goes to Mass, so maybe she will see him again.

Her day is full of preparing for work. Gertrude measures the skirts for hems. She shows Sharon how to take the feathers off the hat and insert lace and ribbons. Sharon washes her lingerie, gloves, and blouses and arranges them on the small porch off the sleeping room to dry. She plans to iron the blouses and other clothing with wrinkles in the evening. Washing her laundry and ironing clothes in the basement is cheaper than having the house staff wash and iron them. Sharon tries to finish early since the nurses need access with their limited time outside the hospital. Many of them, however, either pay the housemaid at the boarding house to wash their uniforms and starch their aprons and caps or take them home on the weekend for cleaning.

As Gertrude and Sharon prepare to go to the parlor before dinner, Gertrude stops on the staircase. She has news and has forgotten to tell Sharon. The Savannah Music Club, which meets semi-monthly from September to May, has asked Gertrude to open their season with a solo piano recital.

"I can't believe they have asked me to play! I am not famous like the pianist Fannie Bloomfield Zeisler. She is so talented that she was hired to make piano rolls of various piano compositions, including Chopin's Waltz No. 11 in G minor! Or Julian Walker, who performed at Carnegie Music Hall in New York! Both of them have been guest artists of the Savannah Music Club."

Sharon listens to Gertrude but is also curious about why an established club asked a young woman to open its season. "Do you belong to the Music Club?"

"No, but I have been asked to fill in for the regular pianist when the chorus sings."

"Then they must know how talented you are."

Gertrude stops on the stairs. "I thought they just needed a free program, so they asked a 'nobody.'"

Holding on to the stair rail for support, Sharon laughs. "Do they not have money?"

Tossing her blond hair, which she has down around her shoulders, Gertrude stands tall on the stairs. "Have you seen their membership roster? They have a hundred members including anyone who is somebody in Savannah. One of the founders was Nobel Andrew Hardee. He was a factor, a commission merchant, and a fertilizer dealer. They have to have money."

"Then they chose someone they wish to sponsor. How lucky for you." Sharon circles her arm through Gertrude's, and together, they walk down the stairs to the parlor. Sharon owes everyone in New York a letter, and the time passes quickly. When Gertrude begins packing up her sheet music, Sharon seals the last of her letters. They enter the dining room, where many of the nurses are already sitting. Mrs. Schultz brings in a casserole dish and hands it to Vivian to pass.

"Mrs. Schultz, what is this dish?" asks Vivian, holding her napkin in front of her face as she looks at the casserole dish.

"It's chicken pudding."

Vivian serves herself and passes the dish. "It's delicious," she says after tasting it. "How is it cooked?"

Mrs. Schultz starts sharing the recipe. "First, roast a whole chicken until done and cut the chicken into chunks. Next, make a bechamel sauce."

Alice interrupts. "How do you make a bechamel sauce?"

Mrs. Schultz pauses, then explains. "To make a bechamel sauce, melt half a cup of butter in a saucepan, whisk in half a cup of flour to thicken, then mix in the chicken stock to cook until the sauce thickens. That's the bechamel sauce."

Vivian interrupts this time. "We call that gravy."

"Yes, I would assume many cultures use the same type of 'gravy,'" says Mrs. Schultz. "To continue—in a separate bowl, beat four large eggs and two cups of milk. Pour this mixture into a pan that you will put into the oven. Add the bechamel sauce and blend. Then add salt, pepper, thyme, and parsley. Add the chicken and mix well. Bake until a knife inserted in the center comes out clean. That's how you make chicken pudding."

The nurses pass the chicken pudding, and each takes a

small spoonful to taste. Bowls of okra and butterbean succotash, pinkeye purple hull peas, and homemade pickles are passed. Sharon enjoys the Sunday dinners since she works late. She misses the camaraderie that is developing among the women. Though she has not spent a lot of time with her roommates, they are cordial and have offered a few pointers for where to eat at lunch or on weekends. They also suggested several pubs where she could go on the weekend, but Sharon has not had the time to take them up on going with them since she has been spending so much time with Lucas. Tonight, though, if they ask, she plans on joining them.

The cake is served, but the women, though they exert a lot of energy at the hospital, are all watching what they eat and take only a small sliver for a bite of something sweet. As soon as they are done, the table is cleared, and the dining room empties.

Sharon disappears up the steps to her room and sees her roommates preparing to go out. The carnation on the table is still vibrant and stands tall. When she enters, Alice says, "We are going out, and you are welcome to come with us if you like."

Sharon sits at the table. "Yes, I will go with you tonight."

The women glance at each other and then back at Sharon. "Okay, but you must not wear a hat. We plan to dance." Both of the women giggle, straighten their skirts, and tuck their hair with numerous pins.

Sharon checks her hair. She wears it in a bun most days. Her black hair hangs so straight that it is difficult to curl around anything; it is easiest to pull it into a bun. She gets her purse and confirms she has cash. There might be a cost for ale or lemonade. She wants to be prepared.

The women walk quickly to the Old Fort Post, where Sean's Bar is located. "The bar is named for the oldest bar in the world," says Alice, "located in Athlone, Ireland, on the banks of the Shannon River in the middle of Ireland, halfway between Galway and Dublin."

Sharon has no idea where this is since she has never been to Ireland. Neither of the women with her have been either; they are just reciting what they have been told. Sharon does not tell them she has been to lunch at the pub with Lucas. Walking a few steps behind them, Sharon notices that Sarah's brown hair is in a French twist, as is Alice's. The women are often hard to tell apart. They do so many things together and resemble each other. Both are slim with pasty white skin, so pale that Sharon's whiteness seems almost beige compared to them.

They arrive at the bar. The women go around to a side door, knock, and are let in. They find a table in the corner. When a server passes, the women all order a glass of ale for five cents. The music has started. The pub looks different at nighttime. It reminds Sharon of the many bars her papa played in on the Lower East Side of New York.

Two young men come over and invite Alice and Sarah to dance the next reel. The two women continue to dance while Sharon sits alone at the table. She is not enjoying being alone. She sips her ale and tries to focus on the music. She watches the people who are dancing and enjoying themselves. She looks down at the oak table top and imagines she is back in New York with her father playing. She is dancing with her friend and boss, Cahey. They dance each tune until they are exhausted. She is caught up in the memory and the music. As she hums softly, she looks up to see the man in the park coming toward her. She ducks her head and waits. Then he is next to her. She can feel his eyes looking at her.

"I like dancing, but I also like singing. Were you humming just now?"

Sharon looks up and sees his eyes smiling. "Yes, I like the tunes."

"This tune goes way back to the Ireland of yesteryear."

"You like old folk songs?"

"I do. And history."

"I was told that this bar was named for the oldest bar in the world. Do you know anything about that?"

"I do." He motions to a chair to ask if he can sit. Sharon nods.

"Sean's Bar goes back to nine hundred AD. It is located next to the ruins of a twelfth-century Norman Castle. It opened as an inn to accommodate travelers on the river who had to cross various fords in a deserted, impassable area. The town of Athlone developed around Sean's Bar as a crossing point. Nearby were ancient monasteries of monks who had been producing whiskey since the sixth century. Thus, Sean's Bar became famous for its quality whiskey."

Sharon listens and hears his heavy Irish accent. "You must be from Ireland."

"Yes, I am." They sit quietly, listen to the music, and watch the dancers.

At the next quadrille, he stands up, gestures for her, and they join another group on the floor. They dance and twirl and then dance again. He is as smart a dancer as Cahey. She does not know where the electricity comes from whenever he takes her hand or touches her arm. All she knows is that the shivers it gives her mix with the dancing and the music. Finally, they take a break and return to the table where Alice and Sarah sit.

"We are waiting for you," Alice says to Sharon as Sarah nods to the man with Sharon. "It's time to leave." They pick up their shawls and head to the side door. "Come on, we have to go," they call back to Sharon.

Quickly, she looks at the man from the park. Sharon can hear the bell chimes and knows they must hurry. "I have to leave. Thank you for sharing the history and for the dance; I very much needed to dance tonight." And with that, she joins her roommates at the door. They hurry down the street to the boarding house. She had wanted to sit and relish his eyes looking at her; instead, she was always hurrying away from him.

Undressing in the dark and then in bed, she lays awake for a long time, remembering his face and going over and over anything he said. She still has no idea who he is. They never got around to introducing themselves.

16

U p early, Sharon dresses and prepares to leave for work. She goes to the kitchen door and sees Mrs. Schultz preparing a biscuit with bacon and a fried egg for her to take since she is leaving early. With the breakfast in hand, she begins her walk to the office. She thinks about the man from the park. She has no idea how long he might be in Savannah, who he is, or even if she will see him again. All she knows is that she likes being in his presence.

She stops and buys apples and pears. She and Tad often need some fortification during the day. She opens the office door with her key and settles in at her desk to eat breakfast and sort through her workbook for notes on the upcoming transition. Tad arrives and greets her. He hurries into his office to do his preparation. Sharon goes to the women's water closet located through the Naval Store. When she returns, she hears Tad talking with someone in his office. She passes near the door and Tad calls out to her.

"Sharon, come in, please. I want you to meet our guest."

Sharon enters and Tad makes the introductions. "This is

Connor Murphy from County Wexford, Ireland. And this is Sharon McGee from New York."

The first thing Sharon sees is his green eyes looking at her. Then she sees his subtle smile. Connor Murphy is the man in the park.

Connor extends his hand to her. "My pleasure to finally meet you. I have heard about the lady accountant from New York."

Sharon reaches out to touch his outstretched hand in welcome. "The pleasure is all mine to work for a company like Graves & Son." She feels a shock when they touch and pulls her hand back quickly. It must be the weather, she thinks.

"Now, let's get to work," says Tad. "There is much to go over. I have arranged for you to work in the conference room." Tad stands and leads the way. He has already piled the ledgers on the table.

Sharon interrupts. "Let me pick up my workbook where I have our transition plan." She leaves the office to go to her desk. She takes a moment to tuck her hair better into her bun and smooth her skirt. Returning to the office, she sees that Connor has removed his jacket and is sitting across the table, not at the head but where a guest might sit. Slowly, she goes around the table and sits in the main chair. For the first time in her life, she feels as if she belongs right where she is at that very moment.

The day goes by quickly. In reviewing the plan that Tad and Sharon had developed, Connor offers a few suggestions of things the County Wexford office needs that they do not use in the Savannah office. Marleen brings them a light lunch. Sharon places the fruit on the table to share. They work through the afternoon, with Marleen bringing tea. At a quarter to seven, Tad steps in to see how the day is going.

Connor stands when Tad enters but turns to Sharon and looks at her with those eyes that tell her exactly what he is thinking. She speaks up. "We have just a few more items to go over to have the map for the transition ready. Once we finish, we can blend the two company ledgers." Though she directs her comment to Tad, she glances at Connor. She feels his eyes looking at her, not Tad.

"That sounds good," says Tad. "I'm going to head home soon. Connor, are you staying at the Pulaski Hotel?"

Connor turns his attention to Tad. "Yes, I am. I will head back there when Miss McGee and I finish."

"Good. Let me know if you need any of the other accountants to work with you. I think you said you would be here most of the fall."

"That's correct. I plan on going back to County Wexford before the holidays." He looks over to Sharon. "I think we are fine in getting this done together. What do you think, Miss McGee?"

Sharon pauses again. She is not used to men asking for her opinion on business affairs. Cahey never said anything. He said he trusted Sharon and his accountant back in Galway to handle his affairs. They should apprise him of what he needs to do or not do. When she worked with the bakery, it was her business with Danielle. And though Danielle's parents worked with them, the two women made the decisions. So, it wasn't like she could not make them, but she didn't expect a company like Graves & Son to be so accepting. She looks at Tad. "We are fine to finish the work. If we need help, I will let you know."

"Great." And with that, Tad dons his hat and says goodnight.

Connor sits back down. "Do you want to stay and finish the map so we can start fresh with the ledgers in the morning?"

She nods and reaches for her workbook when Connor reaches for his notes; their hands pass each other and touch.

Sharon, though it is only momentary, feels electricity up her arm. She has never felt this before. Is she okay? She just barely caressed his hand with hers, yet the shivers up her arm were real. Connor looks at her. She glances down and begins where they left off.

An hour later, they are finished. Sharon readies the desk for the morning, gets her hat and purse, and pauses at the front door, waiting for Connor to join her so she can lock the door. He adjusts his jacket and places his hat on top of his curly red hair. His eyes seek hers. "It is late. I will walk you home."

"It's fine," she protests. "I often work late alone; I am fine."

"So, are you telling me you don't want me to walk with you? You are always hurrying off when I am near."

Sharon smiles. "I'd love for you to walk with me."

The steps they take on the way back to the boarding house are easy ones. She walks slowly by his side. Connor asks why she came to Savannah. After she finishes telling him about her journey, she asks about his. She doesn't dare look at his face, instead looking at the ground in front of her. She sees his polished boots that reflect the evening lamplight.

"My uncle, who owns the company, raised my sister and me after our parents died. He got me into the business early since he had girls and my sister. He and I were the men in the family. We bonded quickly." He laughs.

Sharon glances at him. "Over what?"

"Over having six women in the family. We had to have a unified front. They are a force all their own."

Sharon notices the smile he shows as he thinks about his family. By the time they get to the boarding house, Sharon feels she has known him all her life. Near the front steps, Connor pauses. They are just outside the street light radius. He takes Sharon's hand, brings it to his lips, and kisses her fingers lightly as royal as anyone could. Sharon glows from the attraction that fills her body.

"I look forward to seeing you in the morning," says Connor.

Sharon turns to walk up the steps. On the porch, she looks over her shoulder to see that he is standing where she left him. His eyes motion for her to go on safely. She does as his eyes tell her to do, opening the door with the hand he had kissed.

17

The week passes quickly. She eats, sleeps, attends the Wednesday evening Bible reading, listens to Gertrude practicing for the recital, and feels like her feet barely touch the ground. On Friday evening, as she is alone listening to Gertrude play—Mrs. Schultz has gone to the hospital to attend to some of the nurses' concerns—Sharon finds she cannot write to anyone in New York. What could she possibly write about? All she has been able to think about is Connor. How can she write that she has met the most special man ever, but he is her boss so it will never work? She had been in the same position thinking about Cahey and knows she should not even have romantic thoughts about Connor. He is her boss. How could she write about how comfortable she is with someone she has only known for a week and that she doesn't want him to leave and return to Ireland? She sits listening to Gertrude but not listening. Then she realizes that Gertrude has stopped playing and is standing directly in front of her.

"Is anything wrong?" asks Gertrude.

"No, nothing at all. I'm sorry. I was just a million miles away."

"Or just a mile." Gertrude smiles. She sits on the end of the settee with Sharon. "Tell me about him."

Sharon's pale skin is now scarlet. The heat is extreme. She sips some of the tea that got cold while she was supposed to be writing letters. "Does it show?"

"Does it?! You are so distracted that nothing holds your attention. So, share the details, please."

Danielle and Sharon had talked about Frederick before he asked Danielle to marry him. The love between them had been palpable. Sharon had not talked about Cahey, even though she felt she was in love with him. She knew that Cahey did not feel the same way about her, so there was nothing to discuss with Danielle from Sharon's perspective. But now that there is electricity, that there is the royal finger kiss, that there is a camaraderie not felt before, maybe something is going on.

The two women talk until Mrs. Schultz comes into the parlor at nine-thirty.

"What are you two so engrossed in conversation about that you don't even realize anyone else is in the room?"

Both women sit very still. Mrs. Schultz laughs. "I think maybe this is a conversation about men."

Sharon and Gertrude look at each other and then at Mrs. Schultz. How would she know? Then abruptly, Sharon speaks up. "We are talking about asking if we can have a reception here after Gertrude's recital at the Savannah Theatre on Thursday, September 20. It's only a few weeks away." Sharon looks at Gertrude. "We are sure the Music Club will want to help sponsor something but are not sure where to have it."

Gertrude stares at Sharon, seemingly stunned by what Sharon suggests, but jumps right in. "Yes, that would be lovely."

"What time is the recital?"

"Eight o'clock, and we would be finished by nine-thirty?" Sharon looks at Gertrude to confirm the time. Gertrude nods and looks at Sharon and then Mrs. Schultz.

"Hmmm, that might be too late to have refreshments. Why don't we have a reception before the recital and invite your family and close friends? We could have heavy hors d'oeuvres rather than dinner that night. The reception can be from 6:00 to 7:30 to give people time to get to the theatre."

The three women discuss the details of the reception. The bells chime at half past ten.

"Oh my, we have been talking way too long. I have broken my own rules, my, oh my." Mrs. Schultz hurries off to fasten the front door for the night. Gertrude and Sharon scamper up the stairs, giggling as only women with secrets can do.

Sleep does not come quickly for Sharon. She tiptoes into the room and dresses for bed, but instead of climbing in bed, she goes out onto the covered porch off the bedroom. The August heat is stifling in the room. The screened porch keeps most of the mosquitoes away. Sharon sits where she can see the moon rising above the trees. The moon is full, the stars are abundant, and dreams can come true if only one works to make them happen. As she sits in the moonlight, her thoughts shift from one image of Connor to another. She thinks she has been out on the porch for only a few minutes, but then she hears the bells chime at midnight. With a smile in her heart, she goes into the sleeping room and crawls under the sheets but promptly throws them off due to the heat.

18

One evening after work, Sharon is in the parlor making a list of reception details while listening to Gertrude practice. The Music Club has agreed to sponsor the reception. Mrs. Schultz comes into the parlor and joins Sharon.

Suddenly, Sister Mary Joyce dashes into the parlor in her normal haste, hurrying from one place to another. "I have twenty minutes. What can I help with?"

Mrs. Schultz immediately offers a stack of envelopes and a list of names to address for the invitations. During the early discussions and planning of the reception, some of the nurses wanted to make fabric flowers to decorate the dining room and stage of the Savannah Theatre. They have learned how to make them from women in their families. After getting the go-ahead from Mrs. Schultz, the nurses take over one table in the parlor to stitch the flowers. Other nurses and several of the sisters come in to help.

Amid all the activity, Olivia walks in. She has not been participating in most of the activities at the boarding house since she returned from John's funeral. Sharon looks up and sees her standing at the door. Gertrude stops playing.

"What will everyone be wearing to the recital?" Olivia asks. The women making the flowers stop what they are doing and rush to hug Olivia and lead her over to the flower-making table.

Sharon looks at her two roommates, Sarah and Alice. "What should we be wearing?" she asks them.

They glance at each other, then back at Sharon. "We will be happy to share accessories," says Sarah.

"Or hats," adds Alice, "with anyone." Several nurses gather around Sarah and Alice to chat.

The scene is just what Sharon has been hoping for: the nurses working together, the nuns pitching in, and the satisfying look on Mrs. Schultz's face as she sits in the chair she always chooses to sit in when she leads the Wednesday evening Bible reading. As Sharon enjoys the scene, Gertrude begins to play again. Sharon watches Mrs. Schultz looking out over the women. She crosses to Mrs. Schultz. "Thank you for letting us take over the parlor and plan for the recital. It means a lot to Gertrude."

Mrs. Schultz reaches out and softly touches Sharon on the arm. "I should be thanking you. I so much wanted the women to know one another and to be able to work together, but they were all doing their own thing until you encouraged us to put on a reception and attend to details for the recital. Thank you."

"With all this productivity going on, shouldn't you and I make food plans for the reception?"

"Oh my, yes," says Mrs. Schultz. "All this activity made me forget that we need to feed folks. Yes, we need to create a menu. Then, we need to make a list of the ingredients needed. Last, we need a time plan for getting the food prepared. You are the baker, remember?"

Sharon goes over to get paper and pen from the writing

desk. As the women work in the parlor, one of the sisters, on her way back to the hospital, stops by to speak with Mrs. Schultz. Sharon overhears her question to Mrs. Schultz.

"With all of this energy, after the recital is over, maybe the nurses could work with us on finding ways to help fund the Fresh Air Home at Tybee Island. We need to find money to pay a nurse."

"I will certainly ask. It is such a great project. Thank you for reminding me," says Mrs. Schultz.

The sister leaves to return to the hospital, and Sharon waits for Mrs. Schultz to say more about the Fresh Air Home. Finally, her eagerness to know leads her to ask, "Please, can you tell me about the Fresh Air Home?"

As she takes the list-making materials from Sharon, Mrs. Schultz moves over to a parlor table where they can work. "The home is a way of increasing the health and happiness of under-privileged children," explains Mrs. Schultz. "It was founded by the Froebel Circle, named after Frederick Froebel, a German educator who founded a kindergarten system. The Froebel Circle was organized as a branch of the International Order of King's Daughters and Sons, a religious order. It began in the home of Miss Nina Pape in 1897."

"Who was Miss Pape?" asks Sharon as she pulls up her chair to the table with Mrs. Schultz.

"She was an outstanding civic leader and founder of Pape School in Savannah. It was her idea to have the Fresh Air Home at Tybee Island. Her grandfather has been mayor of Savannah for five terms."

"And the Fresh Air Home is still going forward?"

"Yes. They started with fifty children, and they now have 270! Central Railroad offers free transportation to Tybee for the children. Others donate ice, food, books, medicine, and toys. A trained nurse, matron, assistant matron, and cook care for the children at a new location on the beach.

"How do the sisters think that the nurses can help?"

"First, they want one of our graduates to be the paid resident nurse. Nurses have volunteered, but the hours and transportation have been problems. There is a need for money to run the home, to provide uniforms for the children, and to pay the staff. To raise money, Savannah organizations have sponsored card parties, oyster roasts, and rummage sales.

This new information has Sharon thinking and not asking other questions. She has been so busy planning her career that she has not thought about others. In New York, the time spent making money to feed her big family was all she had to give.

"I'd like to do something," Sharon says. "I'm not a nurse, but maybe through the Music Club, we could organize some events to raise money for the Fresh Air Home."

Mrs. Schultz raises her head to the ceiling and takes an easy breath. Sharon realizes that she is witnessing a prayer.

19

The most difficult thing to work out is for Gertrude to agree on what she will play. "You must decide," says Sharon one evening when deadlines for getting the information in the newspaper and the advertisement printed are looming. "There are so many tunes you have been playing. Can you settle on which ones?"

Gertrude rubs her face with both hands and pushes a strand of blonde hair behind one ear. "Yes, yes, I can tell you now." She stands to walk over to Sharon with a piece of paper and a list of tunes. "Here, do what you want with it." She turns and goes back to the piano and begins to play.

Connor is there with the women in the parlor. He volunteered to handle the printing side of the reception and program, so when he heard Sharon's concern about meeting the deadlines, he asked if he could visit to help encourage Gertrude to decide which music she would perform. Sharon does not know how to think about him being with her in the parlor. To be near him at the office is one thing, but for him to be here with them is a different feeling. Connor looks at home. Sharon reads the list and then shares it with Connor.

After a moment, Connor moves over to sit by Sharon. "This is impressive," he says. "Let's get to work." They interrupt Gertrude to ask who her piano teacher is and if she wants to credit him.

"Yes, I studied under the mentorship of John McDougal, originally of County Wexford, Ireland."

The program includes Amy Beach's "Piano Concerto in C# minor, Op 45," Thomas "Blind Tom" Wiggins' "Water in the Moonlight," Charles Villiers Stanford's "Six Irish Fantasies," and Claude Debussy's "Clair de lune."

Gertrude stops playing at the piano. "I put 'Clair de lune' last in the program. I would like to close with it. What do you think?"

Connor is the first to speak up. "I have not heard of it."

Quickly, Gertrude begins to play. Connor leans back and listens. Sneaking a look at Connor, Sharon observes how immersed he is in the music. She loved the song, especially when Gertrude explained the background. Now, with Connor enjoying the moment, her love of the tune grows deeper, and the power of the music fills her mind and soul.

When Gertrude finishes, Connor is silent. He is still sitting next to Sharon. Looking at Gertrude, he says, "That has to be one of the best tunes I have ever heard. Yes! Play it last!"

Sharon smiles, and, for the first time that night, Gertrude smiles, too.

The *Savannah Morning News* is on Market Square. To get the advertisement in on time, Sharon picked up the advertisement and the programs from the printer near her workplace on Bay Street during her lunch break. After work, she crosses Bay Street and walks to the newspaper office to leave the advertisement. As she enters the newspaper office, Lucas sits at one of the desks. He sees her and immediately stands and approaches her.

"You are a lovely sight to fill my tired eyes this evening. How are you?"

Sharon adjusts the packages in her hands. The programs are heavy and bound by a cord to make it easier to grasp them, but as she shifts her packages, the folder holding the advertisement falls to the floor. Lucas bends to pick it up and sees that it is an advertisement.

"What's this?"

Her tongue is not functioning. Sharon did not expect to see Lucas right away. "It's an advertisement that I wish to place in the newspaper."

"A piano recital? I knew you liked music, but this looks to be all classical and not the Tin Pan Alley of New York."

"My nurse friend, Gertrude, is the pianist. The Savannah Music Club is sponsoring her in their first performance of the season. It has become a special project for the nurses and the sisters at St. Joseph's."

Lucas has not returned the advertisement but is looking at Sharon. "I intended to leave you a note, but since you are here, I am going out to Tybee Island this Sunday on a special assignment and thought you might like to take the train and see what the beach is like."

Sharon wants to go to Tybee to find out more about the Fresh Air Home. A visit to the home might give her ways to help with the fundraising, but she hesitates to reply to Lucas.

"I can see you have some resistance to going..."

But Sharon interrupts him, "Not at all. It's just with the recital coming up, there is still a lot to do for the reception. I am interested in going out to Tybee. I have heard about the Fresh Air Home and would like to see it."

Without missing a beat, Lucas says, "Then let's go the

following Sunday after the recital. I can change my assignment."

"I can meet you at the train depot after Mass."

"That is great. And here is the advertisement. The processing window is over there. I will plan on attending the recital. After all, I can ask to cover it for the newspaper."

"I thought you said you didn't review performances or theatre?"

"I haven't, but I can." He takes her elbow and guides her over to the processing window. "Until later, then."

Sharon watches as he returns to his desk, gets his hat, and leaves the office. But as she moves to the window, she sees Lucas turn to look back at her as he goes out the door.

Sharon concludes her business with the advertisement. The Music Club account will be billed. She walks back to the boarding house the long way. She needs time to think about what she has just agreed to do. She is to go with Lucas to Tybee Island. She wants to see the home. This will be an easy way to see it, but her thoughts are still uneasy. She is unsure as to why, except she keeps seeing images of Connor.

20

Mid-September features perfect fall days. The air is mostly still. Occasionally, a small breeze will pass, but there is no strong wind off the river. Sharon notices that the sun has been coming up later and going down earlier. The shift in daylight hours has her assessing her route to and from work. She has had a lot to do and think about, so she chooses the shortest, most direct route. With the reception planning, accounts transition at work, and accessory exchanges with the women, there has been little outside entertainment for any of the women. Lucas has been seen entering City Hall on occasions. Sharon waves and he dips his hat to her. She sees Connor at work, but as the seven o'clock bell chimes, she is out the door with errands to do on the way back to the boarding house.

One day, during their lunch break, Sharon asks Connor about his evenings. Connor shares that he returns to the Pulaski for dinner, and then he joins a card game in the hotel bar.

"And this is how you spend your free time, playing card games?"

"These are not just card games—men discuss business and new enterprises."

"I see."

"Seriously, these games are important. On November 25, several years ago, the South Atlantic League was formed during a meeting at the DeSoto Hotel. Savannah is one of six charter members."

"Sports?" Sharon asks.

"Not sports," says Connor, "baseball. Great baseball. The Savannah Indians are the league champs. Bill Hallman is the manager. He was a great player and his batting average increased for nine years. That is a record! His last game was in 1903, but it did not end his baseball career."

Sharon is confused. "But how do you know all of this? You haven't been here long."

"The men talk, plus we get the wire reports in Ireland on the games. We do stay informed even if we are forty days away."

Not wanting to be left uninformed, Sharon asks, "Who are these men, and what else do they talk about at these card games?"

"Most of the men are businessmen who come to Savannah regularly from other parts of the South. Savannah is a major port for commerce. Some are from Ireland or New York. Several men with political ambitions who live here have been visiting the hotel to talk with people from County Wexford to gain the support of the local people. They believe that since many of the Irish in Savannah came from County Wexford, those of us from Ireland may have some sway in elections," he tells her. "Everyone goes there, from the police to firemen, mayors, school board members, businessmen, and everyone."

"Why so many?" She has eaten her fruit and is now nibbling on carrots from the boarding house garden and several small biscuit sandwiches Mrs. Schultz saved for her.

"To get concessions for their businesses, wards, family, you name it. Or to be able to move up in their careers."

Sharon hears what Connor says and interjects, "I try to keep up with what is going on, but since I have no vote, then I cannot very well make a difference, can I?" She stuffs her discards and wrappings into her lunch pail.

"Not make a difference? Of course, you can. You can persuade those who can vote. You can create programs and initiatives that bring prosperity to the area. You can support those programs that you feel will strengthen the town."

"My goodness, you seem to take a lot of interest in women's influence."

"Remember, I grew up in a large extended family with six women. These women do not know how to 'not' be political. They have taught me a lot." He stands up to stretch.

Sharon knows the days of sitting and going over numbers and ledgers are hard on the back. Sharon has a fleeting thought of how she would like to rub her hands over his back and make it feel better. She pushes it out of her head. She has to not think about things like that.

"Do you miss your family?"

"Yes, a big yes. The girls are always busy with activities. Aunt Ivy has been active in educational and civic kinds of programs. I miss hearing what they are up to."

Another thing to think about. Sharon thinks about the Fresh Air Home project as well. Her younger sisters would have loved something like that. With money tight, they didn't even get to see the river around Manhattan. Because they lived in the tenements, they were often restricted to the surrounding streets. Sharon saw Grand Central Station for the first time after growing up in New York when she went to apply for maid jobs at the hotels around it.

"What is your favorite memory of growing up with all these

women?" Sharon is fishing for something more than just a memory; she wants to hear what is important to him.

"Ah, that's easy. Christmas in Kilmore, County Wexford, with everyone at Mass on Christmas Eve and dinner the next day. We have a tradition of singing the first of the Kilmore carols at Mass on Christmas Eve. We go as a family and meet up with friends and neighbors."

Sharon does not know the carols and asks for more history.

"There are thirteen Kilmore carols. On Christmas Eve, 'The Darkest Midnight in December' is sung, and then there is a carol for each of the twelve days of Christmas. Dating back some three hundred years, the carols are sung by six men, who divide into two groups and sing alternate stanzas in unison with a single voice starting the first line.

Sharon listens as Connor describes a Christmas she has never had. Once she became an accountant, she gathered with her new friends at Cahey and Frederick's house for Christmas dinner. None of them attended Mass, no one sang carols, and no one participated in the holiday season except for exchanging gifts and having dinner together. She is looking forward to her first Christmas in Savannah with the nurses and sisters at St. Joseph's. Christmas should be different for her this year.

As Connor puts away his lunch and finishes his cup of tea, Sharon asks, "Why begin with 'The Darkest Midnight in December'?"

"It's a simple carol telling the story of Jesus' birth. When I think about this carol, I hear the lyrics and think of hope. If, on the darkest midnight in December, Jesus is born, then there is hope in the world. And when we have dark midnights, we can get through them by thinking of that hope."

His eyes are shining. They are the brightest green Sharon has seen.

Connor looks at her, and the shine does not diminish when

he says, "And hope is something I continually think about. I hope to do well with my uncle's business. I hope to have success in building a family. I hope to find a shared happiness." He turns away from her and looks out the window at the river scene below them.

She again has an urge to go near him and touch him, to reach out to him and agree, but she hesitates, and the moment is gone.

Connor turns and picks up his ledger. "Shall we continue?"

"Yes," Sharon says, but not with enthusiasm.

21

Mrs. Shultz, Edwidge, and Sharon have done everything they could in advance to prepare the food for the guests. With Gertrude's family, the nurses and their guests, the sisters, and a dozen men and women who are Music Club officers, the reception numbers are creeping up to fifty.

Sharon enters the kitchen after a long workday. She has not seriously baked in many months. Danielle sent the recipes for the small cakes she calls petit fours. She puts on an apron, then rummages in the pantry with the recipe in hand and gathers all the ingredients to make sheet-pan pound cakes. In her haste to get the pans prepared, she drops them. The sound reverberates around the high-ceilinged kitchen.

Mrs. Schultz pauses at the door. "Is everything fine?"

"Yes, I am in too big a rush to get the baking started."

"I can help." Mrs. Schultz puts on her apron and waits near Sharon, who is busy measuring flour. Sharon looks up and sees her waiting.

"You're in charge. You need to tell me what you want me to do."

Sharon smiles. "Yes, of course. Please break the eggs into this bowl."

They work together to prepare all the items: flour, sugar, butter, and eggs, and scrape the vanilla pods for the flavor.

"Now we must beat the eggs. It takes a while, so let's divide them into two bowls and start. As they beat the eggs using two forks together, Sharon knows that the five minutes required to beat the eggs can feel like a long time. To make the time pass, Sharon hums a song she remembers from her mother. She looks up at Mrs. Schultz. "Do you know this song?" She begins to sing "Colcannon."

> "Did you ever eat colcannon that's made by
>   spuds and cream
> With greens and scallions blended like a picture
>   in a dream?
> Did you ever scoop the creamy top to make the
>   little cake,
> With the creamy flavored butter that your
>   mother used to make?"

Mrs. Schultz smiles and joins in on the chorus.

> "Yes, she did, so did he, so did you and so did I.
> The more I think about it, it's the nearer I'm
>   to cry.

> "And weren't those the happy days when trouble
>   I knew not,
> When mother made colcannon in the little
>   skillet pot?"

Sharon sings alone.

"Did you ever take potato cake in a bag to the
 school,
Tucked underneath your arm with your book
 and plate and rule?
And when teacher wasn't looking, a great big
 bite you'd take,
Of the floury, mealy, juicy, the sweet potato
 cake."

Again, Mrs. Schultz joins her in the chorus.

"Yes, she did, so did he, so did you, and so did I.
The more I think about it, it's the nearer I'm
 to cry.

"And weren't those the happy days when we did
 have our fling,
Back in dear old Ireland where love is lord and
 king."

The eggs get whipped, and the kitchen gets cheery. Sharon enjoys the camaraderie with Mrs. Schultz. Now, however, concentration is needed to finish the cakes. Once baked and cooled, Mrs. Schultz cuts the cakes into small squares. Sharon makes the icing and then divides the icing into four bowls. She uses natural fruit juices from cherries, blackberries, lemons, and blueberries to dye the icing and add flavor. Then she makes a mixed berry reduction, which will top the cakes and add a sprig of mint from the garden. They will put on the finishing touches before the reception.

 Also left for the last minute are putting pickles and chow-chow on the ham biscuits and making tea sandwiches using cucumbers, radish with anchovy butter, and a fillet of soles with salad sauce. Edwidge puts the vegetables on skewers so that they are ready to put into the oven to roast. She has made the banana fritters and fried apple hand-pies and has baked half a dozen pecan pies. Lemonade in a punch bowl will be at the head of the table. Once all the food is placed, labels will be added to identify the various foods.

Tad offers Sharon half a day off the day of the recital. She's grateful since there are still a lot of food items to finish. As Sharon rushes to the boarding house, listing all the things she needs to do, she pauses. Instead of turning left to go to the house, she goes straight. She needs a few minutes in Forsyth Park to prepare herself mentally. She goes to her favorite bench, the one where she first met Connor. The fountain has become her centering point. As she sits, a Carolina wren perches on the opposite end of the bench and twitches her head back and forth as though trying to get a read on Sharon's mood. Sharon smiles as the bird chirps away and then sails off to a nearby live oak branch.

As she watches the bird, she thinks. Though pleased with how well her work project is going, she is nervous about her relationship with Connor. And then there is Lucas. She has been pining for Cahey for so long that she is unsure how to handle two men. Though she has shared her exploits with Gertrude, she has not shared her feelings. She is not even sure she knows what those feelings are. In some moments, she is floating above the clouds, and at other moments, she wants to cry. The bell chimes the hour, reminding Sharon that she must get to the boarding house to help ready the reception. Her walk is rapid until she nears the house and breaks into a run. Whatever she needs to think through must wait until tomorrow.

Mrs. Schultz is in the kitchen when Sharon dons her apron and begins to make dozens of tea sandwiches. Edwidge is working at the sink, washing the mint from the garden. Mrs. Schultz adds the berry reduction to the top of the petit fours. No one is talking; each knows what to do. Though the hour for the event is fast approaching, there is a steady pace in the kitchen. They work in harmony with an ebb and flow through the space to complete the tasks according to their detailed plans. A list is tacked to the cupboard. Soon, all the items on the list have a line drawn through them.

Edwidge turns to Mrs. Schultz. "I'll take care of the last details."

With that, Mrs. Schultz nods her head, takes off her apron, and turns to Sharon, "We need to change for our guests."

Upstairs, there is chaos. Women are running from room to room. The water closet door is wide open. Women are going in and out. The bells chime. It is a quarter to six. All the chaos seems to end as quickly as it started as each woman walks down the stairs and takes an appointed place in the dining room and parlor. The women have volunteered to help with the serving and cleaning up. Mrs. Schultz is in her best navy dress with a pearl necklace and earrings. Sister Mary Joyce is in a pristine white habit, freshly ironed and starched. The two women stand side by side at the front door to greet the guests. Gertrude is in the parlor pacing. Sharon sees her and gets in step with her.

"What are you doing?" asks Gertrude, picking up her pace.

"Trying to keep up with you," says Sharon.

Gertrude stops, takes a deep breath, and sits in the chair often reserved for Mrs. Schultz. Sharon pats her arm and goes to the kitchen to check in with Edwidge and finish any last-minute details. The kitchen smells fill Sharon's nose. The roasting vegetables, the sugary pecan pies, and baked apples all have wonderful fragrances. She remembers the special dinners hosted at the bakery, though she was not involved in baking or cooking those dinners. She lived on the top floor of the bakery with Danielle and the smells wafted up into their rooms. She also helped at the door with the tickets for payments. Her experience as a baker came with holidays and weddings where all hands were needed in the kitchen. She feels at home in the kitchen and is relieved that the boarding house rule of "never go into the kitchen" did not apply to her.

Edwidge has two of her children helping with the serving and clearing. They are both in starched chef aprons with wrinkle-free white headscarves tying back their curly black hair. Sharon feels she is not needed here and turns to leave but is stopped by Edwidge.

"Miss Sharon, I do need your help." Edwidge walks over to the worktable in the kitchen, where the recipes and lists are kept. She picks up a pile of cards. "I need help with the labels for the food." She looks down at the cards. "I cannot read. Will you help?"

Sharon takes the carefully printed cards. "Of course."

Not everyone can read, Sharon reminds herself. And if she remembers correctly, the lists made and posted were marked off by either Mrs. Schultz or her. If Edwidge had been asked what was left, she answered from across the room, not looking at the list. Sharon has been lulled into thinking everyone in the house could read or write because the nurses are required to be literate. Sharon's sisters, mother, and father cannot read or write. She had been the only one who attended school. She needed to practice when she started working with Cahey's businesses. He relied on her to be able to read letters from the Irish accountant. She would read every night before going to bed. The difficult words that Cahey and Frederick helped her with were placed on a list she kept and memorized. She so much wanted to do well.

Sharon leaves the kitchen and admires the array of food on the dining room table. Standing around the table are the well-groomed women ready to help. She smiles at each and says, "Thank you for helping." She places the cards on the appropriate dishes. On the table, the women have placed herb arrangements from the garden, tied with bright ribbons.

"The herbs are a wonderful touch," she says to everyone gathered around the table.

"They have meaning," explains Sarah, who is standing at the punch bowl with the lemonade.

"How so?"

"The basil is for good wishes. And the thyme is for courage and strength. We hope Gertrude has a successful recital."

"Does the mint on the petit fours have meaning?"

"Yes, mint means virtue. Appropriate for a house full of nurses in training and the sisters of St. Joseph's Hospital, don't you think?"

The women giggle, and Sharon's red blush makes her smile again. Surprisingly, Alice steps forward and, to the amusement of the women listening, recites a poem in a schoolroom voice:

"There is a language, little known,
Lovers claim it as their own.
Its symbols smile upon the land,
Wrought by nature's wondrous hand;
And in their silent beauty speak,
Of life and joy, to those who seek
For Love Divine and sunny hours
In the language of the flowers."

All the nurses applaud and laugh. Sharon, who has never heard of the language of flowers, is intrigued. "Do all flowers have a message?"

Olivia is the first to speak. "There are codes in the flowers as to which ones are given for each occasion and how these flowers might be presented. Take, for example, the flower arrangements in the parlor. Much thought has been given by the women in my ward who have been producing fabric flowers at home for sale in the Exchange House. They have the molds and tools to trim out the flower petals. They tell us that gardenia flowers mean 'you're lovely,' magnolia blossoms mean 'love of nature,' pink roses mean 'happiness,' and violets mean 'modesty and faithfulness.'"

As Sharon listens, she makes a mental note to learn more about the language of flowers. "I saw you assembling the flowers in the parlor, but I had no idea how you got the petals."

"The women in Yamacraw cut them out for us using their molds," says Olivia. "We took the cloth materials from squares that we had cut out of older garments that were stained or torn and could not be worn again. We found muslin, satin, crepe, cambric, and velvet. They trimmed out the leaves and petals, and I picked them up on various visits back to the neighborhood."

The discussion ends suddenly when the first guests arrive. Gertrude shows her mother, father, two sisters, and brother into the room and introduces each nurse. Sharon silently moves through the room and out the door to check on the parlor.

As she enters, she goes to look specifically at the flowers. There are gardenias, magnolias, pink roses, and violets. Some have long stems like roses. Others are grouped in bouquets like the violets. The gardenias and magnolias are dazzling stand-alone blossoms in shallow trays and crystal dishes. She takes a close look at the precision of the trimming and how the petals are layered to make the flower take on a natural look. Several women are at the doorway, ready to do what is needed to make the reception special for Gertrude. Sharon stoops to examine a bouquet of violets but then feels someone standing close to her. She turns and sees Connor's eyes first. His eyes are smiling, but his face is stoic. Sharon realizes they are the center of attention of all the women in the room. Every eye is on her and Connor.

"Miss McGee, I came early in case there were things you might need help with."

"Oh, Mr. Murphy, thank you, we are all set. I am admiring

the handiwork of the women who made the fabric flowers. Aren't they beautiful?"

Connor nods. "They remind me of fashions in Dublin. Many ladies' hats are adorned with flowers like these. I must say the quality is outstanding. The women here made these flowers?"

"Yes, they wanted to make the occasion special for Gertrude. There are special herb bouquets on the dining table. Please, see them and have some refreshments. You must also meet Gertrude's family."

She leads Connor through the parlor into the hallway. At the door, she stops. Gertrude is in tears, standing by the window with her mother at her elbow. As Sharon approaches with Connor, Gertrude wipes her face gently and smiles at both of them.

"Mother, I want you to meet another one of our boarding house residents. She is not a nurse. Sharon McGee." Gesturing to Connor, she says, "This is Mr. Murphy, a work colleague of Miss McGee, who has been kind enough to help with our printing needs."

The smiles and nods are equally distributed as Gertrude's father joins them, and a new round of introductions is made. Connor motions for Mr. and Mrs. Kelly to join him in choosing food at the table. He raises his eyebrow and takes a quick look at Sharon. Gertrude turns to face the window.

"May I help in any way?" asks Sharon.

Gertrude dabs at her eyes. "Tell me that my face is not blotched from crying."

"Your face is not blotched, just damp. Are you all right?"

"I have shared with you that my mother does not like that I am playing at the recital. She says people will think I am putting on airs. No one will believe I am good enough to play at such a location. She says I need to focus on becoming a nurse or else I will never have a family and will be their burden for the rest of my life."

Sharon heard what Gertrude said, but she could not believe a family would say such a thing. Then she remembers how her sisters were horrified at her wanting to focus on a career in accounting and not stay in New York with the family. Her father did not even speak to her until the day she left when he told her to be safe. Her mother cried and carried on, wailing as though Sharon had died and would never be coming to see them again. And though she has written all of them, she has yet to receive a letter from any one of them. In one of her letters to Danielle, she asked if someone from the bakery could check on her family. Danielle sent Frederick with his camera as he could easily go in and out of the Lower East Side and not be noticed as anyone other than a working man. He reported that everyone was just as she left them. Families can be confusing.

Connor turns and glances back at them. Sharon tries to reassure him that everything is fine. She offers a weak smile and nods her head slightly. She takes Gertrude's elbow, and they walk out the door. In the hallway are several officers of the Music Club. Gertrude lifts her chin and walks toward them to express her excitement about playing at their first meeting of the year. Sharon returns to the dining room and finds Connor sampling everything on the table.

"From the pile of food on your plate, it looks as though you have not eaten all day."

"I haven't. And I heard that you were responsible for most of the recipes, especially the petit fours. See, I have four of them, all in different colors. I must try them all."

Despite herself and the moment she just had with Gertrude, Sharon laughs.

"Are you eating anything?" Connor asks.

"I'm too nervous to eat, and I'm not even the one playing the piano."

"Do what you need to do. I think I will take this into the parlor. I know some of the officers of the Music Club from their visits to County Wexford and aim to catch up with them and see how they are doing."

Connor picks up a napkin with silverware tucked inside as he goes to the door. Sharon cannot resist watching him as he walks. He has a soft way of moving through space. His feet glide rather than step. She had not noticed that before. He nods at some of the women as he passes. They, in turn, stare and then lean into each other to share a comment that Sharon cannot hear; she can only guess. Connor is certainly turning a lot of heads tonight. Before she can decide what to do next, Mrs. Schultz comes through the door.

"Some of the guests, specifically the officers of the Music Club, are asking Sister Mary Joyce about the relationship of the sisterhood with the nurses and the boarding house. I thought you might be interested in hearing."

Sharon nods and quickly follows Mrs. Schultz into the parlor. Sister Mary Joyce is sitting on one of the brocade settees at the fireplace. The Music Club officers are sitting on the other settee, an ottoman, and another single chair pulled over to the group.

"About the sisters..." Sister Mary Joyce pauses. "I must start with Sister Catherine McAuley, the foundress of The Sisters of Mercy. In 1841, she came to the United States from Dublin, Ireland, with a group of sisters to establish infirmaries and schools to minister to the poor and sick immigrants. In 1845, the sisters came to Savannah."

Sister Mary Joyce sees that people have stopped behind others in the parlor to hear her historical description. She adjusts in her seat to take in the newcomers. "Hospital training programs are dominant in our work. Formal book learning extends the programs by years, and there has been a growing demand for nurses. So, Sister McAuley supported clinical experience through an apprenticeship as being more helpful."

She pauses here and takes a sip of lemonade from the glass she holds in her lap. She looks around at the women standing nearby, listening to her. "Four nurses graduated last year. This year, six nurses have earned their caps through six months of hard work and perseverance. Six more will reach that milestone in the spring."

The applause from the people listening to Sister Mary Joyce has her pause again. She nods to the nurses. She looks then at the Music Club officers. "Without community support, the Sisters of Mercy cannot do this work. We are forever thankful for the support offered through the Cathedral of St. John the Baptist and through the work of the societies in Savannah that contribute to the hospital."

Another applause ends Sister Mary Joyce's explanation. Murmurs drift through the people listening. Mrs. Schultz leans over toward Sharon. "Now might be a good time to suggest support for the Fresh Air Home on Tybee. Have you given it any thought?"

Sharon hears Mrs. Schultz but is hesitant to speak up. "I do have one idea," she finally says.

Mrs. Schultz waves a hand at the group around Sister Mary Joyce. "Another program the sisters support is the Fresh Air Home on Tybee. Sharon has been learning about the home. She has an idea as to how some of us can help."

Without a pause, Mrs. Schultz turns and looks directly at Sharon, who is not accustomed to speaking in front of so many strangers. She takes a deep breath and looks from Mrs. Schultz to Sister Mary Joyce. "Yes, I have learned that the home needs funds to help pay a nurse. The nurses here made all these beautiful fabric flowers. If we could find a way to sell some of these, we could help put one of the St. Joseph nurse graduates to work this summer."

The nurses look at each other with surprise smiles. One nurse uses her hands in front of her mouth to silence her giggle. Two nurses reach out and touch hands in a sign of solidarity. The Music Club officers begin to move about the room, looking at all the flowers. They pick them up, murmur to each other, and place them carefully back. Each flower is touched and admired. Sharon watches in silence before adding, "These will make lovely additions to a lady's hat, gown, dressing table, front parlor, or a dashing boutonnière for a gentleman. Don't you think?"

There are plenty of nods. Connor, sitting behind the Music Club officers, speaks up. "I believe we have a product here that can be sold. Mr. Nichols, as president of the Music Club, could you see if the club would sponsor a sale of these items and others to benefit the Fresh Air Home?"

Mr. Nichols is an older man, easily the age of Connor's uncle. His white hair is parted off to one side. His dark blue suit is tailored to fit. With one arm draped over the fireplace mantel, his gold cufflinks engraved with a giant "N" glitter in the lamplight. "Yes, Mr. Murphy," he says, "I believe something can be worked out."

Connor grins at Sharon, who is looking at him with raised eyebrows. This man she is working with is full of surprises.

As the time draws near to end the reception and move to the theatre for the recital, Gertrude leaves in advance with her mother, father, and program chair of the Music Club. Other guests finish their refreshments and gather hats or shawls to move on to the theatre. A conversational buzz can be heard as the women clear the dishes and straighten the chairs. The sisters have gone on to the theatre. Left at the end are the Music Club officers and Connor. Mrs. Schultz thanks them for coming. Sharon stands in the foyer and watches the scene unfold. As Mr. Nichols and Connor leave, still in deep conversation, Connor glances back and offers a quick wave to Sharon, who nods but does not move.

22

Edwidge and her two children take over the kitchen and motion for Mrs. Schultz and Sharon to leave. The two women share a smile at the mimed gestures of shooing them away. Both gather their shawls from the parlor and prepare to walk the few blocks to the theatre.

"I think everyone enjoyed themselves," interjects Sharon as they walk along the cobblestone street.

"Thanks to the wonderful petit fours. They were a definite success. They all disappeared."

"Danielle assured me that they would work for us. She is a great French baker. She is the one who suggested using the pound cake rather than a sponge so we could make the cakes in advance."

"They were wonderful. However," and Mrs. Schultz's tone changed from complimentary to concern, "I noticed Gertrude was not in the best mood. Did you talk with her? Is she just nervous about playing tonight?"

"I did talk with her. She says her family has expressed concerns about her focusing on music rather than on nursing."

"I see." Mrs. Schultz slows her walking so that Sharon has

to stop and then start again to match her pace. "I wanted to be a nurse," says Mrs. Schultz. "I had no connections with the medical folks, and unlike the new programs The Sisters of Mercy have introduced for apprenticeship, the Florence Nightingale schools required tuition. I was caring for my younger siblings so that my mother could work. My father died in the war. After the war, the yellow fever took three of my sisters. My two brothers left on a steamship for New Orleans and a new life. My mother was bedridden by that time and I needed to take care of her. When she died, I was at loose ends. My caretaking led me to begin working as a staff person at the St. Joseph's Infirmary. Later, I was offered the job of boarding house matron for the nursing program, but I never got the chance to be a nurse."

Listening to Mrs. Schultz's story motivates Sharon to ask, "Your experiences sound bleak. Have there always been problems?"

"Oh, goodness, no. I have been very fortunate. I had time with my mother that I did not expect to have. I also enjoyed getting to know each of the young women in the nursing program. They have been a delight." She dabs her nose with a handkerchief and apologizes for the fall allergies affecting her. "And I get wonderful surprises like tonight with the reception and now the recital. I have been truly blessed."

Sharon still does not know what happened to Mr. Schultz and thinks that maybe she'll ask her. Her answer might help Sharon figure out how to react to the men in her life. They enter the theatre and discover that all the seats are filled. However, the nurses have seats up front, and Olivia motions for them to join. The flowers the nurses have made are placed on the stage apron with a few long-stem roses in vases grouped at the grand piano's legs. Gertrude's family is in the front row. As Mrs. Shultz and Sharon sit with the nurses, Sharon sees

Connor with Mr. Nichols. He is in deep conversation with Mr. Nichols and does not acknowledge her.

Then, Mr. Nichols is given a nod from the program chair. He stands and walks up on stage. The audience members quieten, and that's when Connor turns to look and sees Sharon. He nods to her.

"As president of the Savannah Music Club, I welcome you to the incredible recital you are to hear. We offer monthly programs from September to May with concerts and lectures for your entertainment and edification. You have the songs and composers in your program. However, as part of her recital and debut, Miss Kelly has chosen pieces to play that will introduce some new composers to our Savannah audience. I have asked our program chair, Mrs. Leo Lynch, to tell us a little about the composers. Mrs. Lynch."

Mr. Nichols extends an arm toward Mrs. Lynch, a trim lady wearing feathers—feathers in her hair, feathers cascading from the shoulder of her formal dress, and a fan of feathers where she shields her notes on the composers. She takes Mr. Nichols' hand as she approaches the last step up to the stage from the audience and waits until Mr. Nichols takes his seat to begin.

"Thank you for coming. The first piece is by Amy Beach, an American female composer of large-scale art music. Her 'Gaelic Symphony,' premiered by the Boston Symphony Orchestra in 1896, is the first symphony composed and published by an American woman."

Mrs. Lynch reads from her cards hidden behind her feathered fan. "Miss Kelly will play Beach's Piano Concerto in C# minor, Op 45, with four movements." She pauses to look out at the audience members, "Now, I would like to introduce Miss Gertrude Kelly."

Mrs. Lynch gathers her skirt and walks gingerly down the steps to her seat in the front row. The house lights dim, but a cascade of lights comes from several directions to highlight the piano bench. Audience members are silent. Gertrude walks on stage in a black skirt and blouse, both glittering with rhinestones. Her blonde hair curled on top of her head is adorned with a single magnolia flower—one that the nurses had made. She comes to the piano and bows to the audience's polite applause. After she sits, she takes a moment and pauses in front of the keyboard. Sharon is amazed—here is a woman who first introduced herself in the dining room as wanting to be a concert pianist, and now here she is in a major theatre filled with people waiting to hear her play.

Gertrude plays the piano concerto with expertise. After much applause and a bow from Gertrude, she exits the stage, and the house lights come up for intermission. Many people stand at their seats while others make a quick dash to the powder room. Sharon stands and observes the people who came out to hear Gertrude.

Savannahians are dressed for the evening. The men are in formal dark grey or black wool suits, some with vests, others with bowties. The women, however, are wearing a variety of styles made from silk, satin, taffeta, faille, moiré, and silk poplin fabrics. Some of the older women wear velvet dresses.

As Sharon looks about the room, she recognizes several male accountants from her office who are with their wives. Then she sees Lucas. He is at the side of the theatre talking with one of the Music Club officers. He is taking notes, so he must be working tonight. The nurses are all chattering to each other and the sisters. Sharon stands, just listening and observing.

Mrs. Schultz stands up next to her. "I have heard Gertrude play these tunes many times, but they sound different in this hall, don't they?"

"Yes, and I find it hard to think of her as a concert pianist even though she is dressed for the part. She is Gertrude to me," says Sharon.

"She is quite talented. I do hope her family will see that after this evening's performance."

"Me, too," says Sharon, looking over to where Gertrude's family members are sitting. They have remained seated through the intermission with no one talking to anyone else. They are simply sitting and waiting. The lights flicker to indicate the end of the intermission. People sit and move in from where they have been standing in the aisles.

Mrs. Lynch climbs the steps to the stage and waits until all are seated and the audience is quiet.

"For the second half of the program, Miss Kelly will play a song by a Columbus, Georgia, native, Thomas 'Blind Tom' Wiggins, who was enslaved and blind from birth but was a music prodigy.

'Water in the Moonlight' is a short but evocative work. The beginning is calm, with a simple melody. However, each section gets bolder until the chords halfway through the piece are robust. It ends with the last chords played boldly, like a last hurrah."

Mrs. Lynch continues, "Next, Miss Kelly will play Sir Charles Villiers Stanford's 'Six Irish Fantasies.' Stanford, born in Dublin, was a composer, conductor, and teacher. He studied at Trinity College, Dublin, and Queen's College, Cambridge. He was known for his orchestral works, which include seven symphonies and five Irish rhapsodies. His music introduced elements of the Irish folk song. The Six Irish Fantasies (or 'Sketches' as they were originally called) were composed in October 1893 and consist of six varying styles of Irish song and dance."

An audible murmur is heard from the audience, and nods and eye contact with friends are made as the program is explained. Mrs. Lynch gives the audience members a moment to absorb the information. "The final part of the program is a new work by Claude Debussy, 'Clair de lune.' Born in France in

1862, Debussy published 'Clair de lune' in 1905. The tune's title, which means 'moonlight' in French, is from an atmospheric poem by the French poet Paul Verlaine, which depicts the soul as somewhere full of music 'in a minor key' where birds are inspired to sing by the 'sad and beautiful' light of the moon."

She lowers her feathered fan. "Let's give a Music Club welcome to our pianist tonight, Miss Gertrude Kelly."

Mrs. Lynch makes her way back down the steps from the stage. Gertrude enters and offers a slight curtsy before sitting on the piano bench. Sharon is lifted emotionally by "Water in the Moonlight." She has heard it repeatedly for the last month, but tonight, the rhythm of the piece reflects not only the talent of the composer but also the talent of the pianist. Gertrude plays with much energy. The audience shows their appreciation for the piece with jubilant applause. Gertrude nods to the audience but focuses on the keyboard. She begins the "Six Irish Fantasies." Again, the audience greets the end of the songs with loud applause. Gertrude nods again and bows her head for a moment. Sharon can see the look on Gertrude's face changing from the spirit of folk songs to the beauty of Debussy's "Clair de Lune."

As Gertrude plays, Sharon finds that she is looking over at Connor. She sees him raise his chin and take a deep breath as though preparing to enjoy the song as much now as he did when he first heard Gertrude play it. Sharon is engrossed in the music but also in Connor, who has taken over her thoughts. Gertrude finishes, keeping her hands slightly hovering over the keyboard for one last moment. The audience members not only applaud but instantly leap to their feet in a heartfelt appreciation of Gertrude's performance and of the songs chosen for the recital. Gertrude stands, offers a bigger curtsy, and exits the stage. The audience continues to applaud. She returns to the stage and takes another bow. Before the applause ends, Mr. Nichols steps up to the stage and beckons Gertrude to join him at the center. Mr. Nichols motions for the audience to quieten, and people return to their seats.

"What a delight it has been to hear you play tonight, Miss Kelly. The Music Club has heard your accompaniment with the chorus when you have stepped in to assist when our regular pianist has been absent. We knew you were talented, but the program demonstrated to the audience how skilled you are. We thank you for beginning our season with such a brilliant program."

The audience members applaud again and Mr. Nichols has to wait to continue to speak.

"To show our thanks, the Music Club wants to present you with a sponsorship. We have contacted our music partners at Brenau College in Gainesville, Georgia, who have offered you a position there to study music in their residential, college-preparatory school for women. As an incentive to get you to accept, they have also extended you a nursing position with Dr. James Henry Downey, who has plans to build a hospital in Gainesville. You will be able to finish your nursing degree and receive a certificate in music education as a gift from the Savannah Music Club."

Another standing ovation from the audience leaves Gertrude with no words. She doesn't even smile. She looks more shocked than pleased. Sharon sees her glance at her mother, who has been sitting through all of the applause. Her mother is now standing, smiling, and clapping as heartily as any other audience member. Gertrude bows her head and offers a slight smile.

As the audience begins to move toward the aisles, talking and laughing, sharing information with friends, the nurses crowd around Gertrude, who has come down from the stage to greet them. Everyone is talking at once. There are hugs and kisses on the cheek. The nurses pause and move back when Gertrude's mother and father come forward. Her mother does not say anything. She stands in front of Gertrude with a placid look on her face. Gertrude mirrors the look. The nurses are quiet. Sharon watches from the periphery of the nurses' cocoon around Gertrude. As Gertrude continues to stay silent, her mother cuts her eyes over to Gertrude's father. He looks at the women, he looks at his wife, and he looks at Gertrude. "Well done," he says, clearing a lump in his throat. Gertrude's mother extends her arms and folds Gertrude into an embrace.

23

M rs. Schultz is in a conversation with several church women, so Sharon slips past her and heads for the theatre lobby. She decides to wait there until some of the nurses or Mrs. Schultz come out to walk back to the boarding house. As she is inspecting the posters advertising the next performances, she feels a hand on her elbow. Lucas is standing close.

"My job improved the minute I saw you," he says.

Sharon's face instantly colors. She feels the blush move up her neck to her face. "I saw you earlier and knew you were probably covering the event for the paper."

"Yes, since it is a one-time event, the regular reviewer willingly let me cover it as a news story. I am happy I did. Gertrude is certainly talented." He paused for a moment. "I know you two are friends. The gift from the Music Club is indeed gracious. How will she handle being so far away from her family in Gainesville, Georgia?"

"Is this for the story, or do you want to know?"

"Both. She could stay here and finish her nursing degree

and still play occasionally for the Music Club. What would be wrong with that? And she could be near her family. Gainesville is three hundred miles away. Trains only travel about forty miles per hour with all the hills heading up to Gainesville, so traveling would take at least a full day."

Sharon does not have anything to say to rebuke Lucas's thinking, except Gertrude wants to be a concert pianist, and playing occasionally is not her dream. She keeps silent, knowing that Lucas has his own opinions about how women and men should be. While she is silent, he reminds her that they are planning on going to Tybee on Sunday after Mass.

"Yes, I will meet you at the train depot and will be prepared to see the beach."

At that moment, Connor walks out with Mr. Nichols. They shake hands, and as Connor sees Sharon, he turns and approaches. Lucas remains close to Sharon. With both men, one on either side of her, she begins to introduce them but is interrupted by Connor.

"I have met Mr. Laurent several times," says Connor.

"It has always been a pleasure, Mr. Murphy," says Lucas.

"Not always," says Connor. "Not when you are pushing for a story that does not exist."

"I ask questions."

"Questions that lead others to think that there is a story when there is not."

"Questions that will encourage one to admit that something is going on."

"Gentlemen, where have you met?"

They answer at the same time. "At the Pulaski card games." Both men are then grudgingly silent.

"Well, then, I know there is more to this than what you have said, but since I have had a delightful evening with Gertrude's recital, I must say goodnight." Sharon turns to leave but hears Lucas say, "See you Sunday."

She pauses as Lucas greets Gertrude, who has come into the lobby with her parents. Connor steps in to match her pace as she begins to leave. "May I walk with you? It is late, and folks are still talking and celebrating."

It is late, and though she had planned to walk with the nurses or with Mrs. Schultz, she just wants to get away from the argument between the men. "Of course, thank you."

Together, they cross the street and move in the direction of the boarding house. They are silent for a while, then Connor speaks up.

"Gertrude was wonderful, wasn't she?"

"Yes."

"All the practice, all the planning. When I first saw the program, I knew we were to be in for a special treat."

"She was fabulous."

They walked a little more in silence.

"By the way, thank you for helping out with the printing. The programs and the advertisements were great. I think people saw the advertisement and came to hear Gertrude."

"My pleasure."

More silence, and then Connor says, "I know we work together, but I was wondering if you would join me for dinner one night? I hear the DeSoto Hotel has a nice evening dinner."

Sharon almost laughs but controls herself. Of all the things that Connor might say to her, she did not expect to be asked to dinner. "That sounds lovely." She is aware that Connor has been watching her as they walk.

"Splendid. Shall we go on Saturday evening? We could go at eight to give you time to return to the boarding house after work. I can meet you there, and we'll walk over. I will make the reservation."

She does not look at Connor but rather looks at her feet as she walks. "Yes, thank you. I would like that."

At the bottom of the steps, Connor pauses as Sharon

continues up the steps. At the top, she turns to see that he has not moved and is watching her with his green, very green, eyes.

24

Friday starts like any other workday except that the nurses are not silent at breakfast. The recital and reception have created a bond among the women. They talk about new fabrics for making flowers for the fundraiser for the Fresh Air Home. More cotton ideas need to be incorporated since Savannah is known for its cotton factors and trade. They talk about the recipes that Sharon introduced at the reception and how they will use them in their family celebrations. They talk about their workday and what they are learning. There is a lot of talk.

Mrs. Schultz, on the other hand, is silently listening. Sharon notices that the crease between her eyebrows has disappeared. She nods and agrees with suggestions yet is silent. As the nurses scamper off to the hospital, Sharon begins to help Mrs. Schultz remove the breakfast food and take it into the kitchen since she now has unfettered access. As they finish, Sharon pauses at the door before leaving for work.

"Mrs. Schultz, will you be in the parlor this evening?"

"I am in the parlor every evening, Sharon. Why do you ask?"

"I would like to talk with you."

"Is everything all right?"

"Yes, yes," Sharon quickly stumbles. "I just need to ask a few questions, but right now, I must dash off to work."

"I'll be there. Come and ask."

Sharon wishes Edwidge a good day and hurries to get her satchel for work. On her walk to the office, she goes over the images she has retained of the previous evening: the reception and Connor trying all the varieties of petit fours, the idea of creating more fabric flowers to sell as a fundraiser for the Fresh Air Home, the amazing music played by Gertrude, how Gertrude and her family reconciled, Connor's invitation to dinner, Lucas and his questions of Connor, and how she will manage two men wanting to spend time with her. There is a lot to think about.

The day goes quickly. Connor and Sharon have an easy working relationship. They think similarly about the shipping company's financial goals. The William Graves & Son Company has been in the business of procuring cargoes, organizing port logistics and paperwork, obtaining ship's stores, providing cash advances to captains, and being the immediate payor of sailors' hospital expenses. The company's link to St. Joseph's Hospital is intentional, and Sharon begins to understand why the company agent placed her in the boarding house with the nurses. As they move through their transition plan, Sharon begins to piece together why the company is making the changes and why Connor has come to Savannah. She does not ask why; she figures it out from the ledgers. What she does not understand is if the company is merging the books, then why did they hire a woman from New York to be a part of the transition?

Connor explains that the original intent of the company was to obtain timber from Georgia, but they also imported cotton. To maintain a full ship, they brought over many Irish immigrants during the last half of the century. The immigration route, though, has reduced its numbers; therefore, the company now wants to expand its mercantile stores. They plan to sell merchandise from American ports in Ross, Ireland, and Liverpool, England, and then turn about and sell woolens and factory goods made in Ireland and England to America. With the expansion of the railroad and with the route already established from Ireland to Savannah, the company plans on using the Savannah port to distribute goods throughout America.

During their discussions, Connor told Sharon that if they were to sell merchandise to a growing town like Savannah, a change would have to happen. Connor sees that Savannah needs to feed the newly developing large-scale industries with petroleum, fertilizers, grain, coal, lumber, ballast, and industrial goods. Additionally, there was a decline in cotton in America after the Civil War, which reduced cotton goods produced in factories in England, lessening the demand and increasing the need to diversify the type of goods sold.

Connor's role, as the nephew of the owner and one who is not yet tied down with a family, is to be in Savannah for several months and make the transition. He has seen that the stores along the riverfront in Savannah are offering hardware, liquor, and rare fineries. There is a pharmacy and an office for the Spanish consulate on the riverfront. Graves & Son management is eager to diversify and create a stronger company to take advantage of the growth.

Sharon hears what Connor says and realizes that she has let her feelings for him go unchecked. He is here for only a short while. He has a task to do. She has a task to do. She needs to concentrate on her work and find a place for herself in Savannah. As they finish for the day and are at the door ready to leave, Connor reminds her that they have dinner reservations for eight fifteen on Saturday night. She nods, locks the door behind them, says goodnight, and hurries down the street to the boarding house.

She barely touches her dinner. She wraps it up to take for lunch on Saturday. She hears the bell chimes for seven forty-five. Instead of going directly to the parlor to see if Mrs. Schultz is there, she goes out the door and heads for Forsyth Park. She needs a moment to clear her head before she talks with Mrs. Schultz.

At the fountain, she does not sit on her favorite bench but circles it, looking at it in the lamplight. At the end of September, the evening starts earlier, and she no longer has the long, wonderful summer evenings to look at all the trees, flowers, and bushes.

As she circles and hears the water splash, she stops suddenly in the pathway. She realizes why her anxiety has grown—she feels alone. She has not gotten letters from New York in several weeks. Danielle did send the recipes for the reception, but her note simply said that she was busy and would write more later. No one in her family has written to her since she arrived in Savannah three months ago. She has gotten some correspondence from Cahey, but he only asked for clarification on some of the New York business accounts that his accountant in Galway could not answer. Filled with loneliness, she returns to the boarding house.

Mrs. Schultz is in the parlor reading the newspaper. When Sharon enters, Mrs. Schultz looks up. "Your reporter friend wrote about the recital in the newspaper."

"I saw him there. He said he was given the task since it was a one-time event. He's not usually a reviewer. How is the article?" Sharon crosses in front of Mrs. Schultz and sits down in the matching brocade chair with only the small lamp table between them.

"It's clear he is not a reviewer nor a music connoisseur. He did a good job, though, of summarizing the program and telling something about the composers. Neither Gertrude nor her family said much to him; there is little about her in the story." And with that, Mrs. Schultz puts the newspaper down on the table.

"Do you know if Gertrude has read the story?" asks Sharon.

"I do not. She had been at the hospital all day, and at dinner, the nurses were so consumed with talking about everything under the sun that Gertrude did not have a chance to say anything. I think she is pleased about the size of the audience and the graciousness of the Music Club. I am waiting to hear more from her as to her plans."

"Me, too. As generous as the Music Club's gift is, I will miss her terribly."

"The two of you have gotten close over the past few months, haven't you?"

"She has been my new friend. I have enjoyed our talks and her music."

Mrs. Schultz fusses with her skirt and pulls at her sleeves in the silence between the two women. Finally, Sharon speaks up. "I have been wanting to ask you but have not found a time to ask, so I guess now is as good a time as any. In the months I have lived here, you have been so helpful with all of the women here. I thank you for your obvious caring about each of us."

Mrs. Schultz folds her hands in her lap and waits as Sharon fumbles with her words.

"I don't know if you want to talk about what I want to talk about, but I will ask, nevertheless." She looks at Mrs. Schultz, who is gazing off into the room, waiting for Sharon to continue. "So, what happened to Mr. Schultz?"

Without so much as a look, Mrs. Schultz gets up and leaves the room. Sharon is startled but realizes that she may have intruded into Mrs. Schultz's private life and rather than reprimand her, Mrs. Schultz has chosen to avoid saying anything. Sharon is frozen in her chair. If she felt lonely before, now she is both lonely and devastated that she has said something that has chased Mrs. Schultz away. Before she can move, Mrs. Schultz is at the door. She has a framed photo in both hands that she holds out to show Sharon. "This is Alfred. Mr. Schultz. Dr. Alfred Schultz."

Sharon takes the photo and stares at the young man in a three-piece suit, his hat in his hand, his arm around a younger Mrs. Schultz. "What happened?"

"I said 'no' when I should have said 'yes,'" explains Mrs. Schultz. She sits in her chair and refolds her hands several times in her lap. "He was a medical student and came to the hospital to do his residency. He was here to finish and then to return to his home in New York, where his family lived. He asked me to go with him. I had my mother to take care of, and he was full of dreams. I said 'no' and he left. My mother died not long after."

"What did you do?"

"After a while, I got in touch with Alfred and told him about my mother, expecting a note in return; he came the next fortnight. We fell deeply in love, and he asked me to marry him. Rather than go to New York to marry, we decided to do it here in Savannah, and then I could travel to New York with him as Mrs. Schultz."

She pauses. When she speaks again, her voice indicates how pleased she is by his choices. "He was a practical man and decided to purchase two horses and a wagon so that I could take some of my mother's items with me to New York. The constable married us. We loaded the wagon, but as he was leading one of the horses over to fasten the straps, something spooked the horse. The horse reared up, and when he came down, he struck Alfred, who fell onto the ground. The horse bounded away. I raced over. Alfred was immobile on the ground. Blood oozed from his scalp. He was very still. I knew then that Alfred was dead."

Sharon remains fixated on the photo in her lap. She is awed by Mrs. Schultz's story but does not have the energy to look at Mrs. Schultz. Finally, the silence and stillness of Mrs. Schultz force Sharon to look at her, and she sees Mrs. Schultz with a smile on her face. Sharon cannot believe she is smiling. Mrs. Schultz looks at the photo Sharon is still holding. "That is a photo of us the day we married."

"How can you be so quiet about this?" asks Sharon. "You have had so many issues in your life. You found the love you wanted, and it ended so quickly. Aren't you sad?"

"Do you mean, do I miss him? Yes, I do, but I am not sad. I had someone love me." She pauses and looks out the parlor window into the darkness beyond. "For me, that will last me a lifetime."

They hear the bell chime at ten o'clock. Mrs. Schultz stands to go secure the front door, but they both hear Big Duke, the fire alarm, going off. Sharon joins her at the front door. The women look out at the street, peering through the trees to see where the fire might be. A bicyclist comes flying down the street and sees them at the door. "The theatre is on fire!" he shouts. Mrs. Schultz and Sharon look toward the theatre.

Sharon is the first to speak. "I will go and see how bad it is. I know you want us all to be safe."

Before Mrs. Schultz can even say, "Be careful," Sharon pulls a shawl kept at the front door for emergencies and rushes toward the theatre.

Sharon knows that the theatre was designed by the renowned American architect William Jay. The recital had been planned because there was no performance scheduled for the theatre for the entire weekend. Thursday nights were usually reserved for a rehearsal for the upcoming performance. Rules were strict at the theatre. Gertrude had shared them with Sharon: absolutely no matches or candles on stage. When Sharon arrives at the theatre, she finds firemen there already.

People in the crowd watching are inching close to the theatre to get a better look. Several thousand people crowd into Chippewa Square, directly in front of the building. Police attempt to keep the spectators back, but the crowds grow quickly as they push in to view the fire and trip over the fire hoses.

Sharon sees Lucas near the front doors. She doesn't want to get near the fire but would like to know if he thinks it will be kept under control so that she can report it to Mrs. Schultz. She slips between people moving toward the side of the building and finds herself only a few feet from Lucas. She calls out to him.

He turns, sees her, and hurries over to her. "What are you doing here?" He takes her elbow and leads her to the far corner of the square, away from the crowd and the fire. He doesn't remove his hand from her arm. "What are you doing here?" he repeats.

"Mrs. Schultz and I heard the fire alarm. She worries about the women in the boarding house and about fires that have leveled Savannah in the past. I volunteered to come and see if you thought the fire could be contained. I expected you to be here."

Lucas pauses. "You came to find me?"

Sharon sees a smile cross Lucas' face. "Yes," says Sharon. "I knew you would know."

"If the police can keep the crowds out of the building, they have a better chance of putting the fire out. Within a minute or two, the flames, which were first seen struggling for air in the rear of the stage, caught up on the highly inflammable stage settings, clambered to the dome, and broke through the windows. I believe the fire will rage for a while, but every fireman in the city has been called. Everything possible is being done to contain it to just this building." Lucas looks over to view the crowd. "I see that Frank Hamilton has just arrived. He is the stage carpenter. He and his wife have an apartment in the theatre. They have been out. I have to talk with him."

"Go. And thank you."

Sharon turns to leave, but Lucas is still holding onto her arm. "Go carefully," he says before releasing her arm.

Sharon returns to find Mrs. Schultz sitting on the porch waiting for her. She sits next to her and shares what she has seen and what Lucas has shared. Both women sit for a while and watch the red glow in the sky above the theatre. Sharon is the first to stand. "I must go and get rid of the smoke on me. I have to be at work early."

Mrs. Schultz nods. "You did not ask more of me tonight. Is there more?"

"No, I am fine for now. See you in the morning." Sharon goes upstairs with her thoughts. She had been hoping Mrs. Shultz's answer would help her figure out what she should be focusing on. Instead, Mrs. Shultz has given Sharon a new question. Will someone love her for just her?

25

S haron sees the *Savannah Morning News* on the table in the foyer when she comes down for breakfast on September 22nd. There is a large story about the fire:

[Frank] Hamilton and Manager [W.B.] Seeskind believed the fire to be of incendiary origin. They spoke of at least two earlier attempts to burn the theater, but nothing was ever proved. Clearly, the ghost that put out the theater's fires had deserted it. Perhaps he no longer felt at home after the rebuilding of 1895. The fire spread rapidly, and all of Savannah seemed to be drawn by "the glow which suffused the heavens."

Within a minute or two after the alarm rang out, the flames, which were first seen struggling for the air in the rear of the stage, caught up on the highly inflammable stage settings, clambered to the dome, and broke through the windows. Hundreds of people were running to the scene of the fire. In their rush, people in the crowd tripped over fire hoses, fell, and got up to hurry on to the best places for watching the fire. The crowd which witnessed the burning of the theater occupied every vantage point on all sides. Chippewa Square, which is directly in front of the building, was filled, and it is estimated that several thousand people crowded into it. On Hull, McDonough, Drayton, and Bull streets, the police had their hands full to keep spectators back. At times, the work of the firemen was impeded by the crowding of the multitude. Some even watched the fire from inside the theater as long as that was possible, "for an hour, nearly. They saw a raging cauldron of flame, more dramatic to the fascinated few who hung over the rail than ever was a spectacle upon the stage now set in fiery splendor."

The next day, Manager Seeskind found the walls strong and in good order and believed the theater could be "rehabilitated." The night of the fire, he believed it to be "a total loss, one felt keenly by most Savannahians. . .. The loss is one that nearly every citizen has a personal interest in, and considers the destruction of this historic old building, where the immortal Booth exhibited his matchless genius, where Jefferson wooed tears and laughter with the witchery of his pathos and the insidiousness of his humor, a personal loss."'

When she enters the dining room, Sharon finds Mrs. Schultz sitting in her usual seat at the table.

"I see you have the newspaper," Mrs. Schultz says.

The nurses are all talking at once and hurrying to finish breakfast. Mrs. Schultz tells Sharon that Sister Mary Joyce has visited and reported there were injuries to people at the scene of the fire from smoke inhalation, abrasions, and a few firemen with burns. The hospital needs the nurses right away. Before Sharon can sit down, the nurses dash from the room to head to the hospital, leaving only Mrs. Schultz and Sharon at the table.

"Well, what a night!" says Mrs. Schultz.

"Did you stay late on the porch?"

"Only an hour later. The glow abated, and I felt it was safe to come inside."

"The newspaper says the theatre will be rebuilt, so that's good."

Mrs. Schultz pours herself a second cup of tea. "The theatre has been instrumental in bringing many great actors to Savannah." She pauses, holding the cup gently near her mouth as she remembers. "My favorite memory is of Joseph Jefferson, who played Rip Van Winkle many times, I am told, though I only saw him once. I heard that he thought Savannah was a lovely city but that he liked it in April the best because it is like a fairyland with the live oaks, magnolias, and gardens with abundant flowers."

Sitting with her cup of tea, Sharon agrees. "My first impression of Savannah was noticing that there was a lot of green. New York has its trees, but everything here is bigger than life, with flowers growing everywhere, even out of the cracks in the sea wall and between the cobblestones on the street. I go to Forsyth Park to soothe my inner self and to enjoy nature."

"I thought I saw you one day recently. I had an errand nearby and you were sitting on a bench near the fountain."

"My favorite place to watch the water and see the birds splash in the fountain. Very soothing."

They sip their tea with a comfort that has been building between the two women. Sharon chooses a few items for breakfast. Mrs. Schultz gets up, picks up the teapot, and brings it to the table, pouring another cup for each of them.

"Another star came to Savannah just before you arrived. She was also interested in birds and bragged that she shot doves and woodpeckers by the dozen."

Sharon gasped. "Oh, no!"

"Yes, Sarah Bernhardt came to Savannah to do a show, and according to the *Savannah Morning News*, she went on a hunting trip to Ellabell, where she reported that she saw a wild boar and fired at it. According to the article, she was firm in her belief that she had done combat with a dangerous animal, but it is said that Capt. John Morrison of Ellabell counted his hogs very carefully the day after Madame Sarah's adventure." Mrs.

Schultz put her napkin to her lips in hopes her laugh did not carry far.

Sharon smiles but asks, "Are there local folks who have performed in the theatre besides solo recitals like Gertrude?"

"Absolutely. Charles Coburn began as a program boy at the theatre and eventually became the box office manager and then the theatre manager, all while in his teens. He left Savannah to become an actor and returned in 1903 to star in Hall Caine's play *The Christian*. Savannahians turned out in force to see 'Charley Coburn.'"

The bell chimes jar Sharon into action. Just because the week has been full of activity and her weekend is busy with dinner tonight with Connor and then off to Tybee on Sunday with Lucas, she has another day of work and must hurry.

When she arrives at work, she finds that Connor left word with Marleen that he would be late. She sees Tad standing in the doorway as she passes his office.

"How is the transition going?" he asks.

She has provided periodic updates to him, and she knows that Connor has left the ledger books in plain sight so that Tad can review them any time he wants. "Good. We have been able to stay with the plan and are making progress. I did want to ask something, though. No one has given a specific deadline when this has to be completed. Do you know?"

"We have a better idea now," says Tad. "We had to wait to see what type of work needed to be done. That is why Connor is late this morning. He needs to telephone the home office and relay information. According to him, you are more than a third of the way through, and if there are no delays, the end date looks to be around the first of December."

"I see," and Sharon did see. She knows that Connor is leaving on the first of December. Her job will be very different when he leaves. She is just hoping she will have a job. She nods to Tad and deposits her satchel and lunch at her desk. She goes to the room

where she and Connor have been working and finds it changed
with him not there. The space he has occupied is empty, and she
feels it not only in the room but also in her heart. Because of their
long hours, Marleen installed a tea service in the room just for
them. She pours a cup of tea and stands at the window, looking
out at the river while the tea steeps in her cup. She remembers
why she came to Savannah in the first place. She came to create a
career for herself so she could take care of herself. That is all. She
should focus on her work and not on a person. She sits and starts
going through the last entries, checking the figures.

At lunchtime, Connor still has not arrived. Sharon takes her
lunch outside. It is a warm September day. She walks along Bay
Street to the lamppost to have lunch. And as she slowly eats,
she sees how green everything is still. In New York, the leaves
would be turning brown and would be covering the sidewalks.
She doesn't finish but closes everything up and heads back to
the office.

Still no Connor. She works through the afternoon. At seven,
when it is time to leave, she packs up and walks slowly to the
boarding house. With no message from him, she is not even
sure they will be having dinner tonight. Mrs. Schultz is in the
parlor and sees Sharon as she passes.

"A letter came for you today," she says. "It is on the table in
the foyer."

"Thank you." The letter is from Danielle, just as she
promised but earlier than Sharon had expected.

Sharon hurries up to her room, closes her door, and goes
out onto the porch. She sits and opens the letter.

Dear Sharon,

    I promised to write and had to put it on the calendar so
that I would be true to my word. Everything has been so busy.
My two sisters have moved into the bakery house, and that

makes it easier to get early starts and help my mother and father in their basement apartment. The changes are going quite nicely to the point that Frederick and I are wondering when there will be a problem; things are too peaceful to be true.

In the meantime, Frederick and I are at the Stiffen House in Murray Hill. Though Cahey is to share it with us, he is more often at the farm in Westchester. Pádraig, son of Seámus, has been up at the farm full-time, so we never see Cahey unless we go to the farm for a visit, which we did. What a delight that young man is. I can see why Cahey wants him to run the farm. He seems to have a lot of book learning. Cahey says that Seámus found a tutor to live in the house with them for room and board; the tutor taught the three children. He certainly knows his horses. Takes after Cahey, he does, even though they are not kin.

I hope the reception was successful and the recipes worked out. The whole event, as planned, sounded wonderful. Please write with the details.

I have some news. I am with child. We are going to have a baby! My goodness, how our lives will change. Cahey assures us that all will be welcome at the Stiffen House, and we plan on turning the parlor into the nursery. That room has always been one that gathers more dust than people. We still congregate around the dining table, work there, talk there, socialize there. We might as well make the parlor into a nursery. I wish you were here to help me plan it all. Do write about any ideas you might have.

Your job sounds like it is occupying a lot of your time. Please write soon and tell me all.

Much love,

Your almost sister,

Danielle

Sharon holds the letter in her lap and gazes out over the treetops. She can still smell the smoke from the theatre fire. There is so much to share with Danielle that Sharon does not know where to start. She hears the bell chime the half hour but does not move. Not hearing from Connor all day, she has no idea what to do about tonight. Mrs. Schultz did not leave her dinner since she had told her she was going to dinner with Connor. Not that she is hungry, but her loneliness and now the news of Danielle having a baby occupy her thoughts. She hears a knock at her bedroom door.

"Yes, who is it?"

"Mrs. Schultz."

Sharon rushes to open the door.

Standing at the door, Mrs. Schultz presents a bouquet with an attached note. "These just arrived."

Her hands shake a bit as she takes the bouquet and turns to put it on the table. She pulls off the note.

Dear Sharon,

Sorry I did not come into the office today. I had much to do with the home office, and it was easier to get it done at the hotel than at the office. I am looking forward to dinner and will arrive at eight as planned.

Yours truly,

Connor

When Sharon turns around, Mrs. Schultz is still at the door, "I think I had better hurry; Connor will be here at eight!" Sharon feels a bit dazed.

Mrs. Schultz walks over and picks up the flowers. "I'll find a vase for these. Wear the light green dress, the one Gertrude embroidered," says Mrs. Schultz. She leaves to let Sharon change and imagine what the evening might be like.

26

As the bell chimes eight, Sharon walks down the stairs. A knock at the door causes Mrs. Schultz to hurry from the parlor to open it. She sees Sharon on the stairs and pauses long enough to say, "You look absolutely beautiful." She is wearing her light green dress with emerald green leaves appliquéd down the side of the skirt, on the sleeves, and smaller ones on the bodice. Her matching hat is angled over her forehead, with the light green netting hanging down over her black hair twisted into a high bun. She holds a cloth bag with the same type of leaves appliquéd on both sides.

Connor enters and greets Mrs. Schultz. Then he sees Sharon on the stairs. She pauses while Connor assesses her, and when he smiles, she moves toward him.

"Please take your time," says Mrs. Schultz. "I have a lot of bookwork to do and will be in the parlor working late." She holds the door as Connor takes Sharon's elbow and guides her down the front steps. Sharon glances back when they reach the sidewalk and sees Mrs. Schultz still standing in the doorway, watching them leave.

Connor apologizes for missing work and explains that he

made the decision to stay at the hotel to handle business because he was comfortable letting Sharon handle the accounts. After she shares where she is in the process, she changes the subject from work to asking about the hotel where they are having dinner. She has not been there but has heard that many famous people have stayed there, including William McKinley, the twenty-fifth President of the United States.

Connor adds what he knows. The hotel was built on the original site of the Oglethorpe Barracks back when the colony was established. However, according to his business friends, the rapid transformation of neighboring Florida into a popular vacation spot caused business people to want to make Savannah a holiday destination. The hotel was opened on New Year's Day in 1890, and everyone calls it "The DeSoto." One of the city's most recognizable landmarks, the city businessmen began referring to the building as the "Dowager Empress of the South." According to his business friends, it has become the center of social life in Savannah.

"The ones you play cards with?"

"The same."

As they approach the hotel, Sharon sees the extensive masonry with the side towers and turrets along the corners of the building's exterior façade. Inside the lobby are squat columns holding up the paneled ceiling. Fabric-covered wing-back chairs and tall trees set in deep blue planters line the back wall behind the columns. A giant tapestry rug covers the lobby floor, and a single round wooden table is in the middle of the lobby. The hotel is as grand as the hotel in New York where Sharon had worked as a maid. She thinks about how her fortunes have changed as she admires the grandeur.

Connor guides Sharon up the carpeted stairs to the second floor. The dining room is over the porch in the south side turret. Each window is in a wide wooden arch. The beveled glass at the top of the window arch is then covered in burgundy

Roman shades that match the wainscot panels halfway up the wall. Midway down the lengthy room is a fireplace with an oversized round mirror hung over the mantel. A green fern shields the reflection from the mirror. Pendant crystal chandeliers hang from the high ceiling. Tables, covered in starched white linen, have two to four solid wooden chairs with seats and backs covered in leather. The room is large enough to hold fifty tables.

Sharon and Connor are led down a center green tapestry carpet to a table at the far end in front of one of three giant arched windows. A waiter removes the "Reserved for Murphy" card from the table, pulls Sharon's chair for her, and guides it in as she sits. Both are given menus. Sharon realizes that her menu has no prices but many choices. She settles in her chair and places her purse on a little stool next to her chair.

"I have seen what you bring to lunch but do not know your preferences," says Connor. "You will need to let me know. But I do suggest that we begin with a glass of wine. Is that good with you?"

"That would be nice, yes. I prefer white wine. If they have a Sauvignon Blanc, that would be good."

Connor's eyes again assess her. "You surprise me."

"Because I have a wine preference?"

"You live in a boarding house of nurses working in a Catholic hospital. How would I have guessed?

Sharon puts the menu down to look directly at Connor. "I have friends in New York, and we dined at some of the best restaurants in the city. I have to admit I know more about ale than wine because ale is more of the Irish liking, but we attended art gatherings. My friend Frederick, who married my business partner, Danielle, is an impressionist photographer, and wine is usually served at the art openings. I got to experience a variety of wines."

"Okay, now we know about your social life in New York. What choices do you have for food from the menu?"

She looks at the menu, reading through the lengthy choices. "I am partial to lamb cutlets," she says.

Connor motions for the waiter. "Please bring two glasses of Sauvignon Blanc. For starters, we will both have the consommé Italianne?" He glances at Sharon for acceptance and she nods. "The lady would like the lamb cutlets, and I will have the salmon."

The waiter nods and shakes out the napkin for Sharon. Then, he does the same for Connor. Water is already in the crystal goblets on the table.

"Tell me about your friends in New York."

There has never been a subject that Sharon can talk about so freely as the friends she left. She describes each: Danielle, Frederick, and Cahey. She tells Connor all about what they do, how they got to America, and how they each met and became friends. The stories go on through the wine and the soup, but as the courses change for the entrees, she pauses, feeling that she may have talked too much.

As they silently digest both the food and the stories, Connor asks, "Why accounting?"

"I have always been comfortable with numbers. Before I began working with Cahey's businesses, I would do all the addition and subtraction in my head. Cahey had his accountant back in Galway school me on processes, and I felt for the first time that I had some control over my work. I discovered that there is a sense of accomplishment when an account is reconciled and balanced. I then figured out that numbers and letters are the same thing; they mean nothing unless they are organized in a way that provides information. A financial statement shows how well or poorly a company is doing. I feel that working as an accountant, I am providing management with accurate numbers so they can make informed decisions."

She is interrupted by the waiter bringing the entrees. The lamb cutlet has green peas nestled on the plate with fresh mint leaves scattered on the side and a sauce drizzled over the lamb. Connor's salmon is served with potatoes topped with parsley and lemon slices. Both begin to eat.

"Your application indicated many different businesses in New York. How did that happen?"

"Is this an interview or dinner?"

Connor's eyes did not leave Sharon's. "Both."

She lowers her fork. "Cahey is quite a businessman. He not only works with horses at Vanderbilt's American Horse Exchange, but he consults as a horse trainer and knows a lot about how to medically treat horses. He purchased a pharmacy, and when he added a soda fountain that served Coca-Cola, he earned stock in the company as well. Then, when Danielle started a bakery, we were all an extended family, and it made sense that I pitch in and do the accounting work she needed for the business. I was a bit out of my comfort zone with some of the accounts, like the stock, so I sought out Christine Ross, the first woman CPA in New York, for advice. I am a quick learner."

"So, I see," says Connor.

"Plus, there is the satisfaction of seeing a nicely prepared income statement and balance sheet. My pleasure matches the same feeling I get when I look at a piece of art."

Connor's face is placid, but his eyes dance all over Sharon's face as he digests her last comment.

"And do you plan on staying an accountant?"

Sharon thinks this is where she should be coy and leave the question open, but she made this giant leap of faith to come to Savannah to have a career. "It's nice having a job no one understands, so they find you useful."

Without looking away, Connor laughs out loud, so loud that the waiter moves toward the table to assist, but Connor motions for him that it is fine. Sharon is abashed. What did she say that he thinks is so funny? She is being honest. She holds her napkin up to her mouth and stops talking.

"My, my," Connor finally says. "I am again surprised."

"That a woman can have a job she likes and feels she is being useful?" Sharon's question had a tinge of disbelief and annoyance.

"No, no, you heard me wrong. I am deeply impressed with your rationale. I see business much the same way and am pleasantly surprised that you feel the same."

She is not sure if he is being truthful with her. Though they have worked together for some time, there is a difference between what they do in the office and being together socially. She needs to think through this and maybe find out more about Connor.

They finish dinner with pineapple pie and, for Sharon, a cup of tea while Connor enjoys a glass of port. A check is not produced, and they leave the dining room with the waiters assisting with both chairs. As they return to the lobby, Sharon asks about the lionhead water fountain. Mrs. Schultz had suggested that she should see it. Connor guides her through the lobby and a side door into a garden. There is the lionhead fountain. She studies the lion's head with water coming out of his mouth.

"You must like fountains. I remember first seeing you at the Forsyth Park fountain. You were singing an old Irish children's song if I remember correctly."

Sharon nods her head two or three times. "I do like that fountain. It has become my place of peace in the city when I need to think."

Suddenly, Sharon is aware that someone has come into the little park with them. She looks over to the gate and there is Lucas.

"Hello," he says, coming through the gate and closing it behind him.

Connor moves to Sharon's side as she greets him. "Hello, Lucas."

"I see you are enjoying yet another feature of Savannah's life, one I have not taken you to."

"Excuse me," interrupts Connor. "Can we be of any service to you?"

"Yes, you can," says Lucas. "You can explain to me why your company wants to control the finances in Savannah and sever the relationship with the factors and other companies who have had long-term business interests with your company."

"What my company does is for the future growth of both the company and others in Savannah."

"Your changes suggest an elimination of many businesses who have grown to rely on Graves & Son as a business partner. How do you explain that?"

"Simply by saying that times make changes. With the growth of the railroads and shipping, there are opportunities for many."

"That's easy for you to say. You will be leaving soon while the rest of us have to stay and pick up the pieces destroyed by your company's decisions."

Connor does not answer Lucas but turns to Sharon. "Shall we go now?" He begins to lead her to the gate. Lucas stands between them and the gate. As Connor approaches Lucas, who does not move out of the way, the two men stand face to face in the path. Sharon does not move but watches the two men in defiant poses, almost nose to nose. Finally, Lucas steps to the side. Connor turns to look at Sharon, who then moves to pass by Lucas.

When she is even with him, he says, "I'll see you after Mass tomorrow." Then he turns and walks into the hotel from the door they had used earlier. Connor holds the gate for her.

They walk silently for a few blocks, and then Connor asks, "If I may ask, where are you going tomorrow with Lucas?"

There is a softness to Connor's question. Sharon notices and makes a note for herself. "I am following up on my interest in the Fresh Air Home located on Tybee Island. If I am trying to promote a sale of the fabric flowers, then I feel I need to see the space to help the nurses and the sisters. You were there when I told the Music Club directors about the home and how we might make more fabric flowers to sell to fund one of our nurses."

"I remember. I asked Mr. Nichols to help with the fundraising."

"That's right. So, I wanted to visit the area and see for myself. Lucas has been an informal guide around the city on Sunday afternoons and has helped me get acclimated to my new city. He has offered to help me with the transportation on the train out to Tybee Island."

Connor is quiet as they walk a few more blocks. "What do you hear from your New York friends?"

"I just got a letter from Danielle today. She shared with me that she is expecting a baby and wished that I was there to help her plan."

"You know something about babies?"

"Very little. My sisters are a lot younger than I am, but they all have children, and I have been the aunt who brought pockets of candy for them when I visited. Danielle and I shared rooms at the house we had purchased for the bakery and became good friends, sister friends."

"I understand. That's how I feel about the women I grew up with in my uncle's house. They all became sisters."

As they walk through the Savannah streets, she is comfortable sharing stories of her family and friends with Connor. When there is silence, it is a good silence of people who are getting to know one another and who respect the other person's right to private thoughts.

The boarding house is in front of them before Sharon is

ready. At the foot of the steps, she pauses. Connor turns to face her. He reaches a hand up to gently touch her face. She looks directly into his eyes. He smiles. "I had a wonderful time at dinner with you," he says.

"So did I."

He continues to hold her face in his hand. She has seen his hand a thousand times at work with pen and ledger sheets yet here is that same hand touching her face. An electric current appears from nowhere and cascades up her spine to her face. She feels a warm glow. Connor slides his hand down her arm and holds her fingers gently. Still looking into her eyes, he kisses her fingers. "I will see you Monday at the office. Take care tomorrow on your venture." With that, he releases her fingers. She turns to walk up the steps. At the top, she does not turn around but feels his eyes still watching her as she opens the door and steps inside. When she closes the door, she leans against it, still feeling the power of his touch.

Mrs. Schultz comes from the parlor and sees her against the door. "Obviously, the dinner was a success," she says.

Sharon feels that the smile on her face originates deep down in her heart.

27

S unday morning comes far too early for Sharon, who spent much of the night replaying Connor's goodbye to her. She floats through the motions of getting dressed, eating breakfast, and preparing for Mass. Gertrude has loaned her a special dress to wear to the beach. It is a light blue seersucker dress with a dark blue four-inch waistband and matching four-inch cuffs below the elbow. Four matching dark blue buttons and trim finish off the bodice. She also borrowed a straw hat from Alice. Gertrude helped refit it with dark blue lace that could hang down and cover her face to shade her from direct sun or be tied around her chin should there be more than a breeze off the ocean. She plans on changing into the dress after Mass.

She and Mrs. Schultz walk together as is their habit on Sunday morning. They sit in their regular place. When Connor enters, he bows toward the women and greets them both with a "Good morning, ladies." Sharon smiles back while Mrs. Schultz answers, "Good morning, Connor." He walks up and sits with Mr. Nichols and his family. Sharon had no idea about the service content that morning. She goes through the motions but does not remember anything the priest says. As soon as the Mass is over, Mrs. Schultz is busy talking with several of her friends, so Sharon begins walking back to the boarding house. She is only a block down the street when Connor catches up with her.

"You walk fast for a lady in heels," he says.

"It's my New York walk. One needs to cover vast distances quickly."

"I see. Well, I have something for you." And he hands her a small package. They stop in the middle of the sidewalk.

She looks first at him and then at the package. "Thank you, but whatever is this?"

"Open it."

She opens the package. Inside is an ornate crystal bottle of *Lavandula Vera* by Charles Flahault, according to the engraved card attached to the bottle.

"The hotel chemist told me that it would be helpful to keep flies and mosquitoes away from a lady should she visit a beach or island off the coast."

Speechless, Sharon holds the bottle gently. Tears came quickly to her eyes. She has never received a gift like this. She blinks back the tears. "Thank you. This is so thoughtful."

"I just wanted you to be safe," he says more with his eyes than with his words. "Well, I know you have a lot to do, so I will let you be on your way. See you at the office in the morning." And with that, Connor turns and walks back towards St. John's.

Sharon hurries to the boarding house with her gift cradled in her arms. She changes into the beach dress. She has not used an expensive perfume like this before. She hesitates, but then she remembers seeing one of Cahey's friends splash perfume on a handkerchief. She pulls a handkerchief out of her bureau drawer and splashes a dab on the linen cloth. The lavender odor permeates the room. She stuffs the handkerchief in her purse and dashes off to the train depot to meet Lucas.

The end of September is a perfect time to go to Tybee, so says the clerk at the train depot as they pay the forty-cent round trip fare. Other folks also wait to board. The platform is full of blankets, towels, satchels, cloth bags, and baskets ready for picnics on the beach. The eighteen-mile train ride is through the marshes and onto the island. Lucas, returning to his role as a tour guide, explains that the Euchee tribe originally occupied Tybee, and in the Euchee language, "tybee" means salt. Claimed by the Spanish but recognized as an important outpost to guard the mouth of the Savannah River, a small fort and lighthouse were constructed in 1736.

The Tybee Island lighthouse has become a symbol of safety to Sharon after seeing it for the first time when the steamship stabilized and she felt they would be safe. She tells Lucas that she would like to see the lighthouse up close. She then listens as Lucas goes off in another direction to explain that the French were interested in Tybee because of its sassafras root, used in tea, which was thought to be a miracle elixir that would cure many ailments. That's when, in the 1800s, Tybee became known to help people with asthma and allergies, and visiting them became known as "taking the salts."

Sister Mary Joyce's information on why the Froebel Circle of Savannah created the Fresh Air Home begins to make more sense to Sharon. If the children were to increase their health and happiness through exposure to the sea, then locating it on Tybee, known for its health benefits, was a good idea.

As Sharon exits the train, she is jostled by children already in their bathing costumes. They are hurrying to reach the sandy beach with their parents urging them to slow down. Sharon notices a steady breeze with salty air filling her lungs. Her small basket with a few pastries and fruits is light compared to some of the beach gear others are carrying. She has been told that there is a café at the Tybrisa Pavilion where they could get something to eat, but Sharon remembers Lucas saying he was on a budget, and she did not want to assume. Lucas takes the basket, and off they go to find the Fresh Air Home.

As they approach the building, it appears empty, but Sharon tells Lucas that it is used primarily in the summer. In the sandy yard, crabgrass grows in patches leading up to the buildings. Raised high off the ground, the house is painted dark green with the same color of green lattice woodwork covering the area from the ground to the porch. Wide wooden steps with white railings lead up to a wrap-around porch trimmed in the same white wood railings as the steps but with support posts. Palm trees on either side of the steps are like sentinels protecting the building. As they approach the house, they see an older woman hanging sheets on a clothesline. Sharon calls out and the woman looks up, shielding her eyes with her hand against the sun's glare. She waves.

As they near, Sharon speaks up again. "Hello, I'm Sharon McGee, and this is my friend, Lucas Laurent. The Sisters of Mercy send their good wishes."

"Ah," says the woman, "good to hear from them. Are you new to the order?"

"No, I am only a resident of the boarding house where the nurses are training at St. Joseph's."

The woman is Sister Mary Ernestine. She is not wearing a habit but a loose cotton dress with an apron. Her hair has been stuffed under a white bandana. After the introductions, the sister offers to show them around the house. At the front door is Froebel's guiding mission, lettered on a wooden plaque: "In so much as ye have done to one of the least of these, my brethren, ye have done also unto me. Matthew 25:40."

They are guided through the house by Sister Mary Ernestine as if they are prospective parents. She points out that the wide porch is used to serve lunch in good weather. Upstairs are large bedrooms with five bunk beds per room and hooks on the wall for the children's uniforms, which are provided. There are several smaller bedrooms for the adult counselors and volunteers who help with the program at the home. Back downstairs, Sharon sees a piano in the dining room and is told that the children are taught songs in the evening and are read stories before dinner.

"Where is the infirmary?" Sharon asks.

Sister Mary Ernestine points to a door to the kitchen. "Through there. Excuse me a moment. I must get the mail. I see the postman coming with a package."

Sharon walks through the kitchen and does not see an infirmary. She goes out to the back porch and sees a locked door with a Red Cross poster on the door.

Sister Mary Ernestine catches up with her by coming up the back steps with her package. "I see you found it. We keep it separate so a sick child will not contaminate others. We keep it locked to protect the supplies." She turns and points out an outdoor shower. "When the children come from the beach, they shower here to wash off the sand and can hang their towels on the clothesline to dry."

Having seen all she needed to see, Sharon thanked Sister Mary Ernestine for the tour.

As she and Lucas exit down the back steps, Lucas remarks, "Okay, so the main goal has been achieved. Let's go to the pier and then the pavilion."

"But what about your assignment?"

"Later. First, I want to show you the sights on Tybee Island."

They walk back to the beach. Their walk through the dunes is slow. Seagulls gather on the sand. As Sharon and Lucas approach, the birds flutter into the air, squawking and calling out, circling low over the water as they fly. Waves gently foam at the shore. Along the edge of the dunes, people sit. Some have laid out their blankets and towels, while others sit in wooden chairs that have little awnings attached to the high-backed chairs to shade them from the sun. Most of the sitters are in dress clothes with street shoes and umbrellas. Sharon studies the bathers' costumes. One has on black silk stockings and ballerina-type shoes with satin ribbons crisscrossing up her ankles to protect her feet and legs from the sand. Sailor-themed bathing costumes are everywhere as part of the fashion. These bathers stand out in their black-and-white striped taffeta suits with sailor-style collars, black silk stockings, and black leather sandals. Sharon is memorizing every detail and plans to write Danielle as soon as possible with the descriptions. She is sure that none of her friends have seen a beach like this.

They get to the pier and slowly walk down the length. Far out into the ocean, the pier finally ends. To observe the view, Lucas leans on the railing and looks out over the water. "There, look there," he says and points out into the water about fifty yards. A graceful black arc emerges from the water's surface and curves up, out, and back down again. A little distance away, six dolphins surface the water and leap in unison. Sharon cannot stop watching. Soon, seven dolphins surface the water and continue on their way. The lone one has caught up. Sharon lets out her breath. She laughs because she did not realize she was even holding her breath.

"That was something, wasn't it?" says Lucas.

"Magnificent. I have never seen anything like that before."

"Have you been to the beach in New York?"

"New York is surrounded by water, but it is river water. And, as easy as it is to get to the ocean from New York, I never had the time, money, or an occasion to go."

"Then I am happy to have the opportunity to show you yet another part of the area around Savannah. The breeze is brisk here, but the sun is bearing down on me. Let's walk back and have a lemonade in the pavilion."

They turn to go, but Sharon pauses. She sees a boat approaching the shore, a small fishing boat with many gulls flying in and around the boat. As the boat nears, she sees that a young man, almost too young, she thinks, is alone in a boat out in the ocean. He rows the boat steadily and comes closer to shore. What concerns her are the waves sloshing the boat about. The boat did not look steady or safe. And in that instant, the young man looks up and sees Sharon. Their eyes meet. She waves to him. He ducks his head and steadies the boat. Seeing that she has been entranced by the young man and not paying attention to where Lucas is, she has to step quickly to catch up with him.

At the pavilion, they purchase lemonades and find a table at the edge where they can feel the breeze off the ocean. Sharon produces the pastries and fruit from her basket. As they watch the people milling about, sitting at other tables, and coming in with fishing poles and baskets to get a little respite from the sun, Lucas pulls his chair closer to the table.

"You work with Connor Murphy."

Sharon quickly looks at him. "Yes, you know I do."

"How much has he shared with you about the changes his company will be making?"

"Why don't you ask him?"

"I did. You heard me last night. I asked, and he did not answer."

"I am not privy to any visions the company might have for its future."

"But from the numbers, you do know if the company is solvent or not."

Too stunned to answer, Sharon looks about the pavilion and sees that a large party has arrived. She changes the subject. "I think we are lucky to have found a table. There is a large group arriving."

Lucas looks up at the new arrivals and then back at her. "So, is the company solvent or not?"

"Lucas, please do not interview me. I have no information for you. I thought this excursion was to be a friend showing a friend something new, not trying to get information for a story." She puts down the plum she had been eating and wipes her hands on a napkin from the basket. She leaves her hand on the table. Lucas reaches out and places his hand on top of hers. Their eyes meet.

"I am happy to hear that you are enjoying my company. After seeing you with Connor last evening, I thought you may not have wanted to come today."

Sharon eases her hand away and picks up the plum. "I am free to do whatever I want and to be with whomever I want."

"Good, because he is leaving soon and probably will not be returning. That is why I need to find out about the company. There are a lot of businessmen who have been having conversations with him at the card games at various times and none of them are sharing any business information. There is a lot of secrecy in what Connor is doing. You do know that he spent the entire day on Saturday at a desk in the lobby of the hotel, going back and forth to answer many phone calls?"

Some plum juice drips on the table and Sharon hastily takes the napkin and dabs at it as though it is the most important thing she could do at the time. Lucas does not look at her but looks out at the ocean. The waves lapping on the shore give a rhythm to the pavilion that will soon be drowned out by the party voices of the new group. One of the men in the group has a guitar. Though the pavilion is famous for its big bands and dances, there is no dancing on Sunday. However, there is no law that says an individual can't play music in public. A chord is struck, and a man begins to sing.

"There's a day we feel gay,

If the weather's fine.
Ev'ry lad feels so glad,
If the sun does shine,
In his best, he is dressed,
And with smiling face,
He goes with his Pearlie,
His own little girlie, to some nice place."

His friends chime in on the chorus. They sing louder than
the soloist. There is no microphone, but with the roof over the
pavilion, the music bounces around. The people in the group
swing each other around, and a few step up on the chairs to
sing the chorus loudly.

"On a Sunday afternoon,
In the merry month of June,
Take a trip up the Hudson or down the bay,
Take a trolley to Coney or Rockaway,
On a Sunday afternoon,
You can see the lovers spoon,
They work hard on Monday, but one day that's
     fun day,
Is Sunday afternoon, on a noon."

The men in the group form a circle around the main singer.
They laugh and link arms, swaying to the lyrics as the singer
continues. He jumps up to stand on a chair.

"Coming home, Starry dome,
With a soft moonshine.
Lover's kiss, oh what bliss,
Oh, what joy divine.
Goodnight Joe, Goodnight Flo,
Don't forget now, dear,

Next Sunday at two,
I'll be waiting for you,
on the old Iron Pier."

The crowd under the pavilion applauds, cheers, and shouts at the end of the song. The members of the party bow, but they are in their own world of singing and having a good time at the beach.

Before Lucas can ask any more questions, Sharon looks out at the shoreline and notices the young man in the boat down below. He is having difficulty with his large number of canvas bags. She stands up. "Shall we visit the lighthouse? I would like to see it after you have given me such a history lesson."

"Yes, and I have something to look into as well."

"You did say you were on an assignment. I forgot to ask, should I wait here for you?"

"No, no, it is just a few blocks from the lighthouse. We can go there after."

They leave the pavilion and exit onto the sand. Sharon sees the same young man she saw earlier, but now he is struggling to haul large bags toward a beachside market. He is about her height but quite thin, too thin to be carrying so much weight.

"Lucas, there's the young man we saw earlier. He needs help. Let's go help." Sharon calls out and waves to the young man, who stops and puts down the heavy bags. He is dressed in tattered tweed pants and a billowing cotton shirt, with a straw hat on his head tied under his chin with a cord. Sharon has seen many young men dressed the same in New York. At one time even her brothers probably looked a lot like the way this young man looks. Sharon cannot let him struggle alone. "Hello, I'm Sharon, what's your name?"

The young man stops and looks at Sharon. "Michael."

"Michael, this load looks heavy for someone your age. How old are you?"

"Fifteen, ma'am." He glances over at Lucas.

"This is my friend, Lucas." After several nods, Sharon continues. "Why all these heavy bags?"

"I have had a really good fishing day and did not want to leave the fish any longer in the boat with the gulls so active."

Sharon looks at all the canvas bags. "You are fishing out in the ocean alone?"

"Yes, ma'am."

"There's no one to help you?" And before Michael answers, Lucas picks up some of the bags, and Michael picks up the rest. Michael steps ahead and leads them to the market. Sharon follows.

As they near the market, a gnarly, sunbaked man comes from behind the stand and shouts out to Michael. "It's about time you got here. We are all out of fish and people have been asking." He removes his straw hat to wipe his forehead and bald scalp with a cloth. He opens a lidded wooden box that has ice in it. "Put them in here." His gruff commands are directed at Michael, who pours his fish into the box. He then takes the bags from Lucas and pours them in as well.

"I'm not paying the two of you, so you don't need to ask," says the man to Lucas.

Sharon speaks up first. "No need, sir. We are happy to help."

The man grunts and moves toward a cash box. He takes a few coins out and pushes them into Michael's hand. The coins that Michael holds make him squint, and then he says, "Sir, you asked for more fish today than last week. I doubled the number, but you have paid me the same as you did last week."

"That's right. I paid you for the fish. I did not ask you to double; I just said it would be nice to have more."

Lucas and Sharon had stepped back from the market to allow Michael to deal with the man. Sharon looks at Lucas. "That's not fair," she says.

"What am I supposed to do? I do not know the boy nor the man. I can't get in the middle of their business."

Both are silent until Michael turns and comes back to them. "Thank you for helping me with the load."

"No problem," says Lucas.

However, Sharon asks right away. "Did he make up the difference in the number of fish?"

"No, ma'am."

"Then let's go talk with him again." As Sharon moves toward the man, Michael stops her.

"Please, just let it go."

"Why? He got more than last week. He should pay more."

"No, please, I need the money and must be able to sell him the fish."

Looking at him, his clothes, his unkempt hair tucked under a straw hat, and the patched but usable canvas bags for the fish, Sharon realizes that he does indeed need the money.

"Do you live near?"

"Everyone lives near; it's an island."

Sharon smiles at her error. "Okay. We plan on walking to the lighthouse. Are you off then?"

"Yes, ma'am. I need to move the boat over to the riverside. Thanks again, mister, for helping me out." With that, he runs toward the water and his boat.

Lucas turns to face Sharon. "Aren't you the good Samaritan! That was a nice thing for you to do. Shall we go now?" He turns toward the lighthouse.

Still watching Michael, Sharon gives Lucas a long look and begins to walk beside him. She is confused as to what Lucas means. Did he think that what they did was a nice thing to do, or did he say so only to please her and her decision to help Michael? He can be so confusing. He seems so helpful with showing her around Savannah and bringing her out to Tybee, but then he says or does things that make her think he is being sarcastic.

They walk leisurely on the sandy beach toward the lighthouse. Lucas explains how important the lighthouse has been to the area. Though it has been destroyed some three times, it has been rebuilt with its height changing from 90 feet to 154 feet. A Fresnel lens displays a light that can be seen at least eighteen miles out to sea. The storm at sea kept her from seeing the light.

On their arrival at the lighthouse, Sharon sees the black base with its white top standing among a group of buildings. One of the buildings, they learn, is the lightkeeper's house, where he and his family live. Another house is for the assistant lightkeeper. The third building looks to be a place to store equipment and materials for the upkeep of the acreage. All in all, she learns that it takes three people to make the light function twenty-four hours a day, every day. Satisfied that she has seen the lighthouse up close, she chooses not to climb the 178 steps to the top.

"Now, where?" Sharon asks.

"To the jail."

"What?"

"Just teasing. I need to check out the new Guard House at Fort Screven. It's just down the beach from here."

They choose to walk on the hard-packed sand nearer the water rather than slosh through the sand and the dunes. Sharon has been cautioned by her roommates to wear sturdy shoes so she is prepared. Soon, she sees a building. It stands out with its buttercream color and its wrap-around veranda that doubles the size of the building.

"See, there it is, the Guard House," points out Lucas. "It's new and we have not written about it yet."

Lucas tells Sharon that the Guard House is at the entrance to Fort Screven, the Army base used for coastal defense. The building will be the headquarters for the soldiers who will guard the post and also serve as a brig for "unruly" troops; that's why he referred to it as "the jail."

As they reach the Guard House and climb the steep steps to the veranda, Sharon sees that workmen are putting the finishing touches on the building. All of the doors and windows are open. Lucas takes out his notebook and begins. Sharon wanders into the first of two rooms. The walls are covered with checkerboard-patterned tin with ten-foot ceilings. The ceilings are covered with ornate pressed tin. Any paint trim in the room is a pastel yellow to match the buttercream exterior.

Lucas talks with one of the workers and locates the foreman. He motions to Sharon that he is going into the other room. She moves back to the veranda to look out onto the ocean. All she sees is water and birds diving for food. Sharon is mesmerized; then she feels someone leaning on the veranda's railing next to her.

"I love to watch the birds play in the water," says the workman Lucas had been talking with earlier.

"Me, too," says Sharon and looks back at the ocean. "Do you know anything about birds?"

"I do. I live here on the island and participate in the Audubon Society's Christmas Bird Count."

"A bird count? Why?" She looks at him, a balding middle-aged man in good physical condition with bulging biceps and defined veins on his lower arms that he has draped over the railing. In his workman's pants and shirt, with his sleeves rolled up tightly above his elbow and wearing heavy boots, he does not look like someone who would spend hours with binoculars looking at birds.

"Ornithologist Frank M. Chapman, an officer of the Audubon Society, proposed that during Christmas, instead of hunting the birds, we count them and identify them in our area. This began in 1900."

"And you do this every year?"

"It tells us when and where the birds migrate and how those patterns may change over time."

Sharon points to a flock of birds sitting in the sand, dozens of them. "What are those?"

"Those are black skimmers. You can tell them from others because their lower beak is longer than their upper beak. Some flocks can be as big as a hundred to a thousand birds. They are here year-round along with the oystercatcher. There, see that bird with the flat red bill? The bird uses that bill to pry open oysters. There is often a purple sandpiper out there; they frequent North Beach. In the winter, because the north beach is at the mouth of the Savannah River, where it meets the Atlantic Ocean, scores of Northern Gannets can be seen circling and diving into the water at the river's entrance. This is also the winter home for loons. Year-round, though, I see terns, gulls, pelicans, and cormorants. It's a busy place."

Sharon continues to look out at the shorebirds. Lucas walks up and nudges in between Sharon and the workman. "What are we talking about?"

"Birds," said Sharon and the workman at the same time, and they both laughed. Lucas looks first at Sharon and then at the workman, who speaks up. "I guess you got all the information you want."

"Yes," says Lucas. "Yes, I did." He turns to Sharon. "Ready to catch the train?" And he takes her elbow and escorts her off the porch. Sharon turns briefly to the workman. "Thank you for the bird information. Have a great Christmas count."

"My pleasure," he says. "Come join us. You'll enjoy it."

Sharon smiles back at him as Lucas guides her down the steep steps to reverse their path and return to the pier.

"We have time now to look at more of the stalls selling souvenirs if you like," Lucas suggests.

There are several souvenir booths featuring items such as photos made in front of a ship on the water backdrop and trinkets as memory tokens. Sharon stops at the booth where necklaces are made from sweetgrass. The weaver has learned from her Native American friends. She tells Sharon that if the necklaces are worn, the fragrances of the sweetgrass will keep away biting insects, especially mosquitoes. She works only with the sweetgrass but has heard that other natural scents like cinnamon, peppermint, cedar, lemongrass, and lavender also work. Sharon takes the handkerchief with the dab of perfume and puts it up to her nose. The fragrance permeates the air around her, and she remembers the lovely gift. The fact that it can keep insects away is secondary.

"Have you had enough sun?" asks Lucas.

"Can we just sit in a couple of chairs and watch the ocean? We may see more dolphins."

Agreeing, Lucas locates a couple who are standing to leave. He moves in to save the chairs. They sit and watch the water as it reaches the shoreline, bounces against the sand, and is covered in white foam, flowing back out again. Sharon watches as a small child with a woman close to her chases the waves. The little girl dances toward the water as it goes out to sea, and then when it turns and begins coming toward her, she staggers quickly away, laughing and running so that the water does not catch her. If the wave gets too close, the woman scoops her up, and the little girl screeches with glee. They repeat this many times.

Neither Lucas nor Sharon pay attention to the chattering that goes on around them. Instead, they both watch the people on the beach as entertainment. Three young men in matching swim costumes kick a ball on the sand, tapping the ball back and forth among themselves. Down the beach, a man with a small boy hoists a kite into the sky. They walk back and forth, letting the twine take the kite up and calling out to each other as they watch the kite go higher.

The sun gets hot, so Sharon suggests they vacate the chairs and head for the depot. Having accomplished her mission of seeing the Fresh Air Home, she is ready to return to the boarding house and prepare for the work week ahead. On the trip back, Lucas returns to being a tour guide, describing the foliage, the advance of the railroad, and how Savannah is growing out and needs additional trolley and rail spurs to accommodate the movement of new folks into affordable houses, much as they had seen when they visited Collins' meadow.

Not wanting to think about Collins' meadow, Sharon remembers the theatre fire. Lucas may have more information. She asks him if he has learned how the fire started.

"No, it is a mystery," he says. "There is speculation that one of the ghosts haunting the theatre did it."

Sharon smiles. "You don't believe that, do you?"

Lucas shakes his head. "No, but it makes for a fun story."

"What will happen now with productions?"

"The Weiss family, who owns the theatre, has confirmed that performances will be held in the Mutual Skating Rink. Sarah Bernhard played there just this year, back in March, so it is the logical place to hold any theatrical performance until the theatre is rebuilt."

"I saw her last December at the Lyric Theatre in New York as Marguerite Gautier in Alexandre Dumas' 'La Dame Aux Camélias.'"

"That is the same play that was performed in Savannah."

"You saw the play? I thought you couldn't afford to go to plays."

"She's French; it was a must-see. Plus, I got assigned to cover it."

"You haven't talked about your family. Are they here in Savannah?"

"My family? No, they are not here. They are in France. I came alone to seek my fortune. Because I can read and write in English, I landed a job with the newspaper."

"Was that your plan?"

"I had no plan; I just needed a job. My family are restaurant owners. We have a long history of chefs in the family."

"So, you cook?"

"No. That's one of the reasons I left France. I cannot cook. Plus, I do not want to run a business where I am inside all day. I want to go about and talk with people."

"Sounds like being a reporter is a good job for you."

"That's what I thought, but the hours are long and the pay is low. I have discovered that the only way to make money in the newspaper business is to own the newspaper."

"Is your goal to own the *Savannah Morning Sun*?"

"Who is being interviewed now?"

"Sorry, I am just curious as to why you have not spoken about your family."

The train whistle signaled their stop at the Savannah depot and interrupted Lucas's answer. Lucas stops Sharon on the sidewalk by placing his hand under her elbow after departing the train. "I had a good day with you. Would you like to get something to eat?"

"Thank you, but no. I have many tasks to prepare for the work week. Thank you for showing me Tybee Island. I have had a holiday and we were only eighteen miles away."

"My pleasure, as always." He moves in close to Sharon. "May I at least walk you back to your boarding house?"

"I'm fine; it is not dark yet." She smiles. "Thank you." She turns and walks quickly down the block and across the street. The day has been filled with many experiences. She has not had time to process the reception, the recital, the theatre fire, dinner with Connor, and now the day with Lucas on Tybee. She needs some time to think.

28

A long weekend of extreme experiences leaves Sharon exhausted but energized. Gertrude's shining performance has produced a camaraderie with the women in the boarding house. Each woman now greets all the others by name and with a smile. Additionally, the women engage each other in conversations about their interests, dreams, and family histories. Even though the women are all from Savannah and many of them grew up in the same neighborhoods, they did not know each other before being accepted into the nursing program. Sharon watches Mrs. Schultz sit at the table with a smile on her face. There appears to be a feeling among the women that they are all in this house for a reason. Even Sharon's roommates, Sarah and Alice, do not go out as often as before.

One evening after dinner, Sharon is in the sleeping room preparing her clothes for the next workday when Sarah and Alice come in. They are chatting away. Before, when they entered the room, they were cordial and would say hello, but then they would silently get their purses and leave.

"We were just talking about how we have to starch our

collars, cuffs, and aprons every night for the next day, and here you are, making wonderful decisions on what clothes to prepare. We are so jealous!" says Alice.

"Don't be," says Sharon. "I don't have your eye to choose the right accessories."

"But you have put together some great ideas, like the dress you wore to Tybee," says Sarah.

Sharon laughs. "It was Gertrude, all Gertrude. She was even the one who suggested buying this hat to change out with feathers, ribbons, and lace."

"Speaking of Gertrude," says Alice, "she will be leaving us in a few weeks. We should do something here at the house, don't you think?"

"Yes, I think that is a great idea. What do you suggest?"

"Well, we don't want to add to the work of Mrs. Schultz or the staff, so maybe we could all come up with a homemade gift for her and have a going away gathering before she leaves," suggests Sarah.

"I love the homemade gifts," says Alice. "I can make a needlepoint cushion to use on a piano bench. I already have most of the needlepoint done. I have not been able to think about what to do with it. Now I do," says Alice directly to Sarah.

"I could make her some sachets for her bureau drawers," says Sarah, looking at Alice.

"And we can talk with the other girls and see what they might like to do," says Alice. Without so much pause, both women are out the door and down the hall to talk with the other nurses.

Sharon makes a little humph laugh with a shake of her head and continues to prepare her clothes and think about what she could make for Gertrude. She has never been good with crafts, just numbers. This will need some thought.

She also remembers dinner with Connor. Each time she thinks about his hand gliding down her arm, a little electricity runs down her spine. What does that mean? This has never happened before, not even with Cahey, whom she thought she cared for deeply. Connor has made it clear that he will be returning to Ireland when their accounting transition is complete, and that goal is the first of December. She knows she should not think about how he makes her feel. On the other hand, it is delightful to have these new feelings. Sometimes, she just wants to break out in a jig and celebrate, but then when she thinks about him leaving, she wants to sit down on her bench in Forsyth Park and feel miserable.

Each workday, when she and Connor sit and prepare the ledgers, she has to push her thoughts away and concentrate on the work to be done. He does not make that easy with his eyes seeking hers. She has to look down hurriedly to avoid sharing how she might be feeling.

And then there is Lucas, the first person she met in Savannah and one who has given her lots of time to see Savannah as her home. Because of Lucas, she knows where to shop for bargains, where to get good but cheap lunches, how to take the trolleys and the train, and more about the city's history than people who grew up here. She has leaned on Lucas many times to ferret out information to accomplish her goals.

Most recently, she asked him who to talk with about selling the fabric flowers. The nurses are busy making the flowers and she must find a way to get them sold. Lucas gives her several organizational names, including the Knights of Columbus and the Ancient Order of Hibernians. As to women's clubs, he suggests that she talk with the Music Club program chair, Mrs. Leo Lynch, who is well-connected in Savannah.

Sharon goes through Gertrude to contact Mrs. Lynch, who invites Sharon to visit her home after Sharon's workday is over. Mrs. Lynch lives in the Old Fort Post section of Savannah. Stopping in after work would be an easy walk for her.

Surprise registers on Sharon's face when she is ushered into

Mrs. Lynch's parlor by the maid. After seeing Mrs. Lynch dressed in feathers at the recital, she is not prepared for her conservative dress. Mrs. Lynch is wearing a long burgundy skirt with a paler burgundy blouse. Her dark hair is streaked with grey along the sides and is pulled back in a bun similar to the style Sharon wears.

"Thank you for seeing me, Mrs. Lynch." Sharon begins as she enters.

"Please, call me Susan. Have a seat. We'll have a cup of tea in a moment." She nods to the maid waiting at the door.

"You've settled in nicely in Savannah, yes?"

"It has been easy to do with well-laid-out streets and squares. And, I could not have found a better place to stay than with Mrs. Schultz."

"Mrs. Schultz has a reputation for having a quality house. The nursing program graduated their first four last year, did you know?"

"I do. And they have six who will be eligible this spring."

"Wonderful." At this moment, the maid brings in the tray with the tea. Conversation stops until the tea is poured, lemon is offered, and napkins are tucked on their laps. "Now, how may I help you?"

With a shallow breath, Sharon straightened her back and presented what she knew about the Fresh Air Home and how the nurses at the boarding house are making fabric flowers to help fund one of them to work in the home during the summer. The camp can offer more experience in which to pursue a nursing position. The idea, she tells Susan, came from the discussion in the parlor during the reception for Gertrude's recital.

"I remember that discussion," says Susan. "I, too, was impressed with the beauty of the flowers the nurses made. Didn't Mr. Nichols suggest that the Music Club might help with the sale?"

"Yes, but we were thinking that if we got more clubs to sponsor, that would help the sales."

"Would you have enough flowers for more to be involved?"

"The women have made quite a few. But we were also thinking that if we sold more than we have, we could take orders and fill them after the initial sale."

"I see." Susan stirs more lemon into her tea, places the spoon on the tray, sips a little of the tea and all the while has her brow furrowed in thought. "Okay, let me tell you what I know about the women's clubs."

Susan is a member of several women's clubs. "Please don't misunderstand me when I tell you that the clubs have opened my eyes to issues I had never been apprised of. Though my husband is a businessman and respected in the city, my role is to run the house, plan our social calendar, and take care of the children. End of discussion." Susan fidgets with her saucer. She smiles sheepishly at Sharon and lowers her eyes. "However, I was raised with tutors in the house and books to read. There is more to learn and I am eager to know. The clubs allow us, as women, to become better educated. We bring all sorts of ideas in for discussion and offer books to read. We share knowledge." She pauses again.

Sharon is leaning forward to hear every word.

"Though we do share knowledge, the members of the club also work to make society a better place through community service. Do you follow what I am saying?"

"Oh, yes," says Sharon. "Please tell me the types of information shared."

Visibly relaxing, Susan enumerates. "We read literature and history as well as study law, music, and the sciences. If a member has another specific interest, we will certainly discuss that as well. Some members present essays or speeches on the current topics we study. Nina Pape..."

"She's the one that got the Fresh Air Home started," interrupts Sharon.

"Yes. She is from a very influential family. Her grandfather, Edward Clifford Anderson, was mayor of Savannah for five terms. Nearly ten years ago, Nina began teaching first grade at the Massie Elementary School, one of our best schools. That's when she created the Froebel Society based on the ideas of philosopher Frederic Froebel. She wants to reach out to the poor children of our city with innovative teaching techniques. She has created seven kindergartens in the poorest neighborhoods of the city emphasizing 'love over harsh discipline, creative play over memorization and treating every child as a unique individual.'" Susan stops when the maid enters to replace the teapot with another. The women sip their tea and stir with their spoons until the maid leaves.

"I am sure that all of our staff knows that things are being shared at our meetings," says Susan, looking at Sharon over the top of her teacup. "But we try not to talk in front of them. We know that we have a privileged opportunity and intend to keep it that way."

Sharon nods, but a tightness between her eyebrows develops into a frown. She might not be staff, but she is not privileged, and she still wants to know more about issues. She sits silently.

"Education is one of the main topics the club members discuss," Susan says. "And, along the way, various projects emerge that will help make our communities stronger."

"What kinds of projects?"

"Establishing kindergartens, libraries, parks, volunteer work. Our club members meet regularly to network, learn about social issues, identify civic problems, and then devise solutions through our volunteer power. Each club is unique and has different goals. We have learned that some clubs in

New York have pushed for women to be admitted to institutions of higher learning."

"Brenau, the college you have gifted a sponsorship to Gertrude, is such an institution?"

"Yes. The Music Club has an annual scholarship, and this seems like the perfect opportunity to strengthen Gertrude's talents and help her meet her future goals. Other clubs have addressed the abysmal conditions of the working girl in factories and have appealed for the end of workplace abuses."

Sharon puts her teacup down. "My sisters work in a shirtwaist factory in New York in the Asch Building. They have much to say about workplace abuses."

"I am sure. That is why the women's clubs are so very important. There is a book . . ." Susan gets up and crosses to her desk. She picks up a copy of Jane Croly's *The History of Women's Clubs in America* and walks back to hand Sharon the book. "This book was published in 1898 and shares information on the General Federation of Women's Clubs. Members swap success stories about educational and reform projects as well as other community projects like improved street lighting, environmental protections, and free milk clinics for impoverished mothers."

Sharon thumbs through the massive book. She shakes her head in disbelief. "I had no idea women were working for these changes. I had heard things about the vote, but not these other issues."

"We may not have the vote—yet, but we can learn and be ready when we do. Many women are joining; the memberships of the clubs are growing every year. We have limited ours to only what we can comfortably fit into someone's parlor. But the women's clubs in the country total nearly 800,000 women members."

Without so much as pausing, Sharon jumps in. "I would

love to be a part of such a group. Your group is full, but are there other clubs that may be accepting members?"

"Yes, there certainly are. And there is no reason why you cannot start your own club and choose who will come and be a part of that."

This time, Sharon paused to think. "In the meantime, would you work with me to get the clubs you are involved with to help the nurses sell the fabric flowers?"

"But of course, and this is how we need to do it."

For the next few minutes, the two women plan their contacts, their out-of-pocket expenses, how to get the message out to folks, and when and where they want to have the sale. "I must say, the hardest part seems to be where to hold the sale. The theatre would have been a perfect place, but with the fire that is out," says Susan.

"Could we have it in a park or square?"

"If we could count on it not raining in Savannah."

"Yes, of course."

"I know," says Susan. "Let's have it at one of the hotels—the DeSoto or Pulaski. We could have it on a Sunday afternoon. After church, there is often a Sunday dinner that is popular with couples. It might be the perfect venue."

"Who do we ask? How can we get access?"

Waving her hands in the air, Susan says, "Not a problem, my husband is part owner of the DeSoto. He is an investor in the Savannah Hotel Corporation, which built the hotel. I will ask him."

Sitting back now with no more questions to ask and so much information shared, Sharon is relieved that all of this went so smoothly.

"I will also talk with Elise and Maude Heyward," says Susan. "They are sisters who are active in several women's clubs and are interested in projects that involve civic improvement."

They sit quietly for a moment. Sharon skims through the

book and finds information on the Georgia Federation of Women's Club, founded in 1896 with 365 clubs and 27,000 members. She finds information on clubs with active Savannahians, like the Opera Study Club, Parliamentary Law Study Club, Thursday Afternoon Reading Club, and the Three Arts Club.

"What does the Parliamentary Law Club do?"

"Those women are eager to share how the democratic process allows individuals to participate and effect change in society rather than being mere bystanders. They have workshops to teach parliamentary procedures and how to participate in public meetings to involve more citizens. Another organization is the Colonial Dames of America. Founded in 1893, Savannah is one of twelve cities with a chapter devoted to furthering an appreciation of our national heritage through historic preservation, patriotic service, and educational projects."

Sharon leans back in her chair with the book in her lap. "I think I need to let the nurses know that we need a lot more fabric flowers."

Both women laugh, fold their napkins, and stand. "Thank you," says Sharon.

Susan nods her head. "Of course. We have a sale to put into place. I will send you a message when I have contacted several of the ladies in different clubs and what Mr. Lynch can offer with hosting it at the DeSoto Hotel."

The walk to the boarding house gives Sharon time to work out exactly what that sale may look like. An appeal can be made to those who host family gatherings around Thanksgiving and holiday community celebrations.

When Sharon gets to the boarding house, Mrs. Schultz is sitting on the porch enjoying the outside air.

"Mrs. Schultz, I have a question for you," says Sharon in greeting. She climbs up the porch steps and sits in a rocker next to Mrs. Schultz, who is poised, listening to what Sharon might ask. "Do you belong to any women's clubs?"

"Yes, to the Catholic Women's Club and St. Joseph's Nursing Auxiliary."

"Do you meet regularly?"

"Every month for a lunch meeting. We often meet here for the Nursing Auxiliary so that the sisters or nurses can attend, even if to drop in for a few minutes."

"And what do you talk about?"

Mrs. Schultz's laughter continues as she explains, "Anything at all. We do have a program of sorts with agenda items we would like to accomplish. One has been the Fresh Air Home and how to fund the nurses."

"I see." Sharon understands now why Mrs. Schultz has been so eager to get Sharon to step forward with ideas on how to raise funds.

29

At work the next day, Sharon finds time to ask Connor if he knows anything about either the Knights of Columbus or the Ancient Order of Hibernians. Connor stands up and walks over to the tea kettle. "This will need a new cup of tea." He pours one for Sharon as well and returns to sit next to her. He explains that the Ancient Order of Hibernians is the oldest Catholic lay organization in America. "It all started with the Church and power. I will give you the story as I have learned it."

Connor explains it this way. "Conflict over religion began early in Ireland when the Church became more materialistic with abuses of power. Reform was needed, but before that reform came, the British Royalty became interested in controlling the Church's wealth and reducing the power of Rome by converting the masses to Protestantism. The monarchy of Henry VIII and Elizabeth I declared that the Church of England, Anglican, would be the state religion. Elizabeth I believed that Ireland was part of her state. The Irish did not. The monarchy outlawed the Catholic Church. As a way to gain control, the monarchy confiscated land and gave that land to supporters who professed the state's religion and governed the population."

He pauses to drink some tea. "Though the Irish fought to protect both their land and religion, laws were passed that disenfranchised Irish Catholics from the political, social, and economic life of their own country. Their religion was outlawed, and their clergy were on the run. Therefore, some men formed an underground society where they could practice their faith in secret. Other secret societies emerged, like the Whiteboys, Ribbonmen, and Defenders, who attacked the landlords but who also vowed to protect the Roman Catholic Church and its clergy. As each of these societies was suppressed, they reorganized under a new name to defend their faith and homeland."

Connor looks at Sharon. "That's what I have learned. There is an American branch of the Ancient Order of the Hibernians. You may need to talk with a member to understand what they do here. All I know is that they provide monetary stipends to immigrants who arrive as members of good standing from the Irish order. They also assist Irish immigrants in obtaining jobs and social services. The Knights of Columbus is an American organization invested in charitable work. I believe there is a group of men at St. John's who belong. You will need to talk with them."

Sharon is listening so intently that her tea has gotten cold. She walks over and gets a new cup. "Well, to sell our fabric flowers to them, I suppose the nurses will need to make sure they have cultural meaning."

Connor laughs. "I suppose so. Make sure they are emerald colored."

Together, they sit and begin focusing on the ledgers. Sharon thinks, based on what Connor describes, that the sale of the flowers will not go far with the men's groups as they seem to be more focused on immigrants. She will need to cultivate the women's clubs once Mrs. Lynch gets back to her.

Mrs. Lynch sends word to Sharon that her husband supports the nurse's use of the DeSoto Hotel lobby to sell the fabric flowers. The nurses spend weeks making the flowers and securing the necessary supplies. One of the hospital auxiliaries provides fabric for the flowers. Another group at St. John's provides thread, needles, and embroidery hoops to hold the fabric flowers for the women to sew on decorations. The date is set. Mrs. Schultz, Sharon, and at least one or two nurses who might not be on rotation that day are scheduled to help at the sale. Other nurses will be there if they are not needed at the hospital.

At work, Connor asks about their plans. "I'll be happy to do the same service I did with the recital," he says. "We can get an advertisement in the newspaper and maybe some flyers to post at the hotel and to have in the vestibule of St. John's after Mass."

Though Sharon wants to distance herself from Connor because she knows he will be leaving soon, she is happy he wants to be involved. "Thank you."

"Why don't I walk you back to the boarding house tonight and we can plan what it is that you need?"

"The Bible reading is tonight in the parlor. Can you come tomorrow night? That will give me time to ask if Mrs. Schultz will be able to join us since she will be working at the sale."

"Of course," says Connor.

"And I can ask Mrs. Shultz if you can have dinner with me in the dining room." Sharon stops abruptly. She could not believe she just asked him to join her for dinner.

"That would be great. Maybe Mrs. Schultz will join us as well. We can plan over dinner."

30

M rs. Schultz is delighted that Connor is coming and will plan for the three dinners in the dining room when they arrive. Sharon shares the information with Connor at work the next day. They get down to their work and the day goes quickly. When they are ready to leave, Tad steps into their office.

"May I see you for a minute before you are off, Connor? It will not take long."

"Of course." He turns to Sharon. "I'll be right back."

Sharon stacks the ledgers and takes care of the teapot and dishes. She goes to the window overlooking the river. It is dark now this time of evening but enough lights are lining the walkways that she can see several boats moored and several anchored out in the river. A ship has arrived late and men are still bustling about unloading and pushing heavy carts into the warehouses down below. Sharon sees a full moon. Suddenly, Connor is at her side.

"Beautiful, isn't it?"

"Yes, see how the moonlight bounces off the river?"

"Did you know that there's a name for each full moon?"

"Really? Do you know what this full moon's name is?"

"A full moon in October is called 'The Hunter's Moon.'"

"Ah, I am not sure what that means."

"It comes from when men needed to hunt game in preparation for the winter. The harvest is over in September, so in October, when the moon is full, they go out and hunt the fatted deer and foxes so their families can eat through the winter."

Sharon laughs. "Here I was getting all excited over the beautiful moon with light to see our way to the boarding house, and all the while, men are stalking game to kill."

Joining her with a smile, Connor picks up his hat. "Let's keep your idea of it being beautiful and lighting our way, shall we?"

They say good night to Tad, who is staying later than usual. Sharon asks Connor, "Is everything all right with Tad? He's normally not here this late."

Connor opens the outside door for her. "He has a lot to think about, I suppose."

On their walk to the boarding house, Connor begins asking Sharon questions. He wants to know if she had certain goals in coming to Savannah. How does she find living at the boarding house? And does she have plans to return to New York?

She answers honestly. "I felt I needed a change of place to see if what I had learned would give me a place in the world, a career. I don't want just a job; I want to be able to grow and develop. As to the boarding house, I have made friends and learned a lot about the nursing profession, but bath times can be a bit rushed with so many women in the house. I have not made any plans to return to New York. I have chosen to relocate, and I must do my best to make it work."

"So, will there be holiday gatherings you will miss?"

"No, my family did not celebrate the season. I had dinner with my friends, but that was about all. I would like to experience a Christmas holiday and hope that might happen at Mrs.

Schultz's. I'm sure there will be something. We have been so busy with the fabric flower sale that there has been no discussion as to the holidays. All of the nurses have family in Savannah, but I do believe Mrs. Schultz will be at the house and I won't be alone. Though the idea of having the bath to myself for long periods is certainly something to look forward to."

Connor laughs. "I see. It's all about the bath, is it?"

"Of course. You may have had several women you grew up with, but I doubt seriously you had to share a bath space with any of them. Right?"

Laughing harder, Connor agrees. "No, my uncle and I had our bath, thank you very much."

"I knew so."

They walk up the steps to the boarding house. Mrs. Schultz is there, opening the door for them.

"Come in. Dinner is in the dining room. Please go on in."

Mrs. Schultz turned on the side lamps in the room for soft lighting and added flowers from the garden, bright red camellias still blooming strongly at that time of year. Dinner is individual ramekins of chicken pot pie with tomato salad on the side, a simple supper but perfect for talking and not having to pass food.

"Tell me what you have in mind for the fabric flower sale," says Mrs. Schultz.

Sharon begins with the idea of having the sale at the DeSoto Hotel. Mrs. Lynch has assured them that it is good but that the majority of club members wanted it to be held during the week and not on Sunday. Now, they need to think about flyers and getting the advertisement in the newspaper specifying how the fabric flower sale is a fundraiser to pay a nurse's salary for the Fresh Air Home. Once dinner is finished, Mrs. Schultz brings paper, pen, and ink for them to draft out what needs to go on the flyer.

Connor remembers reading in a Cork Newspaper a couple

of years earlier about the 50th anniversary of Florence Nightingale's departure from Southampton on the way to Crimea on October 21, 1854. They could use that information to bring importance to the sale.

They start the flyer with the phrase "Celebrate Nurses: Marking 50+ Years of Service. The Fabric Flower Sale will be Thursday, October 25, 1906, from 8 pm – 10 pm in the lobby of the DeSoto Hotel."

Then they add, "The fabric flowers are made by nursing students of St. Joseph's Hospital and are for sale to provide a nurse's salary for the Fresh Air Home summer camps on Tybee Island."

Finally, they have the information grouped and ready to take to the printer and then to the newspaper office. Mrs. Schultz excuses herself and takes the dishes into the kitchen. She invites them to move into the parlor. She refuses their offers to help, so they do as she instructs. However, when they get to the parlor, Sharon is hesitant to choose a place to sit. If she sits on a settee, then Connor may think he has to sit next to her. If she sits in a single chair, then she will distance him. As she hesitates, Connor walks around to the piano and sits down.

"You may not know that I can play a tune or two." He strikes a chord. "Come sit beside me. I know you can sing. I heard you the first day I met you in Forsyth Park."

Connor begins to play and sing.

"Little bird on my window
won't you sing me a song
When you fly over the meadow
will you bring me along
La, la, la, la, la, la."

Sharon joins him on the piano bench.

"There are beautiful flowers to see from up high
will you please take me with you
little bird as you fly
La, la, la, la, la."

They finish the last stanza, and Connor turns to Sharon to say in Irish, "*Is buaine port ná glór na n-éan, is buaine focal ná toice an tosaoil.*"

Sharon has heard little Irish since coming to Savannah. The nurses seem to know Irish but speak in English at the boarding house. The Irish sounds are welcome to her ears. "I agree. 'A tune outlasts the song of the birds; a word outlasts the wealth of the world.' But what word do we use?"

"The truth," says Connor. "The word is always' truth.'"

Connor runs a few chords on the keyboard, and before Sharon can respond, Connor begins another song, a favorite that her father had sung to her many a time as he warmed up to play a gig at a pub. She joins in, and they sing several of the verses.

"Are you going to Scarborough Fair?
Parsley, sage, rosemary and thyme,
Remember me to one who lives there,
She once was a true love of mine.

"Tell her to make me a cambric shirt,
Parsley, sage, rosemary and thyme,
Without no seam nor needle work,
Then she'll be a true love of mine."

Connor smiles and pauses to push his red hair out of his face. It has grown since he arrived and the curls are cascading over his ears and down his neck and hanging on his forehead. There are barbers at the hotel where he is staying, so he must want his hair to be longer. Sharon likes the curls and thinks they are better suited to him in his role as singer and pianist.

"Here's one you may not know, it's called 'The Old Woman of Wexford.'" He begins to play.

"There was an old woman from Wexford,
In Wexford town did dwell.
She loved her husband dearly
But another man twice as well.

"With me rifah loora liddey ay
And me rifah low-rel lay."

The verses of the song tell the story of the woman going to the doctor to get something to blind her husband. The doctor tells her to feed him eggs and marrow bones. The doctor, however, explains what he has done in a letter to the husband. The woman does as the doctor instructs, and the old man says he cannot see the wall and would drown himself, but it would be a sin. The woman offers to help push him in. She steps back to push him in, but the old man steps aside. She falls into the water and swims to the other side, but the old man gets a long pole and pushes her further in.

"Now eggs are eggs and marrow bones
May make your old man blind,
But if you want to drown him
You must creep up close behind."

By the time Connor gets to the end of the song, Sharon is laughing so hard she has to hold on to the side of the piano bench.

At the door, she sees Mrs. Schultz, who has a smile that could bridge the entire ocean from Savannah to Wexford.

"Look what you've done, Connor. You have changed our formal parlor into a pub space. Next thing I know, you may be asking for ale."

"No, ma'am," says Connor, shaking his curly head. "I am just allowing Sharon to see another side of me. I don't know if you know, but we met in Forsyth Park with her singing an Irish children's folk song. So, she's as guilty as I am."

Mrs. Schultz moves to sit down in her favorite chair when there is a loud knock on the front door. As she goes to the door, Connor asks Sharon what other songs her father sings to her. She does not have a chance to answer when Mrs. Schultz returns.

"He says that he has to talk with Sharon." Mrs. Schultz moves aside to let Lucas enter the room. Connor and Sharon both stand and move away from the piano.

"Isn't this cozy," says Lucas. "I hope I am not interrupting anything."

"What can I do for you, Lucas?" asks Sharon, not fully in control of her emotions.

"I learned that the Froebel Circle is having a fundraiser on October 26. I know from our conversation on Tybee Island that this is of some importance to you."

Sharon moves toward Lucas. "Thank you. It is important to know. Mrs. Lynch is contacting Miss Pape, and if we can work together, then I am sure she will make the appropriate connections. She is well aware of what we can do."

"We were just planning the flyer for a fundraiser with several clubs in Savannah," says Connor. "The advertisement will go in the newspaper once the printer has a chance to create it."

"How have you become involved in all of this?" Lucas looks directly at Connor.

"I have volunteered my services, sir, that is all. It is a worthy venture and will benefit the nurses." Connor moves slowly to stand in front of the fireplace.

"You seem to be developing quite a relationship with various enterprises here in Savannah. Do you plan on staying and contributing more to our vibrant society?"

Sharon interrupts and steps toward Lucas. "Thank you for bringing the information. I will contact Mrs. Lynch tomorrow and see how we can work together."

Lucas is not to be deterred and steps closer to Connor. "Is it true that your firm is pulling all of the financials out of Savannah and moving them to Wexford?"

Connor stands easily and rests his hand on the mantle. "The future of our company is connected strongly with Savannah."

"But you are here to duplicate and learn the processes so that they can all be done in Wexford, correct?"

Connor steps closer to Lucas. "How we do our business is of no concern to the newspaper."

Lucas and Connor are now face to face. "It will affect a dozen people who will lose their jobs once you leave, including this lady here." Lucas points to Sharon, who is looking not at Lucas but at Connor.

Connor's chiseled jaw is firmly clasped. His eyes are focused on Lucas and only on Lucas.

"When are you sailing?" asks Lucas.

"When we finish our tasks."

"According to your booking agent, you are scheduled on the November 13 ship to Wexford, correct?"

"Sirs," interrupts Mrs. Schultz, who has moved to stand beside the two men. "It is getting late, and I must close up the house."

Lucas stays rooted to his spot. Connor turns to Sharon. "I'll take this to the printer tomorrow." He picks up the draft advertisement from the piano.

The two men walk to the front door with Mrs. Schultz guiding them. Sharon follows. As the men exit to the porch, Sharon turns to Mrs. Schultz. "May I have just a minute?" Mrs. Schultz steps back into the parlor. Sharon goes out to the porch, where both men are standing at the top of the steps.

She looks directly at Connor. "I would like the truth. When were you going to tell me?"

"Sharon, things are moving fast, and until I had all the pieces ready, I felt I could not share information with anyone."

"Why was I hired to come from New York to work on the accounts if you knew that people would need to be let go?"

Connor is silent. Lucas is absorbing every word.

Sharon turns, walks back into the house, closes the door, and begins to sob. Crying seems to be too soft for how she is feeling at that moment.

Mrs. Schultz approaches her gently. Sharon collapses into Mrs. Schultz's arms and cries, heaving cries that awaken some of the nurses who creep down to the stairway to see what is wrong. As the women gather around the banister, Mrs. Schultz looks up. "Everything is fine, go back to bed." She guides Sharon into the parlor, where they sit together on the settee.

The bell chimes ring out, but Sharon has not spoken. Finally, she takes the handkerchief offered by Mrs. Schultz and breathes in deeply. "Thank you, I am fine."

"No, you are not fine; you have just discovered that the man you have fallen in love with is leaving; you are losing your job, and with that job loss, you also will lose room and board. I don't think any of that makes you 'fine.'"

Sharon smiles through her tears and gives Mrs. Schultz a long hug. "I'll figure something out. I need to write a few letters. May I stay in the parlor a little longer?"

"Of course, just turn off the lights when you are finished. I will lock up." She pats Sharon's shoulders. "Let me know what I can do."

Sharon begins to cry again, and Mrs. Schultz sits back down. "You do know that both young men have feelings for you."

"But is that enough? I want to be loved. You were loved. You know what that means. You told me that it was something that you would take with you for the rest of your life. But neither of these men have said anything that makes me believe they will fall in love with me."

"They spend time with you."

"Is that love? I don't think so. Cahey spent time with me, but he never intended to marry anyone after Micil died back in Ireland. When I figured that out, I decided to come to Savannah."

"I see. Then building your career was not the only reason you wanted to leave New York?"

"Not at all. The job offer was a way to have a new start, to begin again."

"And now those career choices are changing along with the people in your life, and you feel you must act."

"Yes, but I have no idea of what I need to do."

Mrs. Schultz stands to leave but pulls an envelope out of her pocket. "I almost forgot. This letter came today. I put it in my pocket and nearly forgot about it."

Sharon looks at the envelope, which has a New York postmark on it. She feels her heart beating faster. Who would be writing to her now? Though she fingers the envelope, she doesn't want to open it. She can not handle more bad news, not today.

31

S haron looks at her name and address on the letter but does not recognize the handwriting. Since none of her family can read or write, she must open it to find out who is writing. She tears open the letter and skips to the end, where she sees her sister's name. This cannot be good news. She starts to read from the beginning, where the foreman at her sister's employment writes that he is transcribing the letter.

Dear Sharon,

I write to you in hopes you are well, we are not. Papa and Mama have been evicted from their rooms due to non-payment of rent. Mama is sick in bed and cannot sew. Papa is Papa. We have moved them out of their rooms and into our two rooms down the street. With them and the oldest two in the bedroom, my mate and I must be in the kitchen with the baby. We have no bed, just pallets on the floor. None of our sisters can help. They are in tighter quarters, and everyone is working, thank God. We have the eldest children caring for the little ones while we work. We haven't heard a thing from either brother. They have been long gone. We need your help. You are the only unmarried one and the only one with wages to help Papa and Mama. Please come to New York to help us sort this out. You must come.

Your sister,

Eileen

The letter from her sister is the final blow for Sharon to find her place in Savannah. With her job ending and her family's needs, she has to go back to New York. Up in the sleeping room, she cannot sleep. She spends a large portion of the night sitting on the porch listening to the wood frogs, who have come out during their fall awakening. Their croaking is so loud that no one can hear her cry on the porch. At midnight, when the bells chime, she is still not ready to sleep.

She sits for quite a time and watches as the light brightens the sky. Birds are flitting from tree to tree only to dash to the ground and then fly away again, often with food in their beaks or calling out to other birds. The trees are alive with the birdsongs and with the activity of the morning. A wren comes up to the screen, fluttering its wings, trying to find a place to light. On the ledge holding the screen, the bird settles and chatters: cherry-cherry-cherry. Despite her problems, Sharon is drawn to watch the little bird chattering away. She remembers the childhood song of the little bird on my window. She also remembers how she shared with Connor at their first meeting that a bird on your window meant change. What change is coming her way? She already knows that she will be leaving Savannah. What else? She shakes her head in frustration, goes silently into her room, tiptoes past her sleeping roommates, gathers her toiletries, and begins her day, a day she is not looking forward to at all.

Before breakfast, Sharon goes to the desk in the parlor and writes out a telegram to send to Danielle.

Parents need help. Must return to NY. Need job. Please advise.
    Sharon

At breakfast, Sharon is silent. Mrs. Schultz says nothing but keeps looking at her, which just makes her eat faster so that she can leave. Hurrying to the telegraph office before work, she posts the message to Danielle. She slows down as she walks to the office, and just as she passes the newspaper office, Lucas appears.

"Sharon, please stop. I need to talk with you."

She walks on. "I am on my way to work."

"I know." Lucas gets in stride with her. "But there is a weather warning out. A hurricane is approaching Miami and is predicted to cause wind and tidal flooding here."

Stopping abruptly, Sharon shakes her head in disbelief. "What do we do? When will it happen?"

"By nightfall, they say. We got a notice from the weather review. A special edition of the paper will hit the streets shortly."

"What needs to be done?"

"The boarding house is far enough away from the river to not be affected by flooding, but wind can damage the house. I am sure Mrs. Schultz will want to close the shutters and remove anything from the yard that can be blown away."

"Thank you." Sharon turns around to head back to the boarding house.

"Where are you going?"

"I must warn Mrs. Schultz so she can prepare."

"You will be late to work. I'll go and tell her."

Sharon stops and looks at Lucas. Now, it is Lucas who makes her question her feelings. Just when she wants to be angry at yet another man, he does something nice. "You have time?"

"More than you do. Remember, as a reporter, I am free to

move about the city to cover the news. Go to work. I'll see Mrs. Schultz."

"Thank you." Sharon smiles at Lucas.

"That's more like it," he says and quickly walks away.

Getting to the office, Sharon notices an increase in the wind. It's not heavy yet, but it's more than she felt sitting out on the upstairs porch. When she arrives, she finds everyone in place. Connor is already in their office with a cup of tea, and one poured for her. She places her satchel and purse on the table and sits beside him.

"Sharon, about last night."

"We have work to do. Let's not waste any time. You have a ship to catch."

She opens the ledger and begins going over the next section of accounts. Connor continues to look at her. She can feel his green eyes watching her, but she is determined to be poised and professional. She does not look up. Eventually, he, too, begins to work with the ledgers. The morning passes, but Sharon is constantly looking up at the windows overlooking the river. The sky has changed from the morning light to a grey haze. By noon, the rain begins; it is not hard, but it is constant. The sky is dark. She wants to take her lunchtime to go back to the boarding house, but the rain is making the October day dark and gloomy, matching her mood.

"The weather has changed," says Connor as he notices her looking at the windows again.

"There's a storm heading for Miami to make landfall tonight, so says Lucas."

"Ah, he's everywhere. Did he come by the boarding house?"

"No, I ran into him on the street coming into work."

Connor sits up straighter in his chair. "Did he say anything else?"

"Only that the prediction is that Savannah will get wind

and tidal flooding. He volunteered to go tell Mrs. Schultz so she can prepare the house."

When Conner doesn't respond, Sharon glances up at him. He is staring out the window. She takes a long look at him up close. His shaggy red hair is down around his collar; curls cover his ears. His jaw is square and not relaxed at all. He turns and sees that she is watching him. Sharon ducks her head quickly.

"Sharon, about last night."

"Yes, please, tell me about last night."

"I was going to tell you. I wanted to tell you. I should have told you sooner, but I didn't know how. All of these weeks working together have me in turmoil over how I feel about the changes coming soon. I thought I knew exactly what I needed to do and was going to get it done; however, working with you, I discovered..."

They are interrupted by Tad. "Sorry, folks, I have to ask that you secure the ledgers in the vault. We have a warning that severe weather is coming our way. We need to clear out of the office. I hope that the boarding house is far enough from the river to be safe and that though the Pulaski Hotel is near, they have taken all the precautions necessary to secure their guests. Please get ready to leave immediately." Tad departs quickly.

Sharon closes the ledger. "We have worked so hard on these. Shouldn't we move them away from the river for safety?"

"Agreed. There are only five of them. I believe we can get them out of here."

"I will go get a tarp and canvas bag from the navel store next door while you put the original in the vault."

Sharon dashes out and finds two oilskin tarps and a two-handle canvas bag at the naval store. She puts both of them on the company's account. By the time she returns, Connor has cleared the desk and put the original ledgers in the vault. They wrap the other ledgers in the oil skin tarp and wedge them into the canvas bag. Connor starts to lift them, but Sharon picks them up first.

"I am farther away from the river. I will take them to the boarding house."

He nods. "Let's go." As they exit, they see that no one is in the office, and all the desks have been cleared of anything on the surface, all but Sharon's at the far wall. They leave it and exit the building. Sharon locks the door behind her.

Umbrellas are useless in the increasing wind. Sharon covers her head with the second oil skin tarp and heads for the boarding house. Connor accompanies her. The hotel is on their right. "Go in," says Sharon. Connor takes the canvas bag from her. "No, I will get you back to the boarding house first," he shouts into the wind. She shakes her head at him, but he walks ahead, and she must hurry to catch up with him.

The closed shutters on the boarding house make it look empty. Connor is about to climb the steps with her, but she stops him. "Get to the hotel," she tells him. He hands her the canvas bag, nods his head, and turns to go. She stumbles up the steps with the heavy ledgers and slips on the wet boards about halfway up. She doesn't drop the bag with the ledgers but feels her knee is damaged when she hits the steps. Clasping the bag, she staggers the rest of the way up and is on the porch. Mrs. Schultz opens the doors just as she approaches.

"I was watching for you, hoping you would be back during lunchtime."

"They closed the office, and Tad sent us away. I have the ledgers we have worked on. We didn't want to leave them in the office."

"Not even in a vault?"

"We put the originals in the vault. These are the transition ledgers."

"Then we must keep them safe. Let's put them in the back

hallway at the notice board. It is the safest place in the house from wind or water."

Mrs. Schultz takes the canvas bag from Sharon, who needs to loosen the tarp covering her head. She takes it inside since all the chairs have been removed from the porch. As she enters the foyer and closes the door behind her, Mrs. Schultz notices that she is limping.

"What happened?"

"I slipped on the steps."

Taking the oil tarp from Sharon, Mrs. Schultz says, "You sit down in the parlor. I will be right back to take a look at your leg."

Trying not to put too much weight on the knee, Sharon limps into the parlor and sits in the closest chair, Mrs. Schultz's chair. She hesitates before sitting and starts to move to the other chair when Mrs. Schultz returns.

"Sit down there. Let's take a look."

Together, they lift the water-soaked hem of her skirt high enough to see her knee. There are no abrasions but extreme redness. Mrs. Schultz gently leans the leg one way and then another and Sharon does not cry out in pain.

"Nothing seems broken and there are no cuts. Luckily, these long skirts of ours can bring us down but can also protect our limbs when we do fall. But you need to get out of these wet clothes. Can you walk up the stairs?"

"Yes, of course. I am fine."

"Humph, I've heard that before."

Sharon smiles. As Mrs. Schultz stands, Sharon stops her from leaving. "Thank you for all you have done for me while I have been here. I feel like this has been a haven for me to build the courage to take the next steps in my life." She laughs. "I have no idea what the next steps are, but I have courage."

Smiling at Sharon, Mrs. Schultz pats her shoulder. "You will figure it out, I am sure."

With the storm winds coming through and all the shutters closed on the house, the darkness is almost too much for Sharon. She clutches the stair railing rather firmly as she makes her way up to the third floor. She hears nothing. No one else is in the house. All the nurses must be at the hospital. She manages to change and spread out her clothes to dry on a cord her roommates had hung diagonally across part of the room. Changing out their uniform collars, cuffs, and aprons keeps them washing every day. Looking at her knee, Sharon can already see a bruise developing. She puts on a comfortable skirt and blouse, changes her stockings, and cleans her shoes. The door to the porch is closed, and large boards are nailed on the inside to keep the door shut. Sharon feels closed in and goes back downstairs to locate people and something for lunch.

She finds Mrs. Schultz in the kitchen sitting at the work table, busily chopping and cleaning vegetables.

"And how is your knee?"

"Bruising, but fine."

"Good. Do take it easy, though. If you are looking for something to eat, there are some leftover biscuits and bacon from breakfast over by the stove. There is also fruit in the bowl at the sink."

"Yes, thank you. I am hungry."

As Sharon places the food on a plate she gets from the cabinet, she brings it over to the table and sits down with Mrs. Schultz.

"Are you preparing dinner?"

"Yes, I sent the staff home due to the storm warnings, but the nurses will be wanting dinner at five. I decided to make a pot of stew, something warm to stick to our ribs tonight."

"I could smell the beef cooking all the way upstairs."

"I'm not sure what to serve with it. Edwidge usually makes cornbread and biscuits, but I am weary from helping close up the house and getting the last of the fall vegetables out of the garden. At least I got an early start. Thank you for having Lucas come to warn me. I had not heard."

"It was luck that I ran into him. I was crossing near the newspaper office after I posted my telegram to New York."

"A telegram?" Mrs. Schultz stops chopping and looks up at Sharon. "What are you thinking of doing?"

"Yesterday's letter from my sister Eileen gave me more bad news."

Mrs. Schultz continues to give Sharon her entire attention. "And..."

"Mama and Papa have been evicted from their rooms and have moved in with my sister. Things are quite tight and there is no money and lots of children to care for. Mama is not well, so she is not sewing. My brothers have disappeared, and no one knows what to do." Sharon pauses.

"So..."

"So, I sent a telegram to Danielle asking for help. I was thinking of returning to New York to take care of my parents, and if I do, I need a job."

"I see." Mrs. Schultz says nothing more and resumes chopping the carrots and potatoes. Sharon finishes her biscuit.

After a few minutes, Mrs. Schultz says, "Lucas came in and visited for a few minutes over a cup of tea when he brought the weather news."

This time, Sharon is the one who looks at Mrs. Schultz with a furrowed brow. Her look causes Mrs. Schultz to say, "Now, now, it is all good, no more bad news." She moves the vegetables into a large bowl and crosses to the stove to stir the stew meat.

"And..." says Sharon.

"And what?" says Mrs. Schultz.

"Please, tell me what Lucas said to you." Sharon's brow went from furrowed to raised eyebrows and wide eyes, pleading for information.

Taking her time, Mrs. Schultz goes to the corner counter to get the cookie dough. She gathers the baking pans and comes back to sit down.

"Mrs. Schultz!"

"I am simply trying to choose the right words to say."

"Just tell me, please?"

With an audible sigh, Mrs. Schultz says, "He told me that he cares a lot for you and is hoping that you may care for him."

"He just said this out loud without any encouragement?" Sharon could not believe he would say this, especially to someone else and not to her.

"The whole story. Lucas arrived and told me the weather forecast. I ran to get the hospital handymen to assist with the shutters. When we returned, Lucas had gotten the ladder from the outdoor shed and set it up on the front of the house. He assisted the men in securing the shutters. Once they had completed the top stories and moved to the first story, Lucas's help was not needed. So, I invited him in for a cup of tea. He accepted and sat right there." She points to Sharon's chair at the table. "I was working in the kitchen. He sat, drank his tea, and made nice conversation. So, I asked him what his intentions are with you."

"You asked him?"

"Yes, I did. Someone has to ask questions besides him." And she continues working on the cookie dough with determination.

Sharon leans back in her chair, unsure if she should be angry with Mrs. Schultz for stepping in where she is not wanted or relieved that, finally, there will be some clarity as to what Lucas wants.

"And..."

"That's when he said he cares a lot for you and is hoping that you may care for him."

Remaining quiet, Sharon takes her plate over to the sink, washes it, dries it, and puts it back into the cabinet.

Mrs. Schultz stops blending the cookie dough. She takes another deep breath and asks, "How do you feel about Lucas?"

The drying towel is still in her hands. Sharon re-dries her hands, buffing the fingers as she forms the words she has not been wanting to say. "I find Lucas a capable, hard-working man who has a picture of what a woman should be. I believe he is looking to create a family similar to the one he left behind in France with a working father, a stay-at-home mother, and children."

"Are you in that picture?"

"It would not be a bad life. He would put food on the table and a roof over our heads. He took me to a picnic out at Collins' meadow to show me the new neighborhoods and introduce me to the new homes being built in the meadow."

"That sounds nice."

"It is not nice." Sharon tosses the drying towel onto the counter. "A trolley ride from town, no one but the neighbors to converse with, and designed to leave the women alone in the houses as the men go out to work. I want more than that, but if circumstances don't improve, then I may need to lower my dreams of my future and accept my fate as other women have done." She leans against the counter to take some of the pressure off her knee.

Mrs. Schultz raises her gaze to look at Sharon. "How do you feel about Connor?"

Tears start to well up in Sharon's eyes. "He lied to me. He pretended to like me, but I feel he has just been using me to get the task completed so that he can return to County Wexford and another life."

Crossing the kitchen to stir the stew, Mrs. Schultz says, "You don't believe that, do you?"

The memory of how electricity went through her when he touched her face showed instantly on her face.

She looks at Sharon. "I didn't think you did," says Mrs. Schultz.

Sharon changes the subject. "Anyway, with the storm, I don't expect to hear back from Danielle today."

The front door knocker resounds through the empty house. Mrs. Schultz wipes her hands on a dish towel and leaves to find out who has summoned them. Sharon takes the cookie dough and begins to spoon out the cookies in the pan. She has two pans ready and pops them into the oven. She checks the firewood to make sure they have enough to keep the stove hot. Someone had heaped the wood in the bin next to the stove.

"You are wrong; there is a telegram for you." Mrs. Schultz lays the envelope on the table. Sharon wastes no time picking it up and reading.

Wait. Help is on the way. More soon.
Danielle

"Well?"

"She tells me to wait."

"There, see? It will all work out. You need to just be patient and wait."

Sharon is not sure she can wait and work next to Connor, knowing what she knows. And she is not sure that she can hold Lucas at arm's length for much longer. She is not sure about much of anything except that she knows how to bake cookies. She removes the first batch from the oven and prepares another pan.

32

In the afternoon, the wind picks up. Rushing sounds and limbs creaking against the house cause the two women in the kitchen to look up to make sure nothing has crashed into the house. Sister Mary Joyce drops in to check on them and to tell them that the nurses are busy. She asks if there would be any way to do dinner in shifts. The storm is moving toward Miami, and ships are damaged out at sea. Forty-five seamen were picked up by the steamer "Jenny" and returned to Key West. Twenty-four seamen have been brought to Savannah and delivered to St. Joseph's. The news is that the water problem is growing, with three feet of water in the telegraph office in Miami. Storm signals were ordered at 2:40 pm for Miami, Jupiter, Jacksonville, Savannah, and Charleston, with strong winds reported.

Mrs. Schultz shares her thoughts out loud. "If we have three nurses at a time, the stew can stay on the stove. We can serve the bowls and take them into the dining room." She turns to Sister Mary Joyce. "Can you send three women at a time?"

After Sister Mary Joyce leaves, Sharon sits at the kitchen table. "I remember how to make griddle cakes. I just need cornmeal, eggs, baking powder, salt, water, and a little oil. I can fry them in small batches to keep them hot."

As they gather the supplies from the pantry, the electricity goes out. Sharon steps back into the kitchen, where there is little light coming in through the windows that are shuttered against the storm. Though it is only late in the afternoon, the clouds and dark skies make everything dark. The only light comes from the stove.

"Thank goodness the hospital handymen filled the wood bin and brought more into the basement. I believe I remember where I put the candles. I keep an oil lamp here in the kitchen for such a happening. Here it is." Mrs. Schultz lights the lamp so they can see inside the pantry.

Having the chores to do and being able to do them together makes the storm, darkness, and wind bearable. They work in silence in the lamplight. Each of them knows what to do in the kitchen. Mrs. Schultz gathers other oil lamps and candles from the basement storage and places them in the foyer in case the women need to go upstairs during their break. Using a step ladder, she locates two silver candelabras from the top shelf of the pantry.

"These were my mother's," she says. They are simple silver, smooth with no embellishments, each with three holders for candles on a single stem. The women set the dining room table, deciding to put all the dishes in place and simply remove them after the women have eaten. The candelabras are centered along the middle of the table. Sharon disappears with a candle but comes back with a handful of the fabric flowers that she remembered had been left on the piano in the parlor. She tucks them in and around the candelabras. The table in the darkened room is eerily beautiful. Shadows from the candles create odd shapes on the ceiling. The candles flutter with the air pushed through the unsealed window frames and from around the edge of the doors. The house is showing its age in the storm.

Three women come in through the front door from the
hospital. Mrs. Schultz and Sharon are there to help. Sharon has
put an oil tarp on the floor of the foyer. She has placed the hat
tree in the middle. Her idea is that the women could hang the
rain ponchos borrowed from the sisters at the hospital there to
keep the floors dry. Sharon moves three of the dining room
chairs into the foyer so that the women can take off their wet
shoes while in the house. The women chatter loudly and
boldly as they enter the dining room. The energy they share
from having so many seamen brought in and all the frantic
work being done at the hospital carries with them into the
house. Sharon brings in the hot griddle bread as Mrs. Schultz
fills bowls with the stew. In minutes, the food is devoured, and
all three women want to go upstairs. Mrs. Schultz lights the
lamps, and the women stomp up the stairs, still chattering
away.

Sharon and Mrs. Schultz exchange looks. "One group
down," says Sharon.

"Hmph," says Mrs. Schultz.

They clear the table of the used dishes, prepare the batter
for the next batch of bread, and put out the cookies on the
buffet table with a pot of hot tea. They hear the women before
they see them, still chattering away, sharing stories of what the
seamen must have gone through to be in such bad shape.
Without pausing, they woof down cookies and drink their tea.
Crowding into the foyer, they put on their wet shoes, don their
rain ponchos, and, still chattering, exit into the wind and rain
to head back to work.

Standing in the foyer, the two women look at the puddles
and get extra drying cloths from the hall closet to mop up the
water. The process continues until all the women have been in
and out again. Sharon and Mrs. Schultz have been drying the
floor and cleaning the dishes as the evening progresses, but
now all of the women have eaten.

"I have not been as tired since the day my mother died." Mrs. Schultz sits in one of the dining room chairs still in the foyer.

"What happened then?" Sharon is still drying the oilcloth on the floor from the last group of nurses.

"I had spent several months grieving after Alfred left. I was no use to anyone, but I told everyone that I was fine. I worked during the day, took care of my mother, and grieved all night long. By the time she died, I was exhausted. At the funeral, people kept asking how I was. I didn't want to tell them that my heart had broken in two with Alfred's leaving and that now my life was ending with the death of my mother, who had done so much for all of us. So, I simply said I was fine. By the time things were over, I was in bed sick for two weeks. The doctor could find nothing wrong with me and simply said I had a broken heart. When I was able to function, I notified Alfred that my mother had died. He came as quickly as he could. In my mind, though, I have thought often about if I had not been so exhausted, could I have helped him with the horses and saved his life?"

Sharon is jolted by what Mrs. Schultz has shared. "Oh, Mrs. Schultz, there was nothing you could have done." She goes to Mrs. Schultz and takes her hand. "Are you still grieving? You said you have not been as tired since the day your mother died, and you are exhausted now. Are you all right?"

"I am not all right." She puts her hand on top of Sharon's. "I have discovered that I care about all the women who have come into my house as though they are my daughters. And, I have discovered that one of them will be leaving or making choices she does not want to make, or even should make but feels she must make, and it breaks my heart."

Not knowing what to say, Sharon leans in and hugs Mrs. Schultz. "Maybe we can figure this out. I have a little more time, you know? I need to be patient."

Mrs. Schultz smiles and hugs her back.

The dishes are washed and dried. The foyer and dining room have been righted. With the remainder of the stew still on the stove, Mrs. Schultz and Sharon decide to have dinner in the kitchen. As they prepare, they are stopped by yet another knock at the front door.

"When it rains, it pours," says Mrs. Schultz. Sharon giggles. Only gone a minute, Mrs. Schultz returns to the kitchen alone. Sharon looks up from where she is sitting.

"There is someone to see you in the parlor."

Sharon wipes her face with her hands in quick, jerky movements. "Who at this hour and in the middle of a storm?"

"I think you need to see for yourself."

Sharon smooths her hair and tucks some falling strands behind her ears. With a tug on her skirt to level it better and a glance at Mrs. Schultz, she goes to the parlor.

Lucas is standing with his back to the fireplace, watching the door to see when she approaches. "I was at the hospital interviewing the seamen brought in from the storm. I thought I would check on you and see how everything is here."

"Things are fine. We just finished serving dinner to the nurses and are about to sit down and have dinner ourselves. It has been a long day."

"I don't doubt that. I have not stopped for dinner myself. The interviews with the seamen took a long time."

Sharon remembers that Mrs. Schultz shared how Lucas helped with the shutters and what he had told Mrs. Schultz. "Can you wait here for just a minute? I'll be right back."

Into the kitchen to find Mrs. Schultz, Sharon asks, "Can we invite Lucas to have dinner with us?"

Mrs. Schultz lifts her eyebrows in surprise. "Of course, I will set three plates in the dining room."

Sharon returns to the parlor. Lucas has not moved from

where she left him. "Will you have dinner with us? It is simple fare, beef stew with griddle bread."

Relief softened Lucas's face. "I would love to."

They go into the dining room, where the candelabras are still lit, and the flowers offer a peaceful scene. Mrs. Schultz has set three bowls of stew and a small plate of bread.

"Shall we eat?" she asks. As they sit, Mrs. Schultz bows her head. "May this food restore our strength, giving new energy to tired limbs and new thoughts to weary minds. Amen."

Sharon looks up at Mrs. Schultz. "You must be hungry; the blessing is short."

"I'm starved. Please, Lucas, try the griddle bread Sharon made."

33

The storm winds abate and people emerge from their cocooned houses in the early morning light to assess the damage. Sharon awakens to the noise of shutters being unlashed. There is a knock at her door. She opens it to find Mrs. Schultz.

"Please come and help. None of the staff can get here. The trolleys are not running."

"I'm on my way."

Hurriedly, Sharon dresses. She notices her roommates deep in sleep. She vaguely remembers them coming in and stumbling about in the middle of the night. She eases out of the room and closes the door quietly. When she gets to the foyer, she opens the front door to assess any damage. There is debris everywhere. She sees people in the neighboring yards looking at what needs to be done to fix the world they live in. Sharon rushes inside and into the kitchen. Mrs. Schultz is gathering more wood to feed the stove.

"The electricity is still off," she says. "There is no fruit. Edwidge usually brings it on her way in. We have bread for toast and jars of jam I made this summer."

"Do we have milk and eggs?"

"Yes, that we do have."

"I'll make French toast."

"We have honey."

"We're set!"

Mrs. Schultz stops her anxious walking to and from the pantry. "Thank you."

Whereas there had been lots of chatter during the dinner breaks the evening before, this morning, there is silence. Sharon learns that they worked rotating three-hour shifts during the night. The women eat, drink their tea, and leave for the hospital. Sharon is preparing to go to work, not knowing what she will find. There is a knock at the door. Since she is nearest and Mrs. Schultz is in the kitchen, she opens the door to find Connor on the other side.

"I came to see if everything is all right," he says.

"We are fine. How was the hotel?

"They were prepared and had closed everything tightly, ordered a lot of ale, and cooked a lot of food."

Despite herself, Sharon laughs. "I see. That is how we would have done it in New York."

"The office is still standing. I thought I would help you with the ledgers and walk with you. There are a lot of limbs down and tree rubbish on the paths and roadways, so we need to walk carefully."

"I have forgotten the ledgers. I will get them now." Sharon goes to the back hallway and gets the canvas bag. At the door, Connor takes the bag.

Together, they walk through the streets strewn with limbs, leaves, twigs, and items that had not been secured: buckets, clothing still pinned to a roped line, newspapers, overturned barrels, doors off their hinges, screens, and flowerpots. The scene is surreal and makes Sharon pause at some of the debris. Different kinds of noises infiltrate the walk. The birds are quiet.

No trolleys are operating. No wagon, horse, or automobile traffic is on the streets. There are shouts of men working on uprooted trees to clear the roadways and hammering to repair whatever has been wrenched by the wind. It is all Sharon and Connor can do to make their way through the debris and fallen limbs, so they do not talk. Sharon is glad that Connor is leading the way. She has no idea what would be the safest and easiest path to the office.

As they reach Bay Street, Connor speaks. "At the hotel, they told us that there was a surge in the river, but the nineteen-foot wall kept all the water away from town." He stops before crossing the street. "I have already been to the office to see that everything is fine. I need to handle some phone calls, and the hotel has one of the few lines still working. I will be back in the office when I have finished my business there. I trust you. You know what to do."

Sharon does not know what to say. "Okay," she says. He hands her the ledgers, and Sharon crosses the street by herself.

At the office, there is no obvious damage to the building. People are coming and going on errands to repair signs and window sashes, but no structural damage can be seen.

Sharon looks down from the pedestrian walkway to the Factor's Walk. She sees water covering the cobblestones. From where she stands, she can tell that water may have been able to seep into the warehouses on the bottom level. Many of the doors have high thresholds, but others are at the ground level. Inside the office, there are only a few people. Many of the staff travel by trolley from the outskirts of town, and with the trolleys not running, they may or may not be able to get to work. Sharon feels lucky that she can easily walk in.

Though she could take the trolley, the extra steps make her feel better at the end of the day and make her savings grow faster. With the company paying for the room and board and the walk to and from the office, Sharon knows that by only spending money on necessities and extra food and sending a bit home to her parents, she is saving most of what she has earned. She may be able to weather a few weeks to find a new job or even return to New York. She also has the money from the sale of her interest in the bakery, but she does not want to use that until she has to. The question Sharon keeps asking herself is: If the company wants to consolidate the financials into the County Wexford office, why did they go to all the trouble to hire her, a woman accountant, and bring her down from New York?

Not having any idea what has pulled Connor away so quickly, Sharon works on the two sets of accounts. She thinks about what Connor said: that she knows what to do. She has learned a lot about the shipping industry.

From the outside, the shipping industry appears to have a lot of moving parts loosely held together, which isn't remotely true. The industry has a definite structure. There are three parts: the managers of the fleet, the marine supply side, and the finance area. All of these parts have duplicate offices in County Wexford and Savannah.

The managers responsible for recruiting and managing the fleet staff hire the ship masters and skippers who are in charge of a ship, its crew, any passengers, and cargo on the water and in port. The marine supply side includes the purchase and procurement staff. Sharon has learned that an advantage of having their offices next door to the naval store is building a relationship with the store and having quick access to supplies. The women who work in the outer office are the ones making the arrangements using message runners and local teams scheduled in advance. Finally, there is a finance director—Tad McGuire, at their Savannah office. This office organizes the Georgia side for the supply, transport, and handling of goods to be shipped or received.

Early on, before Connor came, Tad explained how insurance is handled by the County Wexford office since it is with Lloyd's and the Institute of London Underwriters. In the spring of 1906, the Marine Insurance Act had been passed and codified the previous common law. That act requires that Tad's office verifies insurance coverage with the Bureau of Navigation. That also means that he has to keep records of inspections and standard-compliance services, towing, dredging, and pilot services. These records have to comply with the Bureau of Navigation as a part of the United States Department of Commerce and Labor. His office also has to keep up with the customs receipts. Tad's job is instrumental in making the company run smoothly on this side of the Atlantic. Sharon understands that his counterpart in County Wexford does the same type of job using Ireland's requirements.

As Sharon is thinking about all she has learned, the rationale for transitioning the ledgers into one ledger begins to make sense. If accounting is to be a useful tool for managerial control, then who controls the books is paramount for guiding any expansion, and according to Connor, the company is expanding into Canada. Georgia has been providing lumber and cotton, but now Canada is competing for the lumber business as well, and the company is looking into what that may mean.

Remembering what she has learned from Christine Ross in New York, Sharon works with the assumption that accounting is the language of business and, thus, is the primary means of communicating business data. However, Sharon thinks about this with just about every entry she makes. Shipping is different from other industries that logically figure their revenues and expenses based on a calendar month. In the shipping industry, the length of a vessel's voyage may span several months. For example, it takes forty days for the company's ship to go from Savannah to County Wexford; therefore, it is difficult to properly apportion revenue and expense items between the completed and the incomplete portions of a voyage. Thus, the logical accounting unit for a steamship company in determining the operation profit or loss of a ship is calculated on each voyage.

This system, where the master of a ship was the fiscal agent, ended long before Sharon began accounting with the shipping company. However, the voyage has been retained as an accounting unit in the shipping industry. And that means that all revenues and expenses are classified by vessel and voyage as a separate venture. Voyages are numbered consecutively.

The final step of the accounting procedure is posting data to ledger accounts, which calls for bringing together all items of like kind, both positive and negative. The chart of accounts provides a sound and logical classification of assets, liabilities, owners' equity, revenues, and expenses.

Sharon is seeing the whole picture. Without a single set of books, the company does not have an accurate account of its holdings. The transition would give the company the knowledge to expand its operations without creating a whole new company. Sharon could also see where many of the bookkeepers would not be needed. The company could also save money by leasing out the work at the dock as well as the procurement of supplies. In streamlining the accounts, the company could probably save a lot of money and be able to quickly assess how to grow the company into other areas. The picture is clear to Sharon, including how she will not be in the picture. What she is still wondering about is why they brought her down to Savannah in the first place.

34

C onnor does not appear in the office all week. Each day, she looks for him, but he does not appear. Tad lets her know that he is working out of the hotel to provide quicker access to the home company. However, the fact that he has made no effort to contact her or be present in any way leaves Sharon realizing how wrong she is about Connor. Her choice of men, first Cahey and now Lucas and Connor, have not led to successful romantic relationships. She is not good at this at all.

Sharon is busy with the ledgers and does not see Tad enter the office. He sits down next to her.

"Can you take a break? I'd like to talk with you."

Throughout the time that Connor has been in the office, she has seen little of Tad. When she looks up at him, what she sees surprises her. Though his white shirt is immaculate, his face is drawn and tight.

"Oh, Tad, I didn't see you come in. Yes, of course." She puts down her ledger and places her hands gently on her lap. She sees his face is missing the usual smile that accents his teeth.

There is a slight frown on his brow. He pauses as though he is not sure how to say what he wants to say.

"I have not addressed your job here, and that has been my fault. With this special project, you and Connor seemed so absorbed in the work that I suspected that everything was fine with what you were doing. Am I correct?"

"Very much so."

"Good. It is obvious that you have taken the lead on this project, and that is welcome since we were unsure how much needed to be done. We had estimated that it would take at least until the first of the year to complete, but here we are at the end of October, and you have almost finished the transition."

Sharon feels as though she knows where this conversation is going. She has never been let go of a job. She resigned from the hotel. The decision to sell her interest in the bakery and take this leap into Savannah was all hers. Now, as she sits and listens to Tad, she expects him to tell her that her work with the company has ended. This is a new experience for her.

"Yes, the project should be completed in the next couple of weeks. Connor will be able to leave on the thirteenth of November as he plans." Seeing the look of surprise and relief on Tad's face confuses Sharon. "Did you know he planned on leaving then?"

"Yes," says Tad. "But I didn't know you knew. That was what I came to tell you. I'm relieved that you already knew so I did not have to break the news." With that, Tad stands up to leave. "You have done an excellent job, and the company is pleased that you joined us."

Sharon stops him. "But Tad, how much do you know?"

"What do you mean?"

"You know that this entire project is meant to consolidate all the accounts into the County Wexford office, right?"

"Yes."

"But do you know that by doing this, the number of employees located here in Savannah will be reduced?"

Tad sits back down. "No, I did not know that. Did Connor tell you? How do you know?"

She takes a deep breath, then lays out all she has learned from the accounts. She adds in the information Connor shared about Canada. "If accounting is to be a useful tool for managerial control," says Sharon, "then who controls the books is paramount for guiding any expansion. That expansion would mean having all the books in County Wexford."

A look of concern is silently conveyed on Tad's face. "How many employees will go?"

"The company will need a link here for sure. I would project that the procurement and supplies would be leased out, as would the receiving and shipping. The smaller staff would send receipts back with the ship master to be posted in County Wexford. That way, the company could easily expand into other areas without creating new offices everywhere they want to do business."

"I see." This time, Tad does stand up. He looks at Sharon. "You figured this out by looking at the accounts?"

"Yes. Why we were making the transition was not clear to me. I looked at the numbers and saw that the procurement and supplies, along with the receiving and shipping, are costing the company far more than leasing these positions out would cost. I got those numbers from two ships; one ship came in late due to the storms in the Atlantic while another ship already in port leased out these jobs to take advantage of the sailing schedule and the supplies on board."

She gives a quick look out the window and then resumes. "Additionally, I noticed that the shipments of cotton and timber have lessened. One would have to talk to the factors to figure out why. I have heard talk that cotton is being driven out by tobacco fields and that timber has been shipped down the river to the Bay Area and is being picked up in New Orleans. Several ships have returned to County Wexford without a full capacity. That creates a loss for the company." Sharon is quiet and looks at Tad, who has not moved.

Tad remains silent, absorbing the news Sharon shares. "Thank you," he says and stands to move toward the door but Sharon stops him. "Tad, who decided to hire me and bring me down from New York?"

He turns to look back at Sharon. "The County Wexford office," he says. "Why do you ask?"

"I think their goal of reducing the Savannah office left them trying to figure out how to do that without giving it away."

Tad looks at Sharon and then looks out the window toward the river. Without another word, he leaves, and Sharon is not sure what she should be doing—finishing the job or packing her desk.

The day is finally over. Sharon packs up her satchel and heads off for the boarding house. As she exits the building, she sees Lucas waiting at the end of the pedestrian walk connecting the office with Bay Street.

She greets him. "Hello, did you have a meeting at City Hall or are you just hanging around downtown?"

"No," he says, "I purposely came to wait for you. I would like to talk with you. May I walk with you back to the boarding house? I assume that is where you are going."

"Of course."

They get in stride. She has walked beside him so often, seeing all the squares and getting to know the city, that getting in pace with him is easy. He waits to talk until they have cleared Bay Street and are safely on the other side of the traffic.

"I want to apologize for being so aggressive with Connor

when you have been around. I should respect your work status and realize that there are times when you need to be with people you are working with."

Confused by his choice of words, Sharon asks, "What do you mean?"

"Just that when you have a job, there are times when you need to be with the people you work with."

"When I have a job?"

"Why, yes. At some time, you may not have a job."

"Like when? When would I not have a job?"

"When Connor leaves and half the people in your firm are let go, including you, or, if you get married."

"I could find another job and still have a job when and if I get married."

"But if you were married, you would not have to work."

Sharon picks up the speed of her walking and Lucas has to hurry to catch up with her.

"Where are you going so quickly?" he asks.

"I'm going away from this conversation."

"Because I suggested that you could marry and not have to work?"

"Yes, and because you do not seem to respect who I am as an independent woman working to establish a career."

"I told you I cared a great deal about you. How do you get that I don't respect your independence?"

"Because you want me to be a homemaker and not work outside the home."

"What's wrong with that? Aren't you working because you don't have anyone to take care of you?"

"How could you think that? Why do you even bring that up?"

"Because you have said that your mother and father can't and your siblings can't. How are you to take care of yourself? You have two options: work and be underpaid or get married."

Sharon stops abruptly. Lucas has to pivot to stop and face her. "You are correct that neither my parents nor my siblings can take care of me. But I can take care of myself. I have a job. I am saving money. I have goals. I have a place to live and food on the table."

"Not for long if Connor does what he says he's going to do. You will not have a job, a roof over your head, or food on the table. Don't you get it? Connor is going to shut down the Savannah office and you will not have a job. They brought you in as a woman accountant, so it would be easy to let you go."

Sharon lets his last remark sink in. She has drawn the same conclusion. "I get that! What I don't get is why you think I can't get another job or find something else to do. Why do I have only one choice left if I lose this job?" Sharon is talking loud and fast. She stops and slows down her speech. "I came to Savannah out of choice, not necessity. I had a job. I co-owned a bakery. I had a roof over my head, food on the table, friends, and a social life. I do not need to marry to have a life. When I do marry, it will be to expand my life to include a family, not because I have to." With that, she turns and walks away.

35

In the evenings at the boarding house, Sharon often finds a nurse who is not at the hospital in the parlor making fabric flowers. They have been spending several hours a night designing, stitching, and talking. It seems as if the women cannot talk enough to each other. Mrs. Schultz comes from the dining room as Sharon stands in the foyer looking into the parlor. Mrs. Schultz's brows raise and she tilts her head to indicate her amusement at how well the nurses are working together. They enter the parlor together.

Gertrude is the first to see Sharon and Mrs. Schultz. "Well, well, well, we finally have more help. Ladies, let's welcome the latecomers to our evening ritual." The women smile and a few giggles are shared at Gertrude's informal way of greeting Sharon and Mrs. Schultz.

"I beg to differ with you," says Mrs. Schultz. "I have checked on you each time you have been working. Who gets the teapot ready when it is empty?"

"But we want hands on deck," says Gertrude.

Mrs. Schultz laughs out loud. "You do not want my hands on a needle messing with your absolutely beautiful creations."

"Nor mine," interjects Sharon. She pauses, looks at Mrs. Schultz for agreement, and says, "I can bake cookies."

"Yes, please," came a chorus of acceptances.

"But first, I have to ask, will we be ready with enough flowers to make a good show at the end of October?"

"Absolutely," said Alice and Sarah simultaneously. Alice continues, "My aunt used her molds to cut out all the flower patterns for us. Now all we have to do is put them together and embellish them."

The women have not stopped stitching. Mrs. Schultz has gone around the room and complimented every flower being worked on. Sharon awkwardly stands in the doorway of the parlor. "Well, then, cookies it is." She turns to go.

Mrs. Schultz joins her. "I'll help. At least this is something we can do to cheer them on."

"Here, here," says Gertrude.

In the kitchen, the two women know what needs to be done. Sharon goes into the pantry and gets the ingredients. Mrs. Schultz locates the large mixing bowl and the baking pans along with the measuring cups and large spoons. They come together at the table and begin making cookies.

"You seemed agitated when you arrived just now. Is everything all right?" asks Mrs. Schultz.

"I had another argument with Lucas on my way back from work. He was waiting for me at the pedestrian bridge. It has been a long day and I did not handle our discussion well. I worked alone all day. Connor has not been around. Then my boss and I talked. I broke it to him that the ledgers indicated a move away from the Savannah office. He did not know. That was awkward. Then Lucas insulted me and my desire to work and be independent. I said a few things that maybe I should not have said."

Sharon is speaking slowly, not so that Mrs. Schultz can

understand her, but so that she can access all that had happened during the day.

"I see."

"It is a relief to come into the house and find the women contributing so much to the sale. I hope my idea works and we make enough money to fund one of them for the summer and begin their careers."

"This project seems important to you."

"It is. I see how hard the women work and the long hours they put in at the hospital to complete their program. I would like every one of them to have an opportunity to do what they want to do."

"Including Gertrude?"

"Especially Gertrude. She has a goal, and with this sponsorship, maybe her goal can be realized."

"And you? Can this project help you?"

"It has already helped me in many ways. I have never suggested such an undertaking. I have never spoken with women like Mrs. Lynch and some of the other women's club leaders. This is a project that will benefit the nurses, not me, but I have learned that to be part of a community, one needs to give back to that community. The nurses have made me feel welcome and part of their community here in this house, and for that, I am very thankful. I just hope we can make it successful for them."

Before Mrs. Schultz can respond, Alice and Sarah are at the kitchen door. They do not come in; they know better. Mrs. Schultz sees them standing with their hands folded in front of them, simply waiting.

"Ladies, how may I help you?"

Alice spoke first. "We want to follow up on Gertrude's going away party."

"Yes," says Sarah. "We have been discussing having it on Friday night after the sale."

"We have made some nice gifts for her," says Alice.

"Vivian has made her a house coat to wear in the dorm at the school," says Sarah.

"And Olivia has finished a needlepoint of The Lord's Prayer, beautifully decorated with flowers along the top and bottom," says Alice.

"Bernice and Katrina have gathered cloth from each of the nurses to make a patchwork quilt and a lap quilt she can use when studying or sitting at the piano. They will ask both of you for contributions as well," says Sarah.

They continue to stand just outside the doorway. Mrs. Schultz sits down and smiles. "I think Friday is a perfect time for a going away party." She glances at Sharon with raised eyebrows. Sharon knows Mrs. Schultz thinks that she should let the women know that she, too, might be leaving the boarding house, but she is silent. Mrs. Schultz audibly sighs. "I will gather a piece of cloth and give it to Bernice and Katrina by morning."

"As will I," says Sharon.

"Great." The women leave together just as they had arrived.

Both Sharon and Mrs. Schultz laugh. "They could be twins," says Mrs. Schultz.

"Aren't they?" laughs Sharon.

Minutes pass as the women put together the cookies and pop the first pans into the oven. Sharon pours them each a cup of tea. They sit at the table while Sharon eats her now very late dinner.

"Back to your discussion with Lucas, what came of it?"

"He suggests that I get married and not work."

"And that is a bad thing?"

"The way he says it! He feels that I have no choice should I lose my job."

"And that does not sit well with you?"

"Not at all. I came to Savannah by choice, not by need. I

have lucked out having an employer who paid for the room and board because my salary is so small in comparison with the other staff members in the office, the male accountants, that having a roof over my head and food on the table is a win. A bonus is the camaraderie I have experienced here in the house with you, Gertrude, and the nurses. Living in a boarding house by myself would have taken considerable money and probably not given me the expanded family I wanted and had in New York. I am grateful the company made the decisions it did."

"You are not the only one who has benefited. You have given me great companionship. I will always be thankful that you came my way," says Mrs. Schultz. She stands and leaves the room.

As she sits at the table, remembering all that has happened to her that day, Sharon feels the tears trickle down her cheek. She dabs at the wetness. Another thing she is thankful for is that she knows how to bake. She stands quickly and goes to take the first batch of cookies out of the oven.

Mrs. Schultz returns with two small platters. They pile the cookies onto them and take them to the women in the parlor. All stitching stops as the women circle the table tops where the warm cookies are placed. New cups of tea are needed and the conversations reach a crescendo. Then, at the door, Sister Mary Joyce enters.

"I saw the kitchen lights on and am just checking to see that everything is all right."

Mrs. Schultz picks up one of the cookie platters and crosses over to Sister Mary Joyce. "Everything is great. Have a cookie and join in the fellowship of the sewing circle at Mrs. Schultz's boarding house."

The women welcome Sister Mary Joyce and make room for her to join them on one of the settees. Sharon recognizes the solidarity among the nurses, the sisters, and Mrs. Schultz as she looks about the room. They are sharing the same warmth she felt in New York with her friends. She hopes that this warmth will radiate out into the community to create a tradition that could continue for many years.

Mrs. Schultz is chatting away with Sister Mary Joyce. Sharon has refilled the teapots. Gertrude moves to the piano and begins to play. It is a song Sharon knows from having attended so many of her father's music fetes. After the first verse, Sharon joins Gertrude at the piano and sings:

"Willie Fitzgibbons,
Who used to sell ribbons,
And stood up all day on his feet,
Grew very spoony
On Madelaine Mooney,
Who'd rather be dancing than eat.
Each evening she'd tag him,
To some dance hall drag him,
And when the band started to play,
She'd up like a silly,
And grab tired Willie,
Steer him on the floor and she'd say:

"'Waltz me around again, Willie,
Around, around, around!
The music is dreamy,
It's peaches and creamy,
O don't let my feet touch the ground!
I feel like a ship on an ocean of joy—
I just want to holler out loud, 'Ship Ahoy!'
Waltz me around again, Willie,
Around, around, around!'"

By the end of the tune, all of the nurses, as well as Mrs. Schultz and Sister Mary Joyce, are keeping time with their feet. Two of the women take to the floor, swing, and waltz around. Then, the women hear the bells chime. It is late. Knowing that the evening has ended, the nurses' mood changes. They begin to gather their sewing and tidy the room. Gertrude pauses at the piano. Then, she begins to play a slower song. Everyone stops where they are. Frozen, in time with the song, the women begin to sing one by one.

"Should auld acquaintance be forgot
And never brought to mind?
Should auld acquaintance be forgot
And days of auld lang syne?

"For auld lang syne, my dear
For auld lang syne
We'll take a cup o' kindness yet
For days of auld lang syne"

In the next verse, the women reach out to each other and offer a hand. Soon, all are connected.

"And there's a hand, my trusty fiere
And gie's a hand o' thine
And we'll take a right gude-willy waught
For auld lang syne"

As Gertrude continues to play, the nurses share silent good-nights, gather their sewing, and make their way up the stairs, softly singing as they climb.

"For auld lang syne, my dear
For auld lang syne

We'll take a cup o' kindness yet
For auld lang syne"

Only Mrs. Schultz, Sister Mary Joyce, Gertrude, and Sharon are left in the parlor.

"Please bake cookies any night, but be sure to invite me," says Sister Mary Joyce.

♦

36

More than two weeks have passed since reaching out to Danielle. Sharon has heard nothing more than the telegram telling her to wait. She has been waiting. She goes to work, but Connor is not there. She walks back to the boarding house and does not see Lucas. The nurses keep their schedules for working in the hospital. Things have been cleaned up and returned to normal after the storm. Tad, her boss, has also been absent from work. Though the rest of the office is buzzing along, there is tension in the air. The men in her office nod politely to her but do not engage in a conversation; not that they had before, but maybe she is just more aware of the silence she is feeling in the office. She gets in early so the "good morning" greeting from Marleen is much later in the morning when she takes a break to go to the ladies' water closet.

And now the flower sale is tonight from eight until ten. She has done all the leg work to get the advertisement printed and then to the newspaper. The flyers were given to Mrs. Lynch, who distributed them to the participating clubs. Sharon checks with the printer, F. E. Purse, located at the wharf and right around the corner from her office. Connor has paid the invoice, so at least he is about. She asked Tad if she could leave early, and he insisted that she leave at lunchtime. That suits her since she is eager to get this sale over. She would like something to go well before she leaves.

She hurries back to the boarding house without eating her lunch. As she crosses the square near the boarding house, she pauses. If she goes straight just a couple of blocks, she will be at Forsyth Park. She thinks it will calm her down a bit if she just sits and watches the birds for a few minutes. Going to her favorite bench, she sits down and begins to watch the birds with their constant little dance of flying in and out of the water spewing from the fountain. She sees the gnarled live oak limbs curving down above the azalea bushes, devoid of their flowers for the fall. The moss moves gracefully with the motion of the breeze off the river. Her first sight of the trees and moss amazed her and made her wide-eyed in wonder, but now she sees them as a part of her solitude and quiet. She may not be in Savannah much longer and wants to soak up all the natural sights she can.

"Good afternoon," says Connor. He has walked up behind her on the bench. "May I sit with you?"

Sharon is surprised. Her awkwardness in moving over to allow room indicates her willingness to see him but also her reserve in what will ensue.

"I went by the office, but Marleen said you left early. You were not at the boarding house, so I came here because I know you like to sit and think while watching the birds."

Not daring to look at him, Sharon looks at the fountain.

"Sharon, I know these past few weeks have not been easy for you."

She looks quickly at him. What she sees in his face is that he is sincere and not patronizing. He reaches over and takes her hand. "I am so sorry that I did not confide in you. I had no intention of making the job any harder than it already is. Please accept my apology."

"Of course," she mumbles. He does not release her hand.

"There is much to share, and I intend to share it all with you. I am hoping you will like what I have to say. But I wish to delay our talk for a little while longer. There are good reasons why. Tonight, you have a much-awaited event, and things are happening tomorrow that may answer many of your questions. Will you give me more time until we talk? I promise you that all of what I have been doing will be clear. May I please have time to talk with you tomorrow after the flower sale?"

Sharon feels a slight clasp of her hand in his. The current racing through her hand and up her arm confuses her. She is not fully paying attention to his words. What is this feeling she is having?

"Will you?" he asks.

She looks straight at him, anticipating his goodbye. "Yes, of course," she says.

Connor stands. "Then I will see you tomorrow. You will have a wonderful sale, I know." With that, he walks away at a rapid pace.

Sharon hears the bells chime and hurries to the boarding house to finish up the details for the fabric flower sale. Her heart beats rapidly, and she feels her face is hot to the touch. As she races up the steps and enters the house, she runs into Mrs. Schultz coming down the stairs.

"My goodness, girl, your face is red. Did you run from the office?"

"I did hurry, and now I must change to finish the details for the sale." She races up the stairs, more to hide her flushing face from Mrs. Schultz than to start on the finishing touches for the sale.

～

Magnolia, azalea, and gardenia flowers are displayed on bright gold cloth (napkins from the boarding house), while the blue spiderwort flowers, purple violets, and yellow and pink sweetheart roses are bunched together in bouquets. In the center of the table are holiday flowers of poinsettias in large, medium, and small bunches, along with baskets of evergreen leaves trimmed in gold and silver threads.

One of the nurses crocheted lapel-size Christmas wreaths, tiny snowmen with red scarves and hats, and petite emerald Christmas trees with red berries and a golden star at the top. Each is displayed on the table, but baskets are holding many more. Vivian has drawn a banner that they place on the edge of the table: "Fabric Flowers for Nurses." Mrs. Schultz is at one end of the table, and Sharon is at the other. Baskets of additional flowers are tucked under the freshly starched pale green linen tablecloth. They are ready. Nurses not required to be at the hospital are grouped behind the table wearing their nursing uniforms and are resplendent in their starched white aprons, collars, and cuffs. They are ready. The bell chimes ring out the eight o'clock hour.

Guests at the hotel, as well as Savannahians from many of the clubs who have been notified, are milling about in the lobby of the DeSoto Hotel. Mrs. Lynch, wearing a fall shade of burnt orange and a matching hat, approaches Sharon. "Are we ready?"

"Yes, we are."

Mrs. Lynch walks around the table and chooses several flowers and a small crocheted wreath. She turns to face the people leisurely standing in the lobby. "Ladies and gentlemen." She pauses while people quieten and turn to face her. "Tonight, we have the pleasure to see the handiwork of nurses at the St. Joseph's Hospital. They have made all of these beautiful fabric flowers." She gestures to the table. "As you can see, the flowers can adorn a hat, a dress, or a lapel. I will demonstrate." She turns to face the table, takes off her hat, and with a hat pin already in the hat, she attaches a magnolia blossom with a burnt orange center. Then she pins another blossom to the shoulder of her dress. She turns to face the audience. "These can inspire you to mix and assemble them for your wardrobe."

Then she smiles and motions for her husband to join her. When he is by her side, she pins a Christmas wreath on his lapel. "And, they are not just for the ladies. Men can wear the seasonal fabric on their lapels or their hat bands if they wish." Little laughs come from the audience as Mr. Lynch grins. "Or the poinsettias can decorate our tables during the holidays without having to refresh them like we must with live flowers, many of which are not available during the holidays. Please come, take a look, and buy. All the proceeds go to fund the salary of a nurse for the Fresh Air Home children's camp on Tybee Island. Should there not be enough flowers to decorate your attire, the ladies at the end of the table will be happy to take your name and place an order. Let the sale begin." She takes her husband's arm, and they move over to the side, greeting people as they go through the lobby.

Sharon takes a deep breath. For the next two hours, she barely gets to breathe. There are questions, money change to be made, donations accepted, orders taken, more flowers from under the table to replenish the baskets, people to meet, conversations with several office staff members who brought their wives, and the ever-present eyes of Lucas standing in the corner of the lobby taking notes in his booklet. Sharon is aware that he does not approach the table.

Hearing the ten o'clock chimes sends a feeling of relief over Sharon as she examines the now empty table. She looks at Mrs. Schultz, who has been keeping up with the money. Mrs. Schultz sees Sharon, raises her eyebrows, and then breaks into a smile that borders on laughing out loud. Sharon smiles back.

The nurses begin folding the tablecloth and gathering the empty baskets.

Seeing that everything is under control, Sharon slips out and walks quickly back to the boarding house. She needs some quiet time. There is still much to do to pack and be ready to leave. She has not heard from Danielle. Her job will end within a couple of weeks, and since she does not have the choice of being married and does not have a talent like Gertrude, she needs to go back to New York to take care of her family. A steamship to New York is leaving on Saturday, which gives her only tomorrow to say goodbyes and finish packing.

37

In the sleeping room, as she sorts through her trunk for items she will forward if she doesn't have room for everything, she hears a loud knock on the front door. She is the only one, to her knowledge, in the house. She hurries down the stairs and opens the door to find Lucas. He is standing with his hat clutched in his hands, folded in front of him.

"Good evening, Sharon. I was going to speak with you before you left the hotel, but you left quickly."

"Yes, I have a lot to do, so I came back. What can I do for you?" She stands in the doorway and has not invited him in.

"May I have a few minutes of your time to talk with you?"

"It's late."

"It'll only take a few minutes."

Sharon sees his frown. "Yes, of course." She steps out of the way and heads to the parlor. Lucas follows. Sharon sits on one of the brocade settees. Lucas does not sit but stands in front of her.

"Sharon, I know we have had our differences, but you must know that I have spent a lot of time getting to know you and being around you." He looks squarely at her. Though she is watching his face, she does not respond. "I am very fond of you and would like to offer shelter to you in this transitional time of yours."

"Shelter?" Sharon asks.

"Well, shelter is part of it, so is food on the table and a job that you like, when you like, and for as long as you like."

Sharon is still watching Lucas's face. He is shifting his hat from one hand to another. "Lucas, what are you offering?"

His face is beet red. "I am asking you to marry me. I have a job. We can find a nice room or apartment. I can even attend Mass with you if you want."

Sharon is silent. "Lucas, please, sit down next to me." She pats the seat on the settee. Lucas puts his hat down on the table and sits next to her. "I have heard from my sister that I must go to New York and take care of my parents."

"How long will you be gone?"

"It is not a visit. I will be returning to New York to live."

"Why? Don't you have sisters and brothers to help?"

"My sisters are overwhelmed, and my brothers are gone, so I must. I cannot abandon my family."

"You left them in New York to come to Savannah. That could be seen as abandonment."

"I left them so I could continue growing my career and be able to help my family when needed. They did not seem to need me at the time I left. Now, they do."

"So, what about me and my needs? Don't I count?" he asks in an accusatory tone.

"Lucas, you have given me so much of your time. I have learned a great deal about Savannah and myself. I have learned that I need to be busy working, creating, growing, and learning. You need someone who will give you the kind of family and home life you imagine. I cannot give you that."

Lucas stands. He looks at Sharon. "I guess that is a 'no.' I will not bother you again." He grabs his hat and heads to the door.

"Lucas, please." Sharon tries to follow him to the door, but he is out and down the steps. As she approaches the door, Mrs. Schultz comes up the front steps from the sale. Lucas passes her without even a greeting. Sharon stands at the door and watches as he leaves.

"I have to assume that the conversation did not go well." Mrs. Schultz enters the house with Sharon and closes the door.

"I need a cup of tea," says Sharon. "Would you like one?"

"Very much so."

The kettle is boiling and cups have been set out by the time Mrs. Schultz removes her hat and gloves, puts them away in her room, and comes into the kitchen. Sharon is sitting at the table with the cup cradled in her hands.

Mrs. Schultz sits down and stirs lemon into her tea. "I did not always use lemon in my tea," she says. "I drank it plain as you do. When we had milk, I did put some milk into it, but then one day, when I was a little girl, I got a cold. My mother made me a cup of tea and put lemon in it. As I got better, I often related to having a cup of tea with lemon as part of my mother's care for me. I think of her often when I have a cup of tea and add lemon."

Sharon looks at her cup of tea. Her early memories are of her mother working in the corner of the room sewing for long hours. Later, when Sharon was older, her mother taught her how to cook and take care of the family's clothing, but she never taught Sharon how to sew. When more money was needed and Sharon was old enough to get a job, she learned why her mother did not teach her to sew. "You have some schooling," her mother said. "You can go out into the world and do things I have never been able to do."

She thinks about her mother and knows that with all the new growth in New York and her experiences as an accountant, she can find a job and not have to return to being a hotel maid or get married, an offer that would not solve the problem of how to take care of her parents. She can do this.

Mrs. Schultz is watching her as she mulls over her tea. Sharon can feel the quiet that has filled the house. After another deep breath, she looks over at Mrs. Schultz. "Lucas proposed to me."

"Ah, and you said no, thus his quick departure."

"I am not the right person for Lucas. I can't accept that marriage is the only choice I have."

"What are your plans?"

"I leave Saturday on the steamship to New York. I have to find a job where I can take care of my parents."

"Do you have to leave so soon? Connor is not set to leave for another few weeks. You'll have a job until then, right?"

'Maybe, but I have finished the project. Waiting will only prolong the pain of leaving. Connor wants to speak with me tomorrow, so being fired by the Wexford Office is imminent." She pauses, "I have enjoyed being here in this house and doing what I have been doing."

Mrs. Schultz stands. "I ask you, as a favor, please don't be hasty. Please wait for just a while longer. You may be surprised what doing nothing at all can do for one's peace of mind."

Sharon smiles at Mrs. Schultz and finishes the last of her tea. She hears the front door open and the crash of nurses' feet in the foyer, along with chattering, singing, and great jubilation. Mrs. Schultz and Sharon join the nurses in the foyer. The women are excited and are taking off capes and coats. All are talking at once.

Finally, Gertrude says, "There will be only five graduating in May since I will be going to Brenau College. Let's hear it for these five women. One of them may be the recipient of a job on Tybee Island in the summer." A loud chorus is heard with lots of hugs to the five women who will be graduating.

At the back of the pack, unseen and unheard, stands Sister Mary Joyce. She raises her hand to get their attention. "Ladies," she calls out in a loud voice. "If you don't get your rest, you will not be prepared to work tomorrow, and that will affect your graduation."

Muffled replies sift through the group of women, but they obediently march up the stairs in groups of two and three, still chattering and talking about the night. Mrs. Schultz and Sister Mary Joyce laugh at their departure. Sharon has too much on her mind to enjoy the laugh.

"I have to assume that the sale was successful," says Sister Mary Joyce.

"Yes," says Mrs. Schultz. "I have the money here in this box." She picks up the box from the foyer table and gives it to Sister Mary Joyce. "My calculations say that there is enough money here to pay for two summers." She looks briefly at Sharon, then back to Sister Mary Joyce. "Will you put the money in the hospital safe since you will be transferring the money to the Froebel Circle to pay the nurse once that nurse is chosen?"

"Of course."

Sharon speaks up. "How will you decide which one will be chosen?"

"I have given it some thought. I think the choice must be based on performance at the hospital. The women are rated during every shift, which is one way we know they are ready to graduate. Additionally, we will consider how a nurse may create new routines that will either reduce the cost to the hospital or increase the care given to a patient. We have several examples of how they managed when we got the twenty-four seamen in at one time. Some of the women were quite resourceful in taking care of so many. And I think we need to consider how willing they might be to spend the summer on Tybee. As excited as they might be, spending a summer with a houseful of young children who have never been to the ocean might be more than some of them are willing to do. I think the women must apply."

"I visited the house on Tybee," says Sharon. "The house is nestled under trees. There is an outdoor shower to cool off from the hot sun after spending time on the beach. And there appears to be a constant breeze off the ocean. It is not as bad as you make it sound."

"But children were not there demanding all of your attention every hour of the day, right? It takes a certain person to work with children, I believe," says Sister Mary Joyce. She moves toward the front door. "Well, I need to get back to the hospital. It was indeed a great sale. Thank you."

"Thank you." Mrs. Schultz closes and locks the front door. With a good night to Mrs. Schultz, Sharon climbs the stairs to finish sorting out her things. She feels Mrs. Schultz watching her, so at the top of the stairs, she turns and looks. Mrs. Schultz waves and walks towards the kitchen.

38

F riday is a day of settling things. Sharon goes to the office to clean off her desk and to tell Tad that she is leaving. No one is about, not even Marleen. She writes a note to Tad explaining her plans. She straightens her desk and leaves. The farewell for Gertrude that evening in the parlor will be her farewell, too.

Stopping by Mrs. Lynch's house, Sharon leaves a thank you note for her help with the sale of the fabric flowers. She writes that the project is considered a success by the nurses, Mrs. Schultz and Sister Mary Joyce, so maybe it will continue with the next group of nurses who come into the program. She heads for the boarding house. She doesn't want to go to Forsyth Park. She is saving it for Saturday before she leaves. No one is at the boarding house when she returns except for Edwidge, who is in the kitchen. Sharon goes up to her room and has a great idea. With no one there, she will take a nap in the middle of the day, a great luxury.

∾

Her roommates awaken Sharon when they come in to change out of their aprons for dinner. They are oblivious to her being in her bed since no one takes a nap unless they are sick. The women enter, chattering about this patient and that patient. Sharon sits up, and Alice, who sees her first, wants to know if she is sick.

"No, just weary and need to rest."

"Did you not have work today?" asks Alice.

"Yes, I went in, but no one was in the office. So, I left and found that I needed to rest."

"We'll be quiet," says Sarah.

"Not necessary. I will dress and come down for dinner."

Sharon gets up and begins to dress, but Alice and Sarah come over to her side of the room and stand side by side.

"Sharon?"

Sharon looks up at them from where she is sitting on the side of the bed, putting on her shoes. "Yes?"

"We just want to tell you that we have enjoyed sharing the room with you," says Alice.

"You brought us all together with the recital reception and the flower sale," says Sarah.

"We were feeling closed in at first," says Alice. "That's why we went out every night to the pub or to walk on Broughton Street."

"Or to get some treats out," says Sarah.

"You gave us all a chance to know one another. Now we enjoy hanging out with the women we work with every day," says Alice.

"We just want to thank you and let you know that all the nurses acknowledge how much you and Mrs. Schultz have created a home for us here," says Sarah.

"Thank you," both women say at the same time and giggle.

Sharon stands. "I love being your roommate. But I have done so little. It's Mrs. Schultz who should be thanked." Sharon opens her arms and both women walk in and are hugged deeply. And for Sharon, their hugs will be remembered for a long time—to be liked by one's peers is important to her.

Dinner is over. A few of the nurses have to go back to the hospital to relieve the sisters for dinner, but they plan to return. The sisters know that there is a special goodbye planned for Gertrude.

At seven o'clock, the women crowd into the parlor. Their gifts for Gertrude, wrapped in cloth and tied with ribbons, are hidden in a basket in the corner beside the desk. Mrs. Schultz is in her chair. Two of the women go up to Gertrude's room and escort her down. She has been told that the women want to share a going away time with her, but she does not know what that will entail. They have her sit in the twin chair on the other side of Mrs. Schultz. Several of the nurses give little speeches about how nice it has been to work with her at the hospital and be a part of the program.

Vivian stands from where she has been sitting in the corner of the room. She has been quiet during most of the presentations and short speeches. "I have a poem to read," she says. "I think it suits the occasion in two ways. First, it is about different ways workers sing and contribute to our society. And second, it is by Walt Whitman, who was a nurse during the Civil War." She clears her throat, stands a bit straighter, and begins.

"I hear America singing, the varied carols I hear,
Those of mechanics—each one singing his, as it
    should be, blithe and strong,
The carpenter singing his, as he measures his
    plank or beam,

The mason singing his, as he makes ready for
    work or leaves off work,
The boatman singing what belongs to him in his
    boat, the deckhand singing on the steamboat
    deck,
The shoemaker singing as he sits on his bench,
    the hatter singing as he stands;
The wood-cutter's song, the ploughboy's, on his
    way in the morning, or at the noon intermis-
    sion, or at sundown;
The delicious singing of the mother—or of the
    young wife at work—or of the girl sewing or
    washing, each singing what belongs to her,
    and to none else;
The day what belongs to the day—at night, the
    party of young fellows, robust, friendly,
Singing, with open mouths, their strong melo-
    dious songs."

She ends by saying, "And the nurse's song—singing through her piano keys."

She backs up to where she has been sitting. The women in the room burst into applause. Alice and Sarah step up next. Alice has the basket of gifts. "Now we each have made a little something for you since we are so into making things in this house." A heartfelt giggle emits from the nurses and Mrs. Schultz, who uses a handkerchief in front of her mouth to muffle her sounds.

Sharon observes Mrs. Schultz's face. Lamplight shows her aging facial lines around her eyes and mouth, but her eyes are shining and alive. With the hues of shadows on her hair and neck, she is regal but relaxed, poised, and lovely all at the same time. Sharon sees how Alfred must have seen her in her younger days.

Sarah places the basket in front of Gertrude. "Choose a gift to open, and the nurse who made it will shout out their ownership."

Gertrude chooses, and it is the needlepoint cushion for a piano bench. Gertrude's tears are about to stain the hand-stitched cushion on her lap, so Mrs. Schultz hands her a hand-kerchief, which she now keeps in the table drawer between the chairs for situations such as this. The women get more excited with each gift unfurled. There are sachet packets and a lap quilt with black and white checkered trim around the sides of the quilt to represent the sisters at St. Joseph's. A satin robe emerges that brings many gasps and desires to hold. It is passed around to the nurses who hold it up to themselves for proper fitting, they say. Finally, Gertrude opens a journal filled with recipes.

"Mrs. Schultz and I thought you might like the memories of what we have been eating. I copied recipes that Edwidge and Mrs. Schultz have prepared for us," says Sharon.

"Is the recipe for chicken pudding here?" asks Gertrude.

"How about the petit fours?" asks Vivian.

"Yes," answers Sharon, "they are, as well as the stew, the griddle bread..."

"And cookies?" shouts out one of the nurses.

Sharon laughs. "Yes, and the cookies."

The nurses all want copies and Gertrude has to hold the journal close to her chest to keep them from absconding with it and keeping it as their own. "Let's name this!" The women shout out different titles, such as "Nurses' Cookbook" and "Eat at Home Cookbook," but then Gertrude says, "I think it should be called 'Mrs. Schultz's Boarding House Cookbook.' The women applaud and agree that the name is appropriate. There is much revelry, and as they crowd around Gertrude to look through the cookbook, Mrs. Schultz interrupts.

"I think there is one more thing that needs to be shared."

The women quiet down and look at Mrs. Schultz. "Another one of our residents will be leaving soon." The women look about at each other and then back to Mrs. Schultz. "Who?" they ask.

Sharon looks first at Mrs. Schultz but then steps forward. "Me." Where there has been much chattering and sharing, suddenly, there is quiet.

Gertrude is the first to speak. "Why?"

The telling should be easy. Sharon has made her decision, but to explain to these women whom she has grown so fond of is difficult. She gives her reasons. "So, excuse me, but I must go and finish packing." Sharon exits the parlor and flees upstairs. She does not dawdle; she packs the remaining items quickly. As she works, Gertrude comes into the room without knocking.

"Sharon, you need to come downstairs."

"No, I need to finish packing."

"There is someone here to see you."

"I am not interested in seeing anyone right now. Don't you see I have to get this done?"

Gertrude walks over to Sharon, takes the dress she is folding, and lays it on the bed. "You need to come with me. I promise you will be fine."

Slowly, Sharon allows Gertrude to lead her back to the stairs. As they descend, she stops when she hears a voice. She races down the last flight. Cahey is standing in the foyer.

"Cahey, how good to see you! But why are you here?"

Mrs. Schultz and Cahey are standing slightly apart. Sharon knows all the women are trying to be inconspicuous in the parlor but are listening carefully and evaluating the handsome red-headed man in a tailored suit who has an Irish accent.

"Sharon." Cahey reaches out and hugs her.

Sharon pushes back from him and says, "It's good to see you, but why are you here?"

"I came because Danielle shared that you needed us." Sharon is still full of questions. Cahey continues, "I visited your family and discovered that they were no longer in the rooms where we had visited them. But through neighbors, I found your sister and them. Things have changed since you left. They were no longer able to make ends meet. We found out that your sister wrote and asked you to return to New York. Danielle, Frederick, and I did not know what to do. So, we thought that if your parents' situation changed, then you would be able to decide what you wanted to do rather than be forced to do what you felt you needed to do. We thought about subsidizing living quarters for your parents, but through conversations with them and with some others on your behalf, we decided on yet another route."

Sharon frowned, trying to understand what Cahey was talking about. "What are you saying, Cahey?"

"I'm saying that I escorted your parents down here with me. They are in the parlor."

Sharon cannot believe it is true. She hurries over to the door, and there on the settee, surrounded by some of the nurses who are offering them cups of tea, are her parents. Sharon envelops them in her arms as tears of joy flow down her face.

Having already given her spare handkerchief to Gertrude, Mrs. Schultz is at a loss for how to help. She takes a napkin from the tea cart and hands it to Sharon.

Following her into the parlor, Cahey tells her that the parents are here to stay if she wants, or they can all return to New York. It's her choice. He has a room for them at the hotel, but he needs to return to his business in a few days. He has left Pádraig running the horse farm but needs to get back.

Amid more hugs and more tears, Sharon learns that they only arrived late that afternoon. Her parents tell her that they are exhausted from their travels. They had been told about the flower sale, so they waited to come over. Cahey offers to guide them back to the hotel after Sharon promises that she will come for breakfast.

In the foyer, as they are leaving, Cahey puts his arms around her shoulders. "Sharon, I hope I have done the right thing to come and bring your parents."

"Yes, of course it is. I just have to figure out what to do from here."

"You are a survivor. You will figure it out. I am sure of that."

Sharon reaches out to hug Cahey once again.

He whispers to her. "You are like the sister I never knew. I will do whatever you want me to do." He hugs her, holding her deeply to his chest. Cahey and her parents leave with many goodbyes from all the women now gathered in the foyer.

Sharon waves and closes the door. A sister, he says. She did have feelings for Cahey, but now she realizes that they are feelings of being a family, not of being a husband and wife. Mrs. Schultz had wanted her to wait, but now Sharon needs to know more from her. Sharon catches Mrs. Schultz's eye. "Can we talk in the kitchen?" she asks. Mrs. Schultz nods and follows her.

Sharon stands in the middle of the room and turns to face Mrs. Schultz. "You knew they were coming."

"Yes, I did. I got a telegram asking me to delay you until they got here."

"And you didn't tell me. Why not?"

"Because your friends and family wanted to surprise you and do something special."

"I have no job, no place to live when that job is finished, and now I need to find a job and a place for all of us to live. That is a surprise! I trusted you." Sharon is gripping her hands in front of her, massaging her fingers as she talks.

"And I trust you to do what is good for you."

"What do you mean?"

"I know you said no to Lucas in marriage. I understand why you did this; he is not the right mate for you, and you want to do right for your family. And, with how you look at Connor and behave after he has left, I knew you were no longer in love with

Cahey. But that you needed to see for yourself. So, with him coming, you would be able to." She pauses and looks at Sharon. "Am I correct?"

Without moving and speaking softly, Sharon answers. "Yes, you are correct. But what am I to do? Connor is leaving in two weeks."

Mrs. Schultz reaches Sharon before she can move and hugs her. "We'll figure it out."

39

B reakfast the next morning is both a delight and a challenge. Sharon is eager to visit with her parents to make sure they are doing as well as they can. It is a challenge because she does not know what she is going to do. Her parents are sitting with Cahey at a table having their first cup of tea when she arrives at the DeSoto Hotel. After hugs all around, Sharon is presented with a menu and needs a few minutes to process all the changes. In her silence with the menu, Cahey continues to talk with Sharon's father, who questions some of the menu items.

Cahey asks the waiter, "What is the broiled Finnan haddie?"

"Haddock smoked in the traditional Scottish manner with green wood and peat," recites the waiter.

"And milk toast?"

"Toast served with a white sauce," he answers while pouring water into the crystal goblets at each place.

"Thank you." Cahey looks back at the menu.

"I'll get a teacup for the lady and then take your order."

Cahey continues to chat with her parents. "I read that the company making the wheat breakfast cereal Egg-O-See distributed the cereal on St. Patrick's Day. That is why the box is a distinctive green."

Sharon sees many foods she has not had since coming to Savannah. The DeSoto Hotel Restaurant is trying to appeal to travelers and not locals, which supports Connor's rationale as to why the hotel was built. There is fruit, a variety of bread, milk toast, hot rolls, homemade biscuits, oatmeal, the Egg-O-See cereal, and shredded wheat biscuits in cream, along with buckwheat cakes with maple syrup or honey. Then there is broiled whitefish, fried fresh cod à la meunière, and the broiled Finnan haddie that Cahey had asked about. Included in the choices are fried veal cutlets with tomato sauce, stewed kidney with mushrooms, sirloin steak, chops, sausages, broiled calf's liver, ham, and bacon. Eggs and omelets can be ordered and come with potatoes that are hashed, browned, stewed in cream, fried, or baked. Not surprisingly, nothing appeals to Sharon. Her stomach feels queasy and her appetite has all but disappeared.

The waiter returns to take their orders. Sharon asks for fruit and toast. She sips her tea as Cahey stops talking and pours more tea for both of the parents.

In the lull, Sharon looks at her mother. She's dressed in a black skirt and beige blouse. The light-colored blouse makes her skin look almost brown. She has never taken care of her skin, and aging has deepened the creases on her face. "Sister writes that you have not been feeling well," Sharon says.

"I have not. But then again, I feel fine right now."

"I see. When did you begin feeling better?"

"The minute I left your sister's house."

Cahey stifles a laugh and hides his smile behind his napkin. Sharon's mother continues. "With losing the rooms, we had no choice but to move into the house with your sister. All the girls work long hours. They want to leave the children with me, but there are too many of them. They are young and need a lot of attention, and it is too much for me to handle. It is one thing to take care of children when you are younger and have to, but quite another to tend to other children. And then your brothers disappeared. Your sisters think they went out to work on the railroads."

"She wrote that you were not working, sewing, that is."

"Have you tried to sew in that cramped household with all those children and no room to stand, much less sit and sew? It is impossible."

Sharon's father interrupted. "She can still sew. She's good at it, she is. And I can still play with fellows at a pub. We just need a smaller city, a place that is easier for us to get around." He looks over at Cahey and takes a hand to clap him on the shoulder. "That's when Cahey, here, came and asked how we were doing and said that he had heard from you. We discussed how coming to see you and figuring out our next move would be the best choice to make since Cahey was being so generous."

"We didn't mean to make trouble or cause you more work than needed," says her mother. "We just had to get out of those crowded rooms and see what choices you might suggest."

Cahey interrupts, "And I will see that they get back to New York if that is what you decide to do."

Sharon listens and looks from one member of her family to another: mother, father, and now Cahey, the brother. The waiter arrives with their food. This gives her time to think, almost. Just as her fruit and toast are placed in front of her, Connor appears at her side. Anger boils up inside of her. How dare he! He has come to take leave of her and to fire her in front of her family? She is prepared to tell him exactly how she feels, but then she hears Cahey greet him by name. Cahey introduces her parents. She looks squarely at Cahey. "How do you know Connor?"

Connor is the one who answers. "Cahey and I talked on the telephone before he came down with your parents."

"I called the office to locate you. Your boss, Mr. McGuire, turned the call over to Connor. I explained all I knew from the telegram you sent to Danielle, but in our conversation, I learned a great deal more," says Cahey.

"What did you learn?" asks Sharon, looking directly at Cahey and ignoring Connor.

Connor, however, kneels beside her. He reaches and takes her hand, holding it gently in his larger hand. He gets Sharon's attention by saying, "He learned that I have fallen in love with you."

She looks at Connor and feels the electricity again cycling through her body. She sees Connor's green eyes, the ones she saw that first day at Forsyth Park, and they are now looking deep into her heart.

"Sharon, will you marry me?"

She is silent and takes a breath. "Are you leaving to go back to County Wexford?"

"Yes."

"And if I marry you, you expect me to go with you to County Wexford?"

"Yes."

"Then how can I go? You must see that I have my parents here now and must see to their welfare."

"I have made arrangements for them to go with us."

"To County Wexford?" Sharon is stunned and looks at Connor's eyes, knowing that they will tell her the truth.

"Yes."

"All of us?"

"Yes. There is a little cottage in the village that I have been inquiring about. And though you haven't asked, I know that you will. What will you do? What about your career? You, my love, will be the head of our new accounting department."

He explains how he knew she was the one for him. He had been put off by women who only wanted his name and station and did not want to be a partner with him in life. She would certainly be a partner. He would be the vice president in charge of the fleet. It was his idea to expand into Canada. He had seen the Savannah accounts and knew a change needed to be made.

"And to your next question, what about the Savannah staff with the changes? That is what I have been doing for the past several weeks. I have taken advantage of the friendships I have made at the hotel playing cards and have succeeded in finding every staff person who would have been let go a new job and a raise!"

So many feelings and emotions have gone through Sharon's mind since the first question Connor asked.

He looks at her with his green eyes, questioning. "If you say 'yes,' I can get off my knees, stand, and kiss you."

She no longer hesitates. "Yes, I will marry you."

Connor stands and pulls her up to kiss her, a kiss that is too long in public in front of her parents and Cahey and yet not long enough at all. The kiss could go on.

Cahey stands as well, hugs her, and shakes Connor's hand. "Plan to visit us in New York, especially since Frederick and Danielle's baby is coming," he says.

"And you, will you come visit us in Ireland?" asks Sharon.

"Of course," says Cahey.

Connor explains that they need to talk about their plans but that he has to call County Wexford and arrange a definite arrival date now that she has said yes. They agree to meet at the boarding house shortly to make their plans. Connor is off, but not before another kiss. He's grinning from ear to ear.

Sharon's parents are surprised but pleased that they will be returning to Ireland. "I never did want to leave; it was just impossible to live there at the time," says her father. Cahey has some businessmen he wants to meet, and her parents want to just wander around downtown and see what there is to see since they will be leaving. Everyone promises to be at the boarding house for dinner. Sharon returns to the boarding house alone, but her spirits are lifted by all the news she has to share with Mrs. Schultz.

She finds Mrs. Schultz in the kitchen. "Can we talk?" she asks.

"Of course, let's have tea in the dining room."

As Mrs. Schultz prepares the tea, Sharon lays out the cups and saucers for the two of them. Mrs. Schultz brings in the teapot and pours. "Well?"

"Much has happened. Connor proposed, and I said 'yes,'" says Sharon. Mrs. Schultz puts down her tea cup. Sharon lays out all the plans they made at breakfast and tells her that she invited all of them to dinner. "Was that all right?"

"More than all right," says Mrs. Schultz. "I knew I could trust you to do the right thing. Getting married, my oh my, that is good. When?"

"That's why I invited them to dinner. We need to plan."

"And we need to let them see the house and where they can stay, temporarily, that is."

"What do you mean?"

Mrs. Schultz explains that she has solved Sharon's housing problem. Gertrude is leaving soon. She shares a room with two nurses. Both of them have agreed to move into one of the other rooms with an added cot to make room for Sharon's parents to stay in Gertrude's room for the two weeks before they leave. "I know it is temporary, but then you don't have to worry about a hotel room for your parents, and they can eat here with us."

What can Sharon say to Mrs. Schultz that will tell her how

much this means to her? Does she have yet another family member? She has a brother in Cahey. Maybe she has an aunt in Mrs. Schultz, who is definitely like family. She tells Mrs. Schultz that she will be back to visit Savannah, and as head of the accounting department, she must come to check on the business.

"Please stay here and not in a hotel," asks Mrs. Schultz.

"I promise," says Sharon as tears keep her napkin busy.

Before long, Connor arrives. He kisses her right away. Sharon feels she will never get tired of that. The two of them sit side by side in the parlor and he shares his plan. If they are to leave on November the thirteenth, they could be married on the twelfth. He has checked with the ship agent and there are rooms available for all four of them. Now, who should be invited to the wedding and where will they be married?

"I'd like to get married at St. John's and have all the nurses and Sisters of Mercy who can get away from the hospital."

"I like that too. I will go and talk with the priest and see if that can be arranged since we are both in good standing in the church, and neither have been married before. I am right about that, aren't I?" Connor looks at Sharon with a twinkle in his eyes. She nudges him with her hand on his arm. He continues, "We can invite the office staff as well since they have new jobs and won't hate me," says Connor. Sharon laughs with him but knows what he is saying is true. She had been angry with Connor when she discovered the real reason for him being in Savannah.

"Things are happening so fast. Are we doing the right thing? What about your family back in County Wexford?"

"I talked with my uncle today. He has known my plans for several weeks."

"Really?"

"Yes, and they are organizing a big dinner on Christmas Day to celebrate."

He kisses her longer and deeper than she has ever been kissed. She shakes her head a bit after the kiss.

"Is everything all right?" asks Connor.

"Yes, everything is fine. I just wonder if the electric current I feel when you touch me will ever stop."

"Let's keep testing it to see," he says and kisses her again.

Dinner is more than anyone expected. Mrs. Schultz pulled out all the silver, the best linen, and put live poinsettias in brass pots on the table. The menu is Savannah red rice, the last of the kale and spinach from the garden sautéed with garlic and anchovy fillets, steamed broccoli, and hot rolls. For dessert, there is a peach cobbler using jars of her canned peaches from the summer. In the parlor afterward, tea is served. The nurses are all chattering with questions, comments, and more questions. Connor, Cahey, and Sharon's parents gather on the settees grouped in front of the fireplace. The women are flitting back and forth, urging Sharon to come here and there. Mrs. Schultz sits in her usual chair. Soon, Gertrude is over at the piano, entertaining them all with songs in her repertoire.

Connor stands and crosses to Gertrude. "May I?" He indicates the piano bench.

"Of course," she says and moves from the bench.

Connor runs a few scales up and down the keyboard. The women stop talking when he begins to play and sing.

"Where Lagan stream sings lullaby
There blows a lily fair
The twilight gleam is in her eye
The night is on her hair
And like a love-sick lennan-shee
She has my heart in thrall

Nor life I owe, nor liberty
For love is lord of all."

During the applause at the end of his song, he goes to
Sharon to kiss her yet again. She definitely can get used to this;
she thinks.

Gertrude asks, "Why leave on the thirteenth? Can't we have
more time to plan the wedding? Sharon and I have to shop for a
dress. I have to decide what to play. I will be playing at the
wedding, won't I?"

Sharon nods and smiles as she enjoys being held in
Connor's arms.

"It is my choice, and this is why," says Connor. "The ship
takes forty days to travel from Savannah to County Wexford.
Leaving on the thirteenth means we should arrive before
Christmas Eve morning. At Christmas Eve Mass, six men sing
the Wexford Carols. This tradition has been celebrated for
three hundred years, and my family has been a part of this cele-
bration for centuries. It helps us remember that in dark days,
there can be hope for what the future may bring. This interpre-
tation is from one of the carols; the lyrics are..." Connor begins
to recite the Wexford Carol "The Darkest Midnight in
December."

"The darkest midnight in December
No snow, nor hail, no winter storm
Shall hinder for us to remember
The Babe on this night was born
With shepherds, we are come to see
This lovely Infant's glorious charms
Born of a maid as the prophets said
The God of love in Mary's arms
"Ye blessed angels join our voices
Let your gilded wings beat fluttering o'er

While every soul set free rejoices
And everyone must adore
We'll sing and pray that God as always
May our friends and family defend
God grant us grace in all our days
Merry Christmas and a happy end."

Connor has been looking into Sharon's eyes the entire time he recites the carol. He then looks at the other people in the room. "So, on the darkest midnight in December, hope is offered for all of us even when things have been dark. That's what I believe. And Sharon is my hope for the future, both for the company and with me, to create a family, a family we both would like to have that includes more than just relatives; it includes the community around us." He looks back into Sharon's eyes. "I love you and fell in love with you when you sang the children's song of a 'Little Bird on my Window' the first time I met you."

Sharon remembers Mrs. Schultz saying that having had someone love her just for her would last her a lifetime. Now Sharon knows how that feels. She reaches and touches Connor's back and rubs her fingers over his shoulders. She has been wanting to do that. She is happy with her choices. If she is looking for a change in her life, as the bird song suggests, then getting married, having a new job, and relocating to Ireland, have to be major changes.

She looks at Connor and says, "*Is buaine port ná glór na n-éan, is buaine focal ná toice an tosaoil.*"

"Yes," says Connor, "a tune outlasts the song of the birds; a word outlasts the wealth of the world. What is the word for you? I had said mine was 'truth.'"

Sharon looks at Connor, and his green eyes smile back at her. Then she looks at the nurses gathered in the parlor, Mrs. Schultz, her mother and father, Cahey, and Sister Mary Joyce.

They are all looking at her with questions on their faces. She nestles closer to Connor, holds him close, and looks deep into his eyes. "I have found my word. I have hope. My word is 'hope.'"

THE END

AUTHOR'S NOTES

When I started thinking about writing *The Darkest Midnight in December*, I began with only a few facts: one, there had been a renowned nursing program at a hospital in Savannah; two, the advance of the railroads led to a need for more accountants near seaports; and three, a large percentage of the early Irish immigrants to Savannah were from County Wexford, Ireland.

According to the St. Joseph's/Candler network, the St. Joseph's Hospital School of Nursing operated from 1902-1969, graduating 741 nurses. These graduates served in the U.S., Philippines, Puerto Rico, West Africa, England, Italy, and Ireland. The story that Sister Mary Joyce tells in Mrs. Schultz's parlor is a true history of the founding of the school. Four students received diplomas and pins in 1905. As enrollment grew, the graduations were moved to the Cathedral of St. John the Baptist until 1968. Participation in the US Cadet Nurse Corps developed during World War II with Mary Margherita Powers as the first Savannah nurse and graduate of St. Joseph's to join the World War II Army Nurse Corps. The largest class to graduate was in 1947, with 33 graduating nurses. The school merged with Armstrong State College's two-year nursing program in 1966.

In 1916, there were only nine nursing programs regulated by the Georgia Board of Nursing. Savannah had four of the programs, St. Joseph's being one of them. All of these programs allowed the nursing students to work alongside experienced nurses in a clinical setting and learn the proper way to care for patients. St. Joseph's was the first nursing program in the state of Georgia and the first in the state to receive accreditation. The motto used on all pins for Saint Joseph's nurses was *Infirmus eram, et visitasti me* (I was sick and you came to visit me). See https://www.sjchs.org/healthcare-professionals/nursing/st-josephs-hospital-nursing-school-history.

The nursing story was a powerful one for me, as was having a woman accountant come to Savannah from New York. Christine Ross got her CPA in 1898 in New York. But the year 1906 was one when the railroads were opening up the country and connecting with seaports like Savannah. In their article "The Railroad Influence on the Development of the American Accounting Profession" (The Business History Conference, 2013), authors Dale Flesher and Gary Previts report that the industry was greatly influenced by the immigration to America of U.K. accountants in the late nineteenth century. America needed accountants.

Finally, the connection between Savannah and County Wexford has been documented through Georgia Southern University's selection of Wexford Town as the site for its first overseas campus due to the historic trade-and-emigration relationship between Savannah and County Wexford. During five years from 1845-1855, approximately 56 percent of direct Irish newcomers originated in County Wexford with a regular, non-stop sailing to Savannah. The research on County Wexford led me to "The Darkest Midnight in December," one of the thirteen Kilmore carols from the village of Kilmore in Wexford County,

Ireland, which are found only in this area and date back three hundred years.

Music and food have always linked me to the cultures of places I have visited and lived. Therefore, it is appropriate that a cookbook should be created to list the recipes from all the food offered in this book. I have created the cookbook to also include a few special recipes. A PDF copy of *Mrs. Schultz's Boarding House Cookbook* will be emailed to anyone who subscribes to my newsletter through my website: lear-arhodes.com.

Thanks go to the following:

- The Traveling Ladies: Freda Scott-Giles, Fran Teague, and Valerie Babb, who went to Savannah with me and were there when Old Fort Press offered to publish my first book, *Spancil Hill.*
- Louise Benjamin, my sister-friend, guided me in things I didn't know about the Catholic Church and led me to contact the Diocese of Savannah with questions about getting married at St. John's in 1906. The Director of Archives & Records Management answered all of my questions.
- Thomas "Tuck" Stephens, my CPA, gave me wise advice on accountants and why they enjoy their work.
- Rebekah Boles, my piano teacher and pianist for the Athens Symphony and the Classic City Band, answered numerous questions on the music used in the book, specifically the recital.
- Donato Palumbo, my son-in-law and retired fireman from Eastchester Fire Department, New York, clarified anything having to do with the fires in the book.

- The Fireside Reading Club: Ellen Stoneburner, Sharon Reber, Nicola Dovey, Ann Puckett, and Judy Capie. These women provided a safe place for me to read my work out loud. I am forever thankful.
- Pam Asberry had already gone the extra mile when she told me that she had recorded a version of the Wexford Carols. https://pamasberry.bandcamp.com/track/wexford-carol.
- John Ebberwein, Savannah River pilot, steered me correctly down the river. Thank you.

I give my heartfelt thanks to my daughter, Jessica, for her encouragement and support. She is there for me in so many ways, as is my publisher. Thanks to Old Fort Press and Leigh Ebberwein for believing in my stories.

SOURCES FOR THE SONGS AND POEMS USED WITHIN THE BOOK:

"Auld lang Syne" is based on a poem written by Robert Burns in 1788. Sir Robert Ayton, who died in 1638, wrote Old Long Syne, a poem that was first published in 1711 and is sometimes cited as Burns' inspiration.

"The Blue Danube," by Johann Strauss (1867) is based on a poem by Karl Isidor Beck (1817-79). The river is not blue and, when the waltz was written, it did not flow through Vienna. Strauss made his American debut in Boston on June 17, 1872, conducting "The Blue Danube" for the World Peace Jubilee. For the occasion, Patrick Sarsfield Gilmore, an Irish bandmaster, assembled an orchestra of 2000 and a choir of 20,000.

"Clair de lune" ('Moonlight') by Claude Debussy is from Verlaine's early collection "Fêtes galantes" (Gallant Parties, 1869).

Colcannon's song, "Little Skillet Pot," by Seán Nolan, known as "The Wicklow Piper," who also wrote "Kerry Long Ago," "Boys of the County Cork," and "My Far Down *Cailín Bán.*"

"The Darkest Midnight in December," Fr Devereux's collection of Kilmore Christmas carols, called "A New Garland."

https://www.youtube.com/watch?v=p9wpXdUJow4.

"Divertimento in D Major," by Joseph Haydn, 1767.

"Faith of our Fathers," by Frederick William Faber, 1849. Written in memory of the Catholic martyrs from the time of the establishment of the Church of England by Henry VIII and

Elizabeth. He wrote two versions of the hymn: one with seven stanzas for Ireland, and another with four for England.

"The History of Women's Clubs in America," by Jane Croly, 1898.

https://www.womenshistory.org/articles/womens-clubs#:~:text=Jane%20Croly's%20massive%20book%20The,numbers%20would%20rise%20until%201926.

"I Hear America Singing," by Walt Whitman, 1860.

"It is Well with My Soul," also known as "When Peace, like a River," by Horatio Spafford and Phillip Bliss, 1876.

"The Language and Poetry of Flowers," London: Marcus Ward & Co.; New York: Pott, Young & Co., 1875.

"Little Bird on My Window," an old Irish ballad, origin unknown.

"Moonlight," by Paul Verlaine, 1869.

"My Lagan Love," collected in 1903 in northern County Donegal. The English lyrics are credited to Joseph Campbell (1879-1944), also known as Seosamh MacCathmhaoil.

"The Old Woman of Wexford," an old Irish ballad, origin unknown.

"On a Sunday Afternoon," words by Andrew B. Sterling, music by Harry Von Tilzer, 1902.

https://www.sheetmusicsinger.com/on-a-sunday-afternoon/

"Piano Concerto in C-sharp minor, Op. 45," by Amy Beach, 1898-99.

"Scarborough Fair." The song's origin can be traced back as far as 1670, alongside the similar Scottish ballad, "The Elfin Knight." Although the title specifically refers to the location of Scarborough Fair, there have been other versions from throughout the 17th and 18th centuries that used other locations.

"Six Irish Fantasies," by Charles Villiers Stanford, 1893.

"Water in the Moonlight," by Thomas "Blind Tom" Wiggins, 1866.

"What the Brass Band Played," by Theodore Morse, lyrics by Jack Drislane, 1904.

"Willie Fitzgibbons," by Will D. Cobb & Ren Shields, 1906.

BIBLIOGRAPHY

Accountants were needed in America. The strong reliance on immigrant accountants was deemed to be the result of the use of skilled immigrants in a situation where there were insufficient home-grown accountants. According to T.A. Lee (2007), *American Accountants in 1880, Accounting, Business & Financial History*, Vol 17 no.: 333-354. See also "Women Accountants in the 1880 US Federal Census: A Genealogical Analysis by Diane H. Roberts, The University of San Francisco, 2010. https://repository.usfca.edu/cgi/viewcontent.cgi?article=1001&context=acct

Beacon Light. The Beacon Range Light was located on the east end of Bay Street in 1858. The Old Harbor Light, which is also known as the Savannah Harbor Rear Range Light or the Beacon Range Light, is a former aide to navigation in Emmet Park on East Bay Street in Savannah, Georgia. The light has the appearance of a giant street light.

Bergamasque or bergamask is a rustic dance originating in Bergamo, Italy.

Collinsville. The Eastside Historic District is significant as a series of subdivisions developed by businessman Jacob S. Collins. Collins was one of the first to receive a franchise in 1890 to provide electric railway service in Savannah. Electric streetcar lines ran through the neighborhood, specifically in the center of Gwinnett and Bolton Streets, and extended from the city market and the river through a rural landscape of fields east to Thunderbolt.

Christine Ross was the first woman to be awarded a CPA certificate in the United States in June 1898. However, Ross did not receive her certificate for another year and a half until the New York Board of Regents decided a woman could receive a certificate at their meeting on December 21, 1899 [Wescott and Seller, 1986]. Following this achievement, Christine Ross practiced from her office at 17 Battery Place, New York City, early in the twentieth century.

Froebel Circle is a branch of the International Order of King's Daughters and Sons, a religious order. The Fresh Air Home was founded in 1897 by Nina Anderson Pape and operated by The Froebel Circle, which still oversees the facility. Thanks to the generosity of several individuals who donated money and property through the years, the Fresh Air Home manages to serve 380 children each summer in four two-week sessions.

George M. Cohan's "Little Johnny Jones" was performed in Savannah in 1906, but Cohan was no longer doing one-night shows, so he was not in the performance. See "The History of the Savannah Theatre, 1865-1906" by Robert Lane Overstreet (Dissertation & Theses, 1970).
https://www.proquest.com/openview/fe6d0af9860426b4695a7f61ded1eed9/1?pq-origsite=gscholar&cbl=18750&diss=y

Graves & Son. The firm of William Graves & Sons owned and operated ships that traded between U.S. and Canadian ports and those in Britain and Ireland. They chartered other ships when needed and were experienced in the carriage of goods such as timber from Canada and tobacco, molasses, and cotton from the United States. In common with other shipping agents, they had become equally experienced in sending those ships back across the Atlantic loaded with people. When famine struck Ireland in 1845, many faced starvations as the potato crop was failing and food prices began to soar. This led to widespread emigration and a huge surge in the need for passenger ships. Entrepreneurial merchants took up the opportunity and fitted their cargo vessels with bunks to meet the extra demand. One such merchant family was William Graves & Son in New Ross, who commissioned the original Dunbrody as well as seven sister ships.
https://www.waterfordvisitorcentre.com/blog/general-news/exploring-our-irish-heritage

Savannah's Irish Neighborhoods. Ryniker, Sarah A. "Savannah's Ethnic Irish Neighborhoods in the Nineteenth Century: A Historical Multimethod Examination" (Spring 2017, Georgia Southern University).
https://digitalcommons.georgiasouthern.edu/cgi/viewcontent.cgi?referer=&httpsredir=1&article=2693&context=etd

Savannah Morning News, September 22, 1906.
https://chroniclingamerica.loc.gov/lccn/sn89053684/1904-12-31/ed-1/
The Savannah Morning News has continued to publish since its beginning in 1850. The paper covered the news of the city in the turbulent years of Reconstruction and the financial resurgence of Savannah through the flourishing export market tied to the city's port in the late 19th and early 20th centuries. There were other newspapers in Savannah at the time. Beginning in 1887, the paper's title was shortened to the *Morning News*

before reverting to the *Savannah Morning News* in 1900. During this period, the paper claimed a circulation of over 5,000 copies covering large portions of southern Georgia and northern Florida.

Savannah Music Club. See *Savannah Morning News*:
https://gahistoricnewspapers.galileo.usg.edu/lccn/sn89053684/1904-12-15/ed-1/seq-7/

Sean's Bar (fiction in Savannah, real in Ireland). In 2004, Guinness World Records issued a certificate to Sean's Bar as the Oldest Pub in Ireland.

Irish:

An áit a bhfuil do chroí is ann a thabharfas do chosa thú.
Phonetic pronunciation: On aw-it a will du cree iss ow-n a hur-fas du cussa huu
English translation: Your feet will bring you to where your heart is.

Is buaine port ná glór na n-éan, is buaine focal ná toice an tosaoil.
Phonetic pronunciation: Iss boona port naw glore na nane, iss boona fu-cal naw tucka an teal.
English translation: A tune outlasts the song of the birds; a word outlasts the wealth of the world.
The proverb reminds us about the important things in life and the importance of music and culture to the Irish people.
https://www.aletterfromireland.com/irish-sayings-is-there-room-for-the-irish-language-in-your-life/#:~:text="Is%20buaine%20port%20ná%20glór,the%20wealth%20of%20the%20world."

IRISH SAYINGS

An áit a bhfuil do chroí is ann a thabharfas do chosa thú.

Phonetic pronunciation: On aw-it a will du cree iss ow-n a hur-fas du cussa huu

English translation: Your feet will bring you to where your heart is.

Is buaine port ná glór na n-éan, is buaine focal ná toice an tosaoil.

Phonetic pronunciation: Iss boona port naw glore na nane, iss boona fu-cal naw tucka an teal.

English translation: A tune outlasts the song of the birds; a word outlasts the wealth of the world.

The proverb reminds us about the important things in life and the importance of music and culture to the Irish people.

https://www.aletterfromireland.com/irish-sayings-is-there-room-for-the-irish-language-in-your-life/#:~:text="Is%20buaine%20-port%20ná%20glór,the%20wealth%20of%20the%20world."

ALSO BY LEARA RHODES

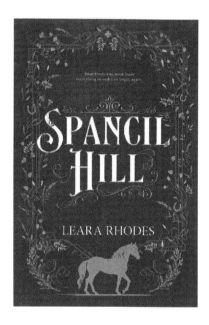

SPANCIL HILL

Leaving behind his friends and a thriving business in Galway, Cahey embarks on a journey to New York and struggles to find his way. He quickly discovers he is not alone. He bands with other Irish, Scottish, and French immigrants to build a life away from everything he once loved.

Being Irish creates many problems, even in New York. Finding out how severe those problems are could change his life forever. His fear is—can his survival skills and love of horses be enough to become the most sought-after horse trainer at the Vanderbilt American Horse Exchange in 1901?

ABOUT THE AUTHOR
LEARA RHODES

Leara Rhodes has been a writer since college in Philadelphia, where she received her master's and doctorate from Temple University. She has been a journalist, editor, freelance writer, and university professor teaching writing. During her academic career, she published three books and numerous journal articles. She was awarded a Fulbright to Haiti and named the first educator inducted into the Georgia Magazine Hall of Fame. Her summer teaching programs included two at the University College Dublin and two at Trinity College, University of Oxford.

Leara lives in Athens, Georgia, and prefers to garden, cook, travel, or spend time with her family and friends when she is not writing. To learn more about Leara, visit her website:

Leararhodes.com.

Made in the USA
Columbia, SC
07 March 2025

54834764R00186